MW01624327

barn burner

A FAKE DATING HOCKEY ROMANCE

SINNERS ON THE ICE
BOOK 2

ANASTASIJA WHITE

This book is a work of fiction. Names, characters, locales, businesses, events and incidents are products of the author's imagination or are used fictitiously. Any resemblance to actual person, living or dead; events; or locations is entirely coincidental.

The author acknowledges the trademark status and trademark owners of various products, and/or brands referenced in the work of fiction. The publication/use of these trademarks is not authorized, associated with, or sponsored by the trademark owners.

Edited by Caroline Knecht, https://reedsy.com/caroline-knecht

Cover Design and Characters Art by Anna Silka, https://www.instagram.com/silka.art/

This book is intended for an 18+ audience.

For content warnings, please visit https://www.anastasijawhite.com

ISBN 978-609-08-0293-9 (ebook)

ISBN 978-609-08-0292-2 (paperback)

ISBN 978-609-08-0366-0 (special edition, paperback)

To the ones who chased a perfect image and set impossible goals out of fear of not being enough.
Do not let other people's opinion rule your life. You don't owe anything to anyone, except the person you see in the mirror.
Love yourself because you are enough, and you deserve the world...and a dirty-mouthed cinnamon roll hockey player, who will do anything for you.

playlist

1. "Heartbroken - Jessie Version" - Diplo, Jessie Murph
2. "Scared to Be Lonely" - Martin Garrix, Dua Lipa
3. "Feels Like" - Gracie Abrams
4. "YOU & I" - Anne-Marie feat. Khalid
5. "Cruel Summer" - Taylor Swift
6. "Halo" - Bethany Joy Lenz
7. "High Hopes" - Panic! At The Disco
8. "Love Like This" - ZAYN
9. "cardigan" - Taylor Swift
10. "Never Let Me Go" - Florence + The Machine
11. "Secrets" - OneRepublic
12. "RUNNING" - NF
13. "Bad At Love" - Halsey
14. "2 Much" - Justin Bieber
15. "One Kiss" - Calvin Harris feat. Dua Lipa

Find the rest of **BARN BURNER** playlist here:

Angie

ONE

snow queen

I GLANCE AT THE CLOCK AND SMILE, SEEING MY ODDLY favorite numbers—12:12. I quickly close my eyes and make a wish for today to turn out well. It's a habit I've acquired over the years, allowing myself to believe in a little bit of magic. Even if it's more of an illusion. Magic has nothing to do with what people are capable of.

The second I let the time sink in, I curse. I'm running late. I have a meeting about my dessert shop's new menu in a little over an hour, and I still need to take Cooper out. He's been a good boy, waiting for me, but even his patience has its limits. For the past forty minutes, my Doberman pinscher has been following my every step, looking into my eyes with an absolutely miserable expression. As if I didn't take him for an hour-long walk this morning. This dog is a manipulative asshole...but I still love him.

I collect my hair into two Dutch braids and twirl around, checking out my outfit. I intend to get in a little run on the way, so I'm wearing a black sports bra and black leggings with red sneakers. Coop sits by the door, eyeing me warily, as if there's a chance I'd run away.

"Come on, Coop, let's go." I grab my keys and his leash from the table and reach for the front door. He always walks out of the house and waits for me, but not today.

As soon as I open the door, Cooper barrels downstairs. His loud barks echo on the street as he charges for the large-as-a-wall guy standing near my Lamborghini Aventador.

"What the hell? Get your fucking dog off me," the guy growls.

Cooper already has his paws on the man's chest, and he keeps baring his teeth, his ears drawn back. I stay planted on the porch, my mouth falling open. Rapidly blinking, I pinch my eyebrows together, and a trickle of sweat rolls down my back.

Oh my God, what am I doing?

I rush down the stairs, tripping over two at once. Then I seize Cooper by his collar and drag him away from the guy. I put the leash on my dog and take a step back. Palm pressed to my rib cage, I try to catch my breath and finally look at the man in front of me. He looks pale, and his dark brown eyes are shooting daggers at me from under etched brows.

"I'm so sor—"

"What the fuck is wrong with you?" he interrupts, making me shut my mouth. "Your dog could've bitten my leg off. Don't you know how to use a fucking leash?"

I made a mistake, and I acknowledge that. Apologizing is the least I can do, but this man won't even let me finish.

"Don't you know how to talk to a woman?" I hiss, furrowing my brow. My gaze roams over his face. I take in his eyes, his slightly crooked nose, and the noticeable stubble on his cheeks. He might be attractive, but he's incredibly far from what I consider my type. "My dog is—"

"Your fucking dog attacked me." The guy clenches his fists. His jaw clamps shut as he grinds his teeth.

If I wasn't so pissed, I'd be intimidated by him. A glance is enough to tell me he's into sports. This man might be an athlete, perhaps a football player like Dad, who's the only athlete I like. I'm not interested in the rest of them.

"I made a mistake letting Coop out of the house without a leash. But I didn't know you'd be checking out my car. He's defending me," I say.

A door slams shut, startling me and making me take a few steps back. Two girls run down the stairs of the two-story house next door with the white facade and large windows. They're headed in our direction.

Did someone buy it?

"I was curious about your car, and I just wanted to have a look. I didn't expect to almost lose my leg in the process."

I blink. "A barking dog is not the same as a biting dog. Maybe try not to gawk at other people's cars next time to avoid problems."

"Avoid problems?" he mumbles, breathing heavily. A vein in his neck pulsates. One of the girls appears in front of him. I focus my attention on her and instantly see that it's Bella.

Eight months ago, when I moved to Santa Clara, Bella worked her magic on the interior design of my house. She's incredibly nice and sweet, and I like her despite the fact that her husband is the quarterback for the California Mustangs. Though Xander is kinda cool; he helped me when I was looking for a tattoo artist four months ago.

Okay, maybe not all athletes are so bad. Maybe I'm being a hypocrite.

"Hey, Evangelina." Bella steps closer to me and kisses my cheek. "How are you?"

Her familiar face is like an instant fix for my mood. I smile, feeling my muscles relax a little. "Hey, Bella. I was great until this little incident. Do you know this guy?"

"Of course. Drake is my client. He bought this house, and I'm helping him decorate it."

My smile slips away, and I absentmindedly touch my earring. "Is he my new neighbor?"

"Yup." The brunette who was silently standing beside the guy takes a step forward and extends her palm to me. "I'm Ava. It's nice to meet you."

"Evangelina." I quickly shake her hand and then let go, stepping back. Her eyes are glued to my face as she stares at me with curiosity. "It's nice to meet you too. Unlike this guy—"

"I did nothing wrong; it was your dog's fault. You shouldn't let him off the leash." His posture is still tense as he bombards me with accusations.

Sighing, I pull Cooper to my side because he's trying to get to Bella. I bet he can smell her dog, Milo, on her. "Listen, I didn't expect him to run at you like he did. He knows how to behave."

A moment passes; my eyes stay locked on this guy. He blinks and shakes his head, muttering, "Whatever."

He stomps to the BMW X6 parked near Bella's car and slams the door so hard Ava flinches. Someone definitely has a problem controlling his anger.

I return my gaze to Bella and Ava. "Sorry about that. He just pissed me off, yelling at me and not letting me apologize to him." Stepping back, I loosen Cooper's leash a little and squint at my watch. "I need to get going."

"Sure," Bella murmurs, hugging me briefly. "See you around, Evangelina."

"See you around," I tell her and focus my attention on Ava. She's gorgeous, and I'm sure I've never seen her with Bella before. If she's this guy's girlfriend, he should be more appreciative of her instead of acting like the biggest child on the planet. "Bye, Ava."

"Bye, Evangelina." She grins at me. My eyes linger on her face for a moment, then I quickly stroll away from my house with Cooper. I can't believe I wasted so much time on that rude guy.

I'M SITTING on the couch in my living room, typing on my laptop, listening to my playlist on Spotify. It's Saturday night, and instead of going out, I stayed home to work. These calm evenings, when I do whatever I want without caring what others think, are exactly what I need.

I glance to my left and meet Cooper's eyes instantly. He's lying in his dog bed, chewing on a big bone I bought for him. Even if he didn't deserve it. No matter what I think about my new neighbor, the way my dog acted toward that dude was not acceptable. He didn't do anything to cause that level of aggression, and I feel puzzled. What the hell happened to Coop?

This guy doesn't look like Asher—the only person Cooper wasn't very fond of. He's more like my dad. Tall and muscular, a good six foot five inches. And Coop loves my father. At this point, I can only hope the situation won't repeat itself. There's no way I'll ever let him out of the house without a leash again.

My phone beeps with an incoming message, but I ignore it. I'm determined to finish the new marketing strategy for my dessert shop. A smile blossoms on my lips when I let my fantasies overwhelm my brain. So many ideas and so many plans. In moments like these, I'm happy I gave up being a runway model. This way, I have more time to myself...even if I loved being a part of the shows. Another huge thank-you to Asher—not. He's my biggest fuckup. If anyone from my family knew *everything* about my relationship with my ex-boyfriend... I'd be dead.

I blink and shake my head, refocusing on my laptop. What's wrong with me tonight? It's like I can't catch a break. I'm constantly switching from one thought to the other.

Getting up from the couch, I proceed to the kitchen. I open the fridge and take out a plate with the last piece of cheesecake I made two days ago. I've been experimenting with flavors, and I love how deliciously sweet this one turned out. Blueberries might not be my favorite, but in cheesecake? It's a ten out of ten. I can't wait to talk to Marcy about adding it to our menu.

I turn on the kettle and move around the kitchen, humming along with Taylor Swift. "Anti-Hero" is my own personal anthem, as my best friend, Nevaeh, said the second she heard me singing it. I'm the problem. Me and no one else. Who in their right mind would start a relationship with a guy knowing he's a cheater and a manipulator? Only Evangelina Jones. Next time I want to prove something to someone, I'll promise to prove it only to myself.

I refuse to ruin my life and body ever again.

Once I settle at the table with my mug of chamomile tea and plate of cheesecake, paws slap on the tile, and Cooper enters the room. I can't even eat in peace with him around.

"Bro, soon you're going to be bigger than the Titanic," I tell him as he comes to the table and sits near my chair, facing me. Cooper won't guilt-trip me into feeding him again. He already had his dinner.

I pop a piece of my cheesecake into my mouth and hear a loud sigh. Someone is definitely trying to get my attention. *Not going to happen, Coop.* With my one hundred and twenty-two pounds against his ninety-nine, he'll be walking me soon, not the other way around. And I hate not being in control.

Another loud exhale leaves my dog's mouth, and he lowers his head onto my lap as I take another bite of my cheesecake. Groaning, I look at him. "What?"

Ugh, Cooper, give me a break. This dog is going to be the death of me. I pat his head and slowly stand up. I step to the cupboard, get a few pumpkin dog biscuits, and offer them to him. He swallows them in the blink of an eye and tilts his head, as if asking me, *What else?* I go back to my seat and finish my cheesecake without paying any attention to Coop's gaze on me. I'm doing it for his own good. He should be grateful.

After I finish loading the dishwasher, I return to the living room with Cooper in tow. He saunters to his dog bed, where he continues to gnaw on his bone.

I should probably watch something, but my mood is all over the place. Debating my next steps, I stare at the ceiling. I reach for my phone, unlock it, and quickly dial Nevaeh's number. There's a good chance she's already clubbing somewhere since it's past nine, but I still want to try. I need company.

"Hey, Nev," I say as soon as she answers. "What's up? What are you doing tonight?"

"Hey, honey," she murmurs sweetly. "Pretty much nothing. I'm on my period, so I'm planning to watch something and cuddle in my bed."

"Do you want to do pretty much nothing with me?" I ask, and she laughs heartily.

"Sounds good. Be there in thirty. You better have something to drink."

"You bet I do."

"See you soon, Angie," she says and hangs up.

Later, I'm sitting on the couch with a bottle of rosé, two glasses, and a cheese plate with olives on the table. I hope it'll be enough for us.

Grabbing my phone from the table, I decide to check the time, and I see the unread message. I'd totally forgotten about it. As soon as I read it, anger fills every bone in my body. The fucker has no idea when to stop.

UNKNOWN NUMBER:

How is my Snow Queen doing? Any chance your heart is warming up to me again? I miss you, Evangelina.

A horde of goosebumps spreads across my skin, and I squirm. Asher makes me hate my name. Any time he's going through another phase, he crawls back. Begging for my attention, asking me to go on a date with him...or just fuck him wherever I want. I don't want any of it.

My third breakup with him left a dent in my confidence and ugly signs of his addiction on my body. I want him to leave me alone, but unfortunately, he doesn't seem to understand. For whatever reason, he believes I still have feelings for him...as if I love him because I'm single. Delusional motherfucker. He's my past, one I don't regret leaving behind at all. Asher needs a reality check.

I block yet another one of his phone numbers and toss my phone onto the table. The doorbell rings, and I push myself from the couch to the hallway. Opening the door, my eyes land on Nevaeh. She's wearing a baggy black hoodie and black sweatpants; her strawberry blonde hair is collected in two cute buns on top of her head. I step away, and she ambles into my house, giving me a loud smooch on the cheek along the way.

A bottle of Moët is the first thing I see when I lock the door and spin around. Nevaeh is grinning from ear to ear as she holds the bottle in front of her. "Will you get drunk with me tonight? Pretty please?"

"As if you had to ask," I reply, and she squeals, jumping into the air like a kid. Shaking my head, I follow Nevaeh into the living room. Now I'm more than sure this night is going to be amazing. Just like it always is when she's around.

Angie

TWO

hot and not

Waking up, I open my eyes and instantly close them again. I lie still, not moving a muscle. If Cooper sees me stir, he'll sit right by the bed, keeping his gaze on me until I get up and take him for a walk. And I'm not ready for that. Especially not after Nev and I went to bed around four a.m.

"Are you trying to pretend you're still asleep because of Cooper?" A loud whisper rings in my ear, and I snap my eyes open, meeting my best friend's blues. She's lying on her right side, facing me. Her hands are hidden under the pillow.

"Kinda," I whisper back. "What time is it?"

"Ten a.m.," she says, fighting a smile. "Coop and I got back from our walk fifteen minutes ago. He's probably in the kitchen."

"What?" I sit up and look down at Nev. "Why did you...?"

"I woke up because of my cramps an hour ago, went to the living room and he followed me. And I just couldn't deal with your dog looking at me with his big puppy eyes." Nevaeh sighs and rolls onto her back, pressing her palm to her lower abdomen with a wince. "I didn't think your Doberman could pull off the Puss in Boots look. Is he always like that?"

"He is. You just weren't paying attention."

Nev smirks and slowly sits up, raising her hands into the air and stretching. "Your dog is growing on me, and it's worrisome. I'm a cat person."

"Why can't you be both?" I laugh, tossing the blanket aside and standing up from the bed. "I love cats and dogs equally."

"And yet you only have a dog," she comments, climbing out of bed as well. "Why didn't your brother give you a kitten too? Why only a dog?"

"Because he wanted me to have someone who can protect me while he and Dad aren't around." I shrug, strolling to my bathroom to wash my face.

"Then why didn't Cooper do anything when Asher—"

"Can you please stop?" I demand, squinting at Nevaeh, who's standing in the doorway, her hip propped against it. She lifts her hands in front of her and takes a step back, leaving my bedroom a moment later. I take a deep breath and turn on the faucet, starting my routine.

My best friend knows my outburst has nothing to do with her and everything to do with my ex. Any mention of what he did can send me flying off the handle quicker than I can snap my fingers. I'm a work in progress, and when I finally deal with all this emotional damage, I'll be able to talk about it with her and anyone else. Including my family. Hiding the *whole* truth from them, the one that never got to the media, is easy while they're away, but it'll be impossible if one of them decides to visit. Or when I have to go home for my grandma's birthday. Another brick in my solid wall of reasons to find a way to deal with Asher and his stalkerish behavior. He needs to realize, the last time I walked away, it was for good.

I need to make him back off...but how?

"I'M SORRY," I say, plopping down on the chair in front of Nevaeh. She's sitting at the kitchen island, flipping through the pages of some magazine and ignoring my presence. "I'm sorry for snapping at you."

That gets her attention, and she looks up. A light tilt of her head tells me she's not done roasting me. As always.

"Thank you so much for coming over last night. I needed it more than you know. Thank you for taking Coop out. And thank you for being such an amazing friend. I don't deserve you."

My best friend sighs and puts her hands on the magazine. "You're just lucky I love you. It's the only reason I tolerate your crap."

"I know." I smile, covering her hand with mine. "Is there anything I can do for you?"

"I have so many ideas," she murmurs with a suggestive smirk. "How about you start with breakfast?"

"Are pancakes with strawberry jam good enough for you?"

"If you also treat me to one of your delicious desserts, I'll be in heaven," she replies, and her melodic laughter fills the kitchen. Shaking my head, I stand up from my chair and go to the fridge. If anything, I love baking. It always helps me clear my head.

"WHAT ARE YOU READING?" I ask, setting a mug of steaming coffee in front of Nevaeh. She takes it and pushes the magazine toward me, grabbing a pancake from the plate on the counter. The second I lower my gaze to the article, I purse my lips.

"I saw your dad's name and decided to buy it. You didn't tell me your photos would be published in *Sports Today*."

"I forgot," I mutter, quickly skimming Dad's interview and checking out the pictures of my family: Mom and Dad, my twin siblings Ethan and Emma, and me. An idyllic image for everyone to admire.

My dad, Logan Jones, retired a long time ago, but his legacy lives on. He has a perfect reputation—a legendary quarterback who brought three Super Bowl championships to his team, a successful kids' coach, a loyal husband, and an incredible father. I love him, and I'll be forever grateful to him and Mom for everything they've done for me and my brother and sister. And yet, he's also the reason I moved to California from Philadelphia. I'm tired of living in his shadow, tired of the high expectations people put on me because of him and my past. At twenty-five, I want to succeed on my own, without his patronage. And articles like this aren't helping.

"How is that possible? It's *Sports Today*, one of the biggest sports magazines in the US!" Nev exclaims, and I pin her with my stare. She quickly sets her mug on the table, her blue eyes narrowed. "I always forget *this* is your normal. I have no clue what it means to have a family like yours."

I close the magazine and lean back against my chair. "You can either enjoy your life and do whatever you want, as the twins do, or you can try to be the perfect kid with perfect grades and all the possible and impossible achievements in sports, in arts, and even in chess. If you pick the first option, your life will be amazing. But if you're stupid like me, you'll be constantly held to some unrealistic standard, and your image of ambitious overachiever will be admired by all your teachers and your friends' parents...while you'll hate every fucking day of your life."

"Until one day you decide to rebel, and everything comes crashing down and no one knows what to do with you," Nevaeh says gently, and I smile at her, nodding. She's the only person in my life who knows absolutely everything about me. Just like I know everything about her. The bond we share is beyond precious, and over years of friendship, it's forged into something out of this world. Meeting her on my first day of college was a blessing. "Too bad you needed to destroy yourself to realize no one is to blame except you."

"I'm learning. It's a long process."

"Too slow. I can't even imagine what happens if you—"

"Not going to happen, Nev. I'm done with this shit. I promised you that time was the last."

"I hope so. The shattered-to-pieces version of you is no fun, and I'm afraid the fourth time would be just too much," she tells me, and I exhale loudly, letting my shoulders drop. My hand instantly flies to my mouth, and I gnaw at the cuticle of my thumb. The memories become too vivid in my head. Asher, the parties, the hangovers. "Angie."

I blink and focus my attention on my best friend. My teeth are still deep in my skin.

"You're doing it again." Her voice is soft, but stern notes make me drop my hand. I grip the table until my knuckles turn white, my jaw set hard. "Are you sure you're alright? I haven't seen you chew on your skin in a while. I thought Dr. Nichols helped you with this."

"He did." I let go of the table and show her my hands. "It's the first time in three months," I drawl, and Nevaeh arches one eyebrow at me. "Asher has been sending me messages again."

"Go to the police."

"And say what? My ex is texting me, wanting to know if I want to fuck him? I'm more than sure they aren't going to do anything unless he *really* starts bothering me."

"He *is* bothering you, Angie. Do you want him to start showing up wherever you go? Considering his usual timing, it won't take him too long." She crosses her arms over her chest, her lips pursed in a tight pout. "Why don't you find yourself a boyfriend?" I snicker, and she rolls her eyes at me. "Or just someone who will make your narcissistic ex back off? He needs to think you're taken. He's too chicken to actually fight for you, and too self-centered to accept that there could be someone better than his cheating ass."

"A relationship is the last thing I need right now," I counter, getting another eye roll from my best friend. "But I'll think about it. Maybe I can hire someone to go with me to a high-profile event or something."

"When was the last time you looked at yourself in the mirror? You're gorgeous. You don't need to hire a man to go on a date with you. You'll have plenty of guys lined up to date you if you just go with me to one of the parties my boss is throwing next week."

"Maybe." I take a sip of my tea. "Can we just enjoy our breakfast? Pretty please?"

Nevaeh nods, motions to her mouth as if she's zipping it, and then snatches another pancake from the plate. Her eyes are full of mischief; she's already planning my surrender. And who knows, maybe it's what I need.

"DID someone buy the house next to yours?" Nev asks as we approach her car. A shiny black Lexus RX Hybrid is parked near my Aventador, and I peek at my neighbor's house. It's dark and quiet, but it doesn't mean no one is inside. It's only seven p.m. I don't turn on the lights this early either.

"Yeah. I met them a few days ago. A prick and his girl."

Nevaeh unlocks her car, puts her bag in the backseat, and then concentrates her attention on me. "A prick?"

"It's a long story. I'll tell you about it some other time."

"Is he at least hot?"

"No." I shake my head, taking a step back and glancing at the house next to mine. "But his girlfriend is beautiful."

"If this is your new neighbor, then I don't agree with you," Nev says in a breathy whisper, and I snap my head in her direction. She's not looking at me. Her dilated pupils are focused on something behind my back.

Slowly, I turn around, and my gaze instantly clashes with a heavy glare. My neighbor is scowling at me. His cheeks are bulging as he grinds his teeth together. Is that his usual facial expression, or does he just scowl when he sees me? Something is telling me the second option is way closer to reality.

I frown. My fingertips are itching again. As I drag my gaze down his body, I finally realize what Nev is staring at. The guy has only shorts on. His rippled muscles are glistening with sweat, and his six-pack flexes with each step he takes. His running shoes and the backward hat on his curly hair make me think he's coming back from a run. And dammit, his legs are to die for—strong and muscular. All my annoyance suddenly disappears.

Jesus, what sports is he into?

Drake

THREE

sneaky

"Why are you going for a run this late?" My sister is breathless. I fix my earbuds to hear her better.

"Why did you take Maya for a walk this late? It's almost ten p.m. in Michigan," I tease, and she sighs loudly. Tenderness swells in my chest, and I slow down, starting to walk instead. "She couldn't sleep again?"

"She's teething, and it's exhausting."

"Move in with me. Come here to Santa Clara, and move in with me. I'll help you with anything you need." The words rush out. It's the plea I've been making every time we speak since her dickhead boyfriend packed his things and left. I hate the idea of her being all alone.

"Drake, you just moved to Santa Clara yourself. You need time to settle in, to adjust to your life in a new city, to your new team. Maya and I will be a burden," Layla says quietly.

"I already moved into my own house. The team didn't make it into the playoffs, so I'll have a lot of free time on my hands. The season is almost over. We can adjust to the city together. We can look—"

"Moments like this make me regret calling you," my sister exclaims, raising her voice an octave higher. "Mom and Dad are helping me. Yes, they can't be here every day, but when Mom has a spare minute, she's always at my place. Dad takes Maya for a stroll when he has days off. I'm doing fine, and I want the same for you. Start living. Go on dates, have some fun. Be the big brother I always looked up to."

She's deflecting. It's so obvious I want to laugh, though this situation is rather sad. Layla is still hoping Eli will return. That he'll come around, realize how much he loves her and their daughter. He won't. The last I heard, he was chilling with his friends in Vegas, and a new chick was hanging off his arm every night. That musician was never the right person for my little sister. Too bad she wasn't able to see it.

I turn my hat backward and wipe sweat off my forehead. There's no point in getting into another argument with her. Layla isn't ready to listen to anyone—not me, and not even her best friend. I try to be optimistic, but so far it's been one big disappointment. I miss her and Maya terribly.

"Fun, I can do," I reassure her after an awkward pause, and my sister giggles. "The barbecue on Friday was great, even if I never thought I'd be making friends with California Mustangs players. Colt never really mentioned he was hanging out with the football crowd."

"Tell me more?" she asks, and I grin. She definitely sounds more like my little sister, as curious and nosy as she's always been.

I talk to Layla for a while and hang up only because Maya starts crying again. The sound makes my skin itch and my heart ache, so I turn up the volume. "Ride" by Twenty One Pilots resonates in my ears. Taking a deep breath, I swivel around and take off, running back toward my house. My plan for tonight is simple: have a hot shower and find something bingeworthy on TV. A very pleasant evening... even if it's a lonely one also.

I need to start making new friends. It's not that easy at twenty-seven, but I don't want the Thompsons to babysit me all the time. Ava is already having too much fun poking and taunting me with her little jokes. If I keep hanging out at their place, I won't hear the end of it.

Even from afar I see a white BMW convertible still parked near my car, though that's not what makes me frown. My neighbor is here. I recognize her immediately, even if she stands with her back to me. Her dark brown hair is collected into a bun on top of her head, giving me a perfect view of her neck. My gaze easily trails down her shoulder blades and lower, to her ass in tight black pants. She's tall and fit, and curvy in all the right places. *And fucking hell, what am I thinking?*

My first time meeting her turned into my worst nightmare, making me relive memories from my childhood in graphic detail. My neighbor's dog breaking free from the leash and charging at me when I was throwing the ball in my driveway flooded my mind that day. Although the scar on my calf has faded and is barely visible now, I still remember the sharp pain from the Rottweiler's teeth sinking into my skin. I'm not afraid of dogs anymore, but hers made me lose my shit for the first time in my adult life. I've never been that rude to anyone, especially a woman, but that day, I didn't even care what was coming out of my mouth. The fear her dog planted affected me way more than I wanted to admit.

I need to apologize...but I don't really want to. At least, not now.

As if feeling me watching her, she slowly whirls around. My scowl deepens as I grit my teeth. There's a blonde behind her, but I don't pay her any attention. My staring competition with my neighbor is way more important. I don't blink, trying to pierce her with my eyes. Not successfully, because her gaze drops to my chest and abs. The second it slides down my legs, I pinch my brows together. What is she doing?

"Well, hello there." The girl behind my neighbor steps aside and heads in my direction, diverting my focus to her. Her blue eyes roam over my face and down my body, and a playful smirk forms on her full mouth. She blocks my way and halts me in my tracks. "I didn't know my friend finally got herself a neighbor. A very handsome neighbor." She extends her palm to me. "I'm Nevaeh."

I take her hand, noticing how comically small it is in mine. "Nice to meet you, Nevaeh. I'm Drake."

"You too, Drake." She lets our handshake linger, not breaking eye contact. "Have you been in Santa Clara for long?"

"A month," I reply, taking a step back and pushing my hands in my shorts pockets. Her look is messy. Her baggy clothes hide her body, and yet it's so easy to see how gorgeous she is. "Moved here all the way from Michigan."

"Really? I've never been to Michigan before. Me and my friend over there are Philadelphia girls, but we're loving our life in California." She looks over her shoulder. "Right, Angie?"

"Right," my neighbor grumbles. And suddenly I want to stay and talk to this blonde...just to spite her friend and keep her quiet.

"So, you love running," Nevaeh states, her eyes tracing the lines of my body. "And probably going to the gym. Did you move here for work?"

"You could say that." I don't elaborate, keeping things to myself.

Some of the guys I play with would've used this opportunity to brag about their career in the NHL, to show off and feed their ego. I've never done that. Not because I don't have anything to brag about or I feel I'm not good enough. No. I just believe my game is the best evidence of my talent. Even when it comes to getting a beautiful girl in my bed. Been there, done that, and I'm not interested. I want them to want me for me, not because they crave a life full of fancy events, publicity, and money.

Nevaeh is stunning, but she also reminds me of my ex. Her flirtatious smile and the pinkish-blonde hair cascading down her shoulders make her look way too much like Janelle, and it's too soon. My level of trust dropped below zero after that breakup, and I'm not ready to go down that road again. Not in the foreseeable future, for sure.

"Well, Drake, I hope to see you around. It was a pleasure."

"The pleasure is all mine." I glance at my neighbor, and our eyes meet for a split second before I look away. "Bye, Nevaeh."

She nods and strolls back to her friend. I look ahead as I walk toward my house. The voices behind me grow louder. The words "hot," "gorgeous," and "sexy butt" make me smile. I'd pay a lot of money to see the look on my neighbor's face. Is she angry? Exasperated? Or just annoyed? We're definitely not each other's favorites, so I highly doubt she liked Nevaeh acting friendly with me.

Maybe I should've stayed, should've made an effort. Maybe I should've asked for Nevaeh's number. I'd love to play on her friend's nerves after her behavior the day we met.

Damn, this isn't me. I'm not mean to people. I don't use them for my benefit. And I don't hold grudges. Being cordial with the woman next door is way better than being her enemy. At least, I hope so.

Sitting on the couch, I stare at the TV, scrolling through the list of shows. Nothing catches my attention, and I sigh, feeling defeated. Why is it so hard to find something to watch? It was never a problem before.

I turn off the TV, toss the remote onto the couch, and grab my laptop from the side table. Unlocking it, I open my browser and hesitate. I have no clue what I'm doing, or what I want to do, for that matter. It's just plain stu—

My fingers freeze, hovering over the keyboard. It would be sneaky and unfair, but do I care about that? I chew on the inside of my cheek for a moment, trying to convince myself to change my mind. There's a high probability I'm not going to find anything. And truthfully, I don't need to know anything about her. It's not like I'm going to use the information...but fuck it.

Layla isn't the only curious Benson in our family.

I remember what Ava told me before, about my neighbor and her dad, the famous Philadelphia quarterback Logan Jones. I quickly type "Evangelina Jones" into the search bar. The second the results appear, my face becomes long. Talk about YOLO—my neighbor follows that motto to a tee.

The more I read about her, the more mixed feelings I have. She's the same age as my sister, and what she also has in common with Layla is her taste in men. All her boyfriends were musicians, and every single one of them did her dirty. Cheating, public arguments at clubs, her checking her last boyfriend into rehab. It doesn't make any sense, considering the family she has. Is she on a rebelling spree or what?

This girl isn't as simple as I thought. The change in her look from four months ago is astonishing. And it's not even about the tattoos on her left arm or the weight loss. The gleam has faded from her eyes, and they've become glassy and lifeless. As if life drained all the color from her. Something changed, and now I really want to apologize to her.

Just because.

Drake

FOUR

just what i needed... not

I PUSH MY BAG AND MY STICK INTO MY TRUNK AND CLOSE it. Practice today was exhausting but great. Coach is very attentive to team cohesion, and it pays off. I had my doubts, joining this late in the season, but so far, all my worries have been pointless. Being on the same team with my best friend also makes things easier.

"Any plans for tonight?" Thompson asks, leaning against his car. His brown eyes are trained on me as he drags his palm down his beard.

"Bath to soak my sore muscles, and then sleep. We have two more games before the season is over. I want to be in my best shape."

"You're playing awesome," Roman Pashkevich, the right defenseman, comments. "I don't like to make predictions, but I'm confident next season will be great for us with you on board."

"Think we can make it to the playoffs again?" Colton folds his arms across his chest. "Winning the Stanley Cup would be a dream come true, because playing in the finals was definitely a once-in-a-lifetime experience."

"With this guy?" Pashkevich chuckles, nodding at me. His blue eyes are scanning me from head to toe. "I think our chances are good. Who knew your best friend would be such a cool addition?"

"I did." Thompson and I exchange a glance, grinning at one another. "I've been saying it for years."

"Yeah, yeah. I've only been here for two seasons, and I've heard that story like...a thousand times already." Roman laughs heartily. "We just need your goalie friend from the Hawks to make the dream team complete, right?"

"If only it were that simple, Rodgers would've been here a long time ago," Colton says, and then looks down at his watch. "I better go. I promised Ava I'd pick up Michael from his swimming class. She rescheduled it for today so they can come to the game tomorrow night."

"I love when your son comes to cheer for us. He's something else." Pashkevich opens his car door, sliding inside. "The biggest fan of the California Thunders, and me."

"He loves you too, especially when you teach him new words in Belarusian." Thompson grins, and then gestures at me. "Though now the competition is tough. Michael loves his Uncle Drake."

"That was cruel, Thompson." Roman starts the engine, looking between us with a broad smile on his clean-shaven face. "But I know how to win. I'm naturally good at it."

Pashkevich's car takes off, leaving Colton and me alone. We share a snort and simultaneously climb into our cars. I can't believe that guy's ego. It's bigger than his fucking home country, but he still manages to be absolutely amazing. From time to time.

Thompson rolls down his window. "See you tomorrow, Drake."

"See you, Colt," I reply and start the engine, watching his car drive away.

Two more games, and then I'll get one of the longest breaks I've had since I graduated college. It'll be a good opportunity to get used to the city, to meet new people and make some friends. I definitely hope I'll be able to persuade my sister to come live with me, but I need to be patient with her. Maybe when she knows I'm settling into my new place just fine, it'll be easier for her to make a decision.

I drive home with "High Hopes" by Panic! at the Disco booming. I hum along, nodding to the rhythm. My mood after being on the ice is always light, no matter how rough things are or how tired I feel. There's something freeing about it. Hockey is the best fix for all my racing thoughts and worries. The second I step on the ice, my mind shuts down, and being a team player is the only thing I focus on. It was even a cure for the worst heartbreak of my life. I'll be forever grateful to my dad for taking me to my first hockey game. It was love at first sight, one that stayed with me throughout the years. It's a blessing.

I park near my neighbor's yellow Aventador, then jump out and get my bag with my gear and my hockey stick from the trunk. Rolling back my shoulders to ease the tension in my muscles, I head to my house. A bath at this point is a must. I won't survive without soaking my body in hot water.

As I'm nearing the porch, my neighbor's front door opens, and she steps outside with her dog on a leash. Well, it looks like she learned her lesson. I absentmindedly slow down, watching her lock the door and twitch the handle to make sure it's secure. I could ignore her and go inside, but I could also use this chance to apologize. It's not like I'll die if I say I'm sorry. At least, it might help make things less awkward next time we see each other.

She turns around, noticing me. Her face stays emotionless, and I realize she's not so easy to read when she's not fuming. Holding my gaze, she walks down the stairs and stops only when she's a few feet away from me. I stop too, keeping my eyes on her face.

"Hey." Her voice is soft and melodic, and quite different from the way it sounded when we first met.

"Hey," I echo her cautiously.

"You probably hate my guts, and you have every right to be pissed at me for not controlling my dog. But I still wanted to say I'm sorry. How Cooper acted toward you that day was absolutely unacceptable, and I should've never let him out of the house without a leash, even if he never did anything bad before. A positive experience in the past doesn't mean there will never be failures." She pauses, taking a deep breath. "Can we please move on?"

I shift from one leg to the other, fixing my bag on my shoulder. "Absolutely. It'd be nice to bury the hatchet," I say, and a smile spreads across her puffy lips. A small dimple on her right cheek draws my attention. "And you're not the only one who needs to apologize. The man you met that day isn't me. I was an insufferable jerk to you, and I don't talk like that to anyone. Ever. So, really, I'm sorry for how I treated you and how I spoke to you. You didn't deserve it."

She wraps the leash around her right hand, tugging the dog to her leg, and steps closer. The scent of her perfume reaches my nostrils, and I inhale, enjoying how nice it smells. There are notes of cinnamon and vanilla, and something flowery, but I can't quite figure out what it is.

"I'm Evangelina."

I blink, refocusing on her face and then on her outstretched hand. I take it, my fingers circling hers.

"Drake." I shake her hand. The smoothness of her skin against mine makes me feel hot. The handshake is firm, but at the same time incredibly gentle. "Nice to meet you."

I take a step back, fix my bag again, and then drop my eyes to my neighbor's dog. There's no trace of hostility. On the contrary; he wags his tail, watching me. "You said his name is Cooper, right?" I ask, and his tail moves faster. "Looks like he doesn't think you're in danger in my company."

"He's wagging his tail," Evangelina mutters quietly. Her eyebrows knit together as she stares at her dog. "He rarely does that." She looks up at me. Her green eyes, framed by thick black eyelashes, remind me of a forest during a rainy day in the middle of summer. A deep and mesmerizing color. "I'm so confused right now."

"If you're confused, then I totally don't know what to think of your dog. First he scares me to death, now he looks at me like I'm his best buddy."

Evangelina gasps, and I bring my eyes back to her face.

"Oh my God, I should've figured it out earlier." She shakes her head, and her ponytail bounces left and right. "Coop thought you were him because of how you look...and then he ran at you, realized he was wrong, and he... Jesus, I feel like the biggest idiot. His reasons were all there, and I was dumb not to piece them together."

"Care to explain?"

She points her finger at me. "You look like my dad. I mean, your height and your build. And Cooper adores him. My only guess is he thought you were him when he noticed you that day. And when he saw you weren't Dad, he became hostile and aggressive."

"When you put it that way, it makes sense. I think," I say, grinning, and her face lights up with a smile. "Well, I'm glad he doesn't hate me for whatever reason."

Evangelina raises her hand, tucks her hair behind her ear, and looks at her dog. I slowly drag my eyes down her body. She's wearing a sports bra, black leggings with a red stripe, and red running shoes. She's dressed like she's going for a run, and everything about her makes my skin warmer, sending a rush of heat to my dick.

Damn. The last thing I need is a boner for my neighbor.

"Drake?" I snap out of my thoughts and meet her gaze. "Any plans for tonight?"

"Not really, unless taking a bath and going to sleep early counts. I have a game tomorrow."

Evangelina licks her bottom lip, and my enchanted eyes follow the motion. "Well, have a nice evening then." She backtracks and tilts her head to the hockey stick in my hand. "Good luck with your game."

"Thanks. Bye, Evangelina." I step aside and start climbing stairs.

"Bye, Drake." She veers right and strolls away from our houses with Cooper in tow.

Unlocking the door, I throw a glance behind my back and instantly regret it. My neighbor has a perfect ass in addition to her feminine body, and now I have a boner to deal with. Just what I needed...not.

Angie

FIVE

were you googling me?

Going for an early morning run is one of my favorite things to do. The air isn't too hot, there are way less people on the streets, and the sounds of the city are quieter. It's the best way to clear my head, to shoo away the remnants of sleep, or even just to collect myself and prepare for a long and busy day. And today is promising to be exactly that. Long. Busy. And so boring. I hate when I need to deal with paperwork. It's the worst.

At my dessert shop, I don't mind helping in the kitchen, being a cashier, or even serving customers. Literally anything where I don't need to sit and read documents, sign contracts, or check the bills. I'm constantly on the go. My parents even have an inside joke about me. They say I have a family of hedgehogs up my ass, always pushing me to move, not letting me spend even a minute of my time sitting. It's not like that, but the narrative is kinda truthful.

I slowly come to a stop and put my hands on my knees, catching my breath and trying to calm my heartbeat. I should've brought Cooper with me instead of going for a walk with him an hour ago. My stomach grumbles, and I purse my lips in an annoyed pout. Why did I think separating Coop's walk and my run was a good idea? I should've stuck to my usual routine, dammit.

My head bobs back, and I close my eyes, turning my face toward the sun. The rays gently warm my skin, and little by little I'm smiling. The light breeze gets caught in my hair, my ponytail swinging back and forth and tickling my neck. My grin grows bigger, and I begin to lip-synch to the song exploding in my ears. Finding positivity in even the smallest things always helps me fix my mood.

Being happy is an art, and I'm learning how to master it.

Opening my eyes, I pivot to my right and take a step forward, intending to continue my run—not successfully, because I instantly bump into a solid male chest. I stumble back, and my mouth opens as I gasp, recognizing my neighbor.

"Jesus, what are you doing here?" I ask, pulling out my earbuds.

He presses his lips together, trying hard not to smile. His eyes are failing him, twinkling with mischief. "Same as you." He gestures around. "I went for a run."

And you ran into me? What are the odds? Though, with my luck, I shouldn't be surprised at all.

I smirk, reaching for my phone and switching off my music. "Sorry, that was a weird question." I stash my phone and my AirPods back in my belt bag and focus on Drake. "How are you?"

"Good. I'm officially on vacation, so I have plenty of free time." He turns his hat around backward. "Trying to figure out my routine for the next few months while also staying in shape. Fun times."

Drake rolls his lips together, wiping sweat off his forehead. He taps his right foot on the ground, one of his hands pressed to his abs as he evens out his breathing. His white T-shirt makes a good contrast to his sun-kissed skin. A smattering of small freckles on his nose and cheeks make him look boyish. Playful, even.

"What about you? Where is Cooper?"

"Coop already had his morning walk." I fix my ponytail, tying my red scrunchie tighter. "I was heading home."

"Mind if I join you? I was on my way home too."

I shrug. "Why not? Though, honestly I'm tired, so I'm planning to just walk."

"Okay."

We start to stroll in the direction of our houses. I keep silent, thinking about the meeting with my accountant in two hours. My dessert shop is doing great, and I'm looking forward to getting the sales report from her. Yet the competition is strong, and if I want to stay afloat, I need to be smarter and more creative. That's why I'm having a quick lunch with my marketing specialist to discuss the strategy I came up with. That meeting is probably the part of my day I'm looking forward to the most.

"I've been meaning to ask. Your friend Nevaeh..." I whip my head toward him, my brows pinching together. "Why are you looking at me like that?"

"Like what?" I deadpan as we turn the corner. The honking of car horns intensifies. Nev is a night owl, so the mention of her at eight a.m. on a Friday feels almost foreign to me.

"Like I said something incredibly stupid." Drake suddenly places his hand on my lower back. "Sorry, but let's just switch places." He guides me to my right, taking my place on the sidewalk, closer to the road. "That's better."

My mouth hangs open, and I gape at this guy beside me. He knows the sidewalk rule? I don't remember anyone, except my brother and my dad, who ever exchanged places with me. My head starts spinning. It's all too much for this early in the morning.

"Okay, Evangelina, I give up. Forget I said anything. You look weirder and weirder by the second, and I honestly am starting to wonder if I did the right thing asking to join you."

"Stop saying I look weird," I tell him sternly and follow it with a smack on his forearm.

"But you do." Drake laughs. "You're spacing out and not paying attention to where you're going."

"I kinda didn't expect the question about Nev." I look him up and down with a knowing grin. I've yet to meet a guy who's immune to her charms. "You're not exactly her type, but she thinks you're hot."

"I heard that." A smug smile crosses his face, and I can barely hold myself back from rolling my eyes. "She said I have a sexy butt."

"And also a huge ego, from what I can see," I say sarcastically. "Is that common for hockey players? Or is it just a personal thing? Trying to figure out the pattern, you know."

"The pattern? It sounds like you think you know what to expect from a jock, no matter which sport he's into. I don't judge anyone based on my past experiences with people like them. It's kinda hopeless, because everyone is different, and it's strange to make assumptions without knowing their story."

No matter the sport, they're all the same once they know who my father is. No exceptions.

The change in my mood is drastic, and I stop smiling. My index finger circles my thumb, and I want to get rid of this raw and damaged skin. I ball my fists to stop myself from gnawing at my cuticle again. "What did you want to know about Nevaeh?"

Drake frowns, and his steps slow down. "Did I say something to upset you? I thought we were just—"

"Don't you have a girlfriend? The girl I saw you with, Ava?"

"Ava?" he asks. A puzzled look crosses his face. I nod, arching an eyebrow as I wait for him to answer. "She's my best friend's wife, and my sister's best friend. We're not together."

"Oh, okay. Well then, Nevaeh is single, if that's what you wanted to know."

"It's not—"

"Then what?" I mutter in annoyance, stumbling forward and landing awkwardly on the ground. My ankle twists, and pain strikes through my whole leg like lightning in the night sky. I close my eyes, shutting my mouth to bottle up the scream. "Fuck."

"Hey, what's wrong?" He wraps his palm around my elbow, helping me find my balance, and I take a hesitant step forward. I wince; the pain only intensifies. "Did you sprain your ankle?"

"Fuck if I know." I open my eyes, biting the inside of my cheek. "Sorry, that was rude. I don't know, Drake. It feels like it, but..."

My neighbor lets go of my hand and turns his back to me. "Hop on."

"What?" My eyes are probably the size of saucers as I watch Drake in astonishment.

"I'm giving you a piggyback ride. Have you never had one before?" he asks, lowering himself in front of me as he bends his knees slightly. "Just grab my shoulders and hop on. I'll do the rest," he instructs me, sneaking a glance at me. "It'll be fine. I promise."

I'm probably losing my mind, but I take a step forward and wrap my arms around his shoulders. He reaches straight back, hooks his arms underneath my legs, and slowly rises. My chest is pressed tightly to his broad back, and I feel every muscle move as he slowly ambles toward our houses. It's intimate, and a horde of tingles spreads across my skin. Good ones. They allow my body to relax a little, even if my brain tries to take control of the situation to make me feel more distant.

"A sprained ankle can hurt like hell, and you'll need to ice it to limit swelling, but overall I think you'll be good. I'll help you. I've definitely had one."

His voice reverberates through my body, sliding deep under my skin to my very nerves. I lock my hands against his chest, digging my nails into my skin. I'm not used to guys talking to me like that, so it feels almost fake...while it's the realest thing that's happened to me in a long time. Just a man who takes care of me without any ulterior motives. Without wanting anything to happen between us. Just because he's a good guy.

But wait...will he help me? What's going on? And why am I nodding at him? Did I lose my sense of reality along with spraining my ankle? It looks like a possibility at this point.

"Did you have plans for today?"

"Yeah, I need to see my accountant and my marketing specialist," I drawl, keeping my eyes in front of me. This closeness isn't good for me. It feels foreign, makes me nervous. "Why?"

"You're going to let me check your ankle, and I'll tell you if you need to reschedule your meetings."

So authoritative. Is he my dad or what?

I snort. "I don't think that's for you to decide. I'll go to the dessert shop, meet with Amelie to discuss the marketing strategy, and then I'll go see the doctor. Only in that order."

"The internet says you're twenty-five, but you sound like a five-year-old. Wait, no—my friends' kid is almost five, and he's more reasonable than you."

Our cars come into view as we near our houses. I should be sighing in relief, but I'm too stunned to speak. My jaw drops, and I'm unable to produce even a sound. There are so many things I want to say, so many things I want to ask. But I end up with the most pathetic one: "Were you googling me?"

Drake climbs the stairs to my house. Cooper's huffs and barks reach my ears instantly. I slowly unlock my hands, sliding my arms down his shoulders as he lowers me to my feet. He turns around and extends his hand to me.

"Let me help you."

I look at him from under my lashes, my lips pressed together tightly. I etch my eyebrows together and tilt my head, eyeing him suspiciously.

"Did you google me, Drake?"

His ears suddenly turn red as he shifts his weight from one leg to the other. Taking a deep breath, he crosses his arms over his chest. "And what if I did?"

Right. Another cocky asshole.

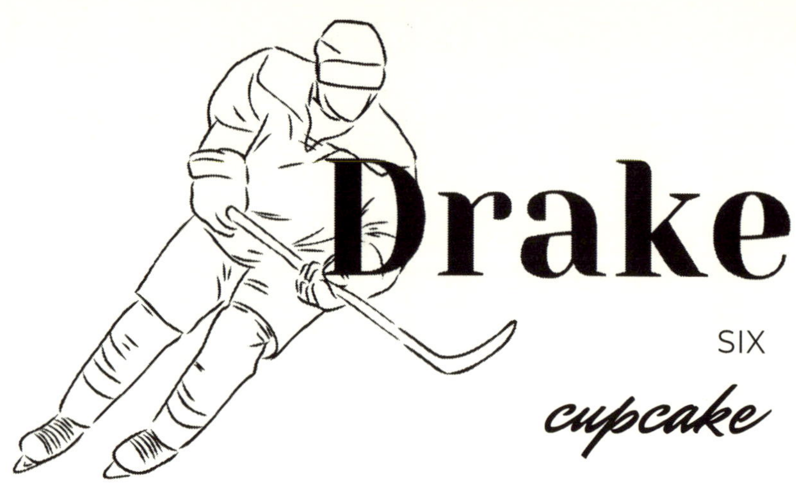

Drake

SIX

cupcake

Admitting I googled her wasn't my brightest idea. But her demanding tone sent a chill down my spine, and I couldn't keep quiet any longer. It's kind of a dick move on one hand, but on the other hand, she's a public figure, and I don't feel bad about doing it. Anyone can google "Drake Benson" and read stuff about my early years in hockey, my professional career, and even my dating history. It's not fucking secret material, stacked in the depths of the FBI. I did nothing wrong.

"Was it entertaining?" Evangelina asks, mirroring my stance and crossing her arms over her chest. "Did you have a good laugh reading all the gossip about me?"

Laugh? There was nothing funny about it. If anything, I felt so fucking sad for her, a sadness I didn't expect would be possible.

"I only read about your family, about your dad," I lie, not wanting to admit I read way more.

Her scowl becomes more prominent, and I suddenly realize that might be an issue. Sports guys and mentions of her father are triggers for her. Why?

"Evangelina, look, I'm sorry. I only did it because I couldn't figure you out. No other reason." I offer her a smile, dropping my hands to my sides and then sliding them into my back pockets. "It was just curiosity."

I shouldn't be staring at her like I am now. And yet her dark green eyes look tempestuous while she continues to glare at me. Her nostrils flare, and she presses her lips together. The bottom one is puffier, and it makes her mouth look fuller than it is. She's very different from the girls I've been with in the past eight years, but I can admit one thing easily: she's stunning. And I kinda like looking at her.

She breathes out a long, exasperated sigh and drops her arms to her sides too. "Whatever."

I extend my hand again, but she ignores it, limping to the front door. Following her closely, I let my eyes coast over her body. She definitely works out. Her sleek, toned back is the best evidence of hours spent in the gym. Her defined and narrow waist flows effortlessly into round, curvy hips. She's sporting an absolutely mouthwatering ass and legs that are so long, my mind drifts to a totally indecent image... of her legs resting on my shoulders.

Damn it.

I should probably start using my brain instead of my other head. It'll save me from a lot of troubles. Especially when it comes to my neighbor. I don't think she's a very levelheaded person. "Fiery" and "passionate" are two words that come to mind. Definitely not "calm" and "sensible".

"Coop, let me in," Evangelina says with a hiss, trying to push past her dog. Cooper doesn't even budge, just presses his head into her leg to make her pet him. She groans, but she puts her palm between his ears and rubs his fur. "You're such a good boy, aren't you? Just happy to see me back home. Did you miss me?"

He barks, and I instantly tense, squaring my shoulders on instinct. Jesus Christ. One dog is all it takes for my fears to come back? This is not even fucking funny. I take a deep breath and exhale through my mouth, watching Evangelina and Cooper. The way this huge dog shows his affection toward his owner calms down my rapid heartbeat and evens my breathing. It must be nice coming home to someone who's always happy to see you. I've never experienced anything like that, not even with Janelle when we lived together. It says a lot about how miserable my dating life has been...without me even realizing it.

"Why are you still here?" I snap out of my thoughts and look down, meeting Evangelina's gaze. "I don't need your help."

"Let me see your ankle, and I'll leave."

"What part of 'I don't need your help' didn't you understand?" she grumbles, but she turns on her heel and takes a step forward. The pained whimper that springs from her mouth doesn't leave me any doubts. I roll my eyes and close the door, stepping inside. "I don't—"

Wrapping my arm around her waist, I pull her to my side. "You do. Stop fighting me on this, please. I'll help you and will be out of your hair in no time. I promise."

She stares at me from under furrowed brows for a moment, and then she nods. Draping a hand around my neck, she presses her hip to mine. The scent of her perfume envelopes us both, and I wonder how it's possible for someone to smell and look so nice after a run. It's fucking illegal, I swear.

"Where do you keep your first aid kit?" I ask, shooing away the impulse to look down at her cleavage. I'm here to help.

"In the kitchen." She points toward a hallway.

We cross the living room with Cooper following our every step, and she leads me into the kitchen. Hugging Evangelina's shoulders, I help her sit on a chair, then I step back and observe her. She bends down and takes off her sneaker and her sock, grimacing till it hits the floor. The corners of her mouth drop as she touches her ankle with her fingertips. She pinches her eyebrows together, closing one eye when she pokes at her ankle a bit harder.

"Dammit," she mutters, slowly straightening her back. "It hurts."

"Of course it does," I snort and earn a nasty look in my direction. "Can I?"

She huffs but stretches her leg in front of her. It takes all my willpower to hold back my laughter. She wouldn't appreciate it, and she would try to argue with me again. I don't need that, because I really want to help her.

I kneel in front of her and take her leg in my hands, gently examining the swollen area. It's nothing serious, from what I can see, but I still would prefer for her to stay home today. It'll heal rather quickly if she lets herself rest, icing it and wearing a bandage to provide compression.

"Well?" Evangelina asks, her voice sounding hoarse. "What's the verdict?"

"You sprained your ankle," I reply, my eyes roaming over her foot. Her toenails are painted red. Red nails, red sneakers, red scrunchie in her hair. At this point, I wouldn't be surprised if she likes wearing red lipstick too. I'm sure it's fitting for her. "Do you have some ice?"

"Yeah. Is that all?"

"You'll need to wrap some ice in a towel and keep it on your ankle for twenty minutes every two hours. Elevating your leg also helps, along with some tight bandages." I slowly put her leg on the floor and stand up, hovering over her. "I can help you with anything if you want—"

"No, thank you. I'll deal with all that on my own," she says. She keeps staring me in the eyes, and I hold her gaze, not even thinking about leaving. "What?"

"Promise me you won't go anywhere? That you'll cancel your plans?"

Evangelina shifts in her seat, freeing her hair and letting it spill over her shoulders. "People are counting on me. I can't let them down."

"You can, and you should." I crouch in front of her again, putting my hand on her knee for better balance. "I play hockey, and for several years it was one of my worst nightmares ever. Spraining my ankle. So simple, and so bad at the same time. Just give yourself a day to rest and you'll see how quickly you bounce back."

She lowers her gaze to my hand on her knee, chewing on the inside of her cheek. Her dog sits by my side; his eyes are trained on her. Strangely, I don't feel intimidated by his presence. As if having a dog around is the most natural thing in the world.

"Fine, I'll stay home. Just need to make a few calls to reschedule."

"Good." I stand up, glancing around her kitchen. "Do you have an elastic bandage in your first aid kit?"

"I don't think so. I've never needed one." Evangelina shrugs, twisting her lips into a scowl when she takes off her other sneaker.

"I'll bring you one," I say, and she looks up at me. "I have a few at home, so it's not a problem."

She hesitates, tucking strands of hair behind her ears. "Thank you, Drake."

"Don't mention it." I take a step back, then turn around. "I'll be back."

As I return to her house, I head to the kitchen, but I stop short when I find Evangelina in the living room. She's sitting on the couch, her leg propped up on the table in front of her. Her phone is pressed to her ear, and she's listening to someone talk. Cooper lifts his head, noticing me, and stands up from his dog bed. He slowly advances toward me. His tail wags slightly, and I extend my hand, rubbing the fur between his ears. His shiny, short fur is sleek and soft to the touch. His chocolate-brown eyes focus on me, and I don't feel even an ounce of fear. A huge difference from the first time we met.

"Thank you so much, Amelie.... Yeah, it's definitely unfortunate.... See you tomorrow. Bye." Evangelina ends the call and tosses her phone on the couch.

Our eyes meet for a moment, and I smile at her. She's way nicer than I thought, and it's a pleasant surprise.

"I think he likes me." I gesture at Cooper as I take my hand off his head. He steps away from me and goes back to his dog bed. "Would've never guessed it after our first encounter."

"He's an incredibly sweet dog, and I'm glad he's showing that to you now."

I nod, looking away from Cooper. Stepping forward, I lower my gaze to her leg on the table. There's a little towel wrapped around her ankle. "How does it feel now?"

"Way better. Your advice about the ice was the best."

"I've done this way too many times, especially in high school." I grin, extending the elastic bandage I brought for her. "Here. It'll help with compression."

"Thank you so much, Drake." She takes it and puts it on her lap, eyeing me with a smile on her face.

And just like that, I don't have any reason to stay.

"Did you reschedule your meetings for the day?"

"Yup. Luckily they both have time to meet me tomorrow. Though my lunch with Amelie will turn into quick coffee at my dessert shop."

I blink. "Dessert shop? *You* own a dessert shop?"

She frowns. "Now you sound way too judgy. Why can't I own a dessert shop?"

My eyes roam over her perfect figure, and I arch an eyebrow. "You don't look like someone who eats desserts."

"I not only eat desserts, I also love baking them," she exclaims, pointing her finger at the kitchen. "See those cupcakes on the kitchen counter? I made them."

I whip my head to where she's pointing, and my jaw drops. A plate of cupcakes is sitting on the kitchen island, and they look delicious. "Can I?"

"Be my guest. Let it be my thank-you for your help today."

Sauntering to the kitchen island, I examine the cupcakes. Some look like chocolate, others have colorful frosting. I reach for a chocolate one, pick it up, and carefully take a bite.

A thousand different flavors burst in my mouth, making me instantly close my eyes. It's sweet and mouthwatering. I devour the cupcake, forgetting where I am and what I was doing just a moment ago. This dessert is like an orgasm, and, damn—I already want another one.

"You can take a few if you want, or all of them." Her voice rips me out of my orgasmic oblivion. I swallow the last bite and meet Evangelina's gaze. "Did you like it?" she asks.

"I did." I stroll back to the couch. "It was tasty."

"Just tasty?"

I smirk, hiding my hands in my pockets. "Just tasty," I confirm and tilt my head toward her leg. "Don't forget to change the ice. Once you get rid of the swelling, you'll need to do some warm compresses or hold a heating pad to your ankle."

"Thanks, Doc. I'll manage. Dr. Google will know what to do. Don't worry." Evangelina mocks me with a taunting smile on her face.

I shake my head, padding out of the room. "Whatever you say, Cupcake." Stopping in the doorway, I look over my shoulder. She's gaping at me with her jaw dropped. "Bye, Evangelina."

When I walk out of her house, I can't stop myself from smiling as I go down the stairs. With Evangelina around, my vacation will be more fun than I initially thought. And I think I like it.

Angie

SEVEN

i need a boyfriend

"HONESTLY, THANK YOU SO MUCH FOR AGREEING TO MEET me today," I say to Amelie when she stands up from her chair. "I can't wait to see what you come up with."

"Your dessert shop is a banger," she comments, looking around with a smile. "I like coming here myself, and not just because you're my client. You've got delicious desserts, incredible employees, and an interior design that doesn't make me want to scratch my eyes out with how cute everything is."

I chuckle, leaning back in my chair. Amelie loves punk music, black clothes, and accessories that often make me wonder where she finds them because of how old-school they are. She has tattoos covering her neck and trailing down her shoulders and arms. Her platinum blonde hair is collected in a neat bun, revealing her shaved temples. A beautiful girl with a creative side that she isn't afraid to show.

"At first I was skeptical when you said you prepared a marketing plan for me to take a look at." Amelie meets my gaze, and I tilt my head, expecting her next words. "But I actually kinda like it. It shows how invested you are in your business and how much attention you pay to the things we talk about. When clients interfere with my job, it's usually a nightmare. With you? I believe we make a great team."

"Are you gently preparing me for when you show me the final proposal and I won't see any of my ideas there?" I ask, bursting into laughter. "I figured it out the second you rubbed the bridge of your nose when I showed my mockups for ads."

"That's why I enjoy working with you." She flashes me a smile and takes a step back. "I'd love to stay longer, but I have another meeting in thirty."

"Of course." I stand up from my chair and give her a brief hug. "Bye, Amelie."

"Bye, Evangelina." She kisses my cheek and strolls to the door, throwing a wink to my cashier, Alana, on her way out. "Bye, beautiful."

Quirking an eyebrow, I watch Alana's cheeks go red. *Interesting*. I slowly come closer and prop my hip against the counter, leaning on my elbow. Silence stretches between us, and only the customers' chatter fills the space.

"Spill," I urge.

Alana snickers, looking at the ceiling. "You're impossible, Evangelina."

I press my hand to my chest, gasp loudly, and knit my brows together, feigning offense. "What did I do to deserve that? I'm only ever nice to you."

"And also nosy," she adds, setting her elbows on the counter and inching toward my face. "I think I like your marketing lady."

"I think my marketing lady likes you too," I whisper knowingly. "She never shows her affection if she's not interested."

Alana bites her bottom lip, gawking at me in silence. "Do you think I'm her type? She hooked up with your best friend, and Nevaeh is a fucking goddess."

"I'll pass the compliment on to Nev, but in all honesty, you're focusing on the wrong thing. They hooked up, and that's all there was to it. We all hung out a few times after that, and if I didn't know, I'd have never guessed something happened between those two." I put my hand on hers. "If you like her, go for it. You'll never know if someone is your type or not until you try."

Her dark brown eyes roam over my face, and then she nods. "You're a gem, Evangelina. Thank you so much for this pep talk. I needed it."

"Always." I push myself away from the counter and straighten my back, stepping aside to let a couple take my place.

I head back to my table, looking around. An open-concept space combines the industrial style with the welcoming aura of a cozy shop. The vintage pendant lights hanging from the high ceilings cast a warm glow over the place. The walls are covered with artistic graffiti and eye-catching murals.

Against one wall is an exposed brick backdrop with shelves of books of different genres, from children's books to thrillers to romance. There are plush leather booths, wooden tables, and sleek metal stools. The whole place is painted in rusty red, earthy brown, and neutral gray colors. It has a soul, charismatic and sometimes witty, and I love everything about it.

As soon as I hear the couple ordering margarita-inspired cupcakes, my memories instantly drift to my neighbor. The guy is a mystery to me. I have no clue what's on his mind most of the time, but my hesitance has nothing to do with him. I'm not used to trusting jocks. My gut instincts are on high alert when he's around, but it's looking more and more like a false alarm.

There's something different about Drake...and I can't say I don't like it.

I stop in my tracks. The reality of this situation is dawning on me. All my years of experience with athletes, pieces of my broken heart and the buckets of tears I've cried, are disappearing from my mind just because one man was kind to me? It sounds like a joke. I know better than to trust a dude blindly, without even getting to know him.

And why the hell do I need to get to know him? This is insanity, and all goes back to my past, to me allowing my exes to treat me like dirt. It's the only explanation I have for my sudden interest in him. The guy was just kind enough to help me with my sprained ankle.

I slowly limp to the chair and plop down onto it. Taking my phone from my pocket, I unlock it and type a message to Nevaeh. We had plans to go out tonight, but my ankle is clearly saying "fuck no" with how swollen it is again.

ME:

hey babes. I'm staying in :(my ankle is killing me

NEV:

what do you mean you're staying in? The party tonight is going to be amazeballs. I need you there

NEV:

hey

ME:

I won't be able to dance. Come to a party to just sit? No thanks

NEV:

your sprained ankle won't be in the way if you're going to have sweaty, hot sex

ME:

I'm not going to have sex

NEV:

but Travis is bringing his friend Luca. I wanted to introduce you to him

ME:

your fwb can always invite his friend again. It's not the end of the world

I watch three dots appear as my best friend types. She's perfectly aware I'm not going to change my mind, and yet she's not giving up. It's one of her most annoying and also admirable character traits. This girl has the determination of a bulldozer, and most of the time she gets what she wants. Unless it's me. My stubbornness matches her determination in every way.

The scent of mint, lemon, and mandarin orange hits my nostrils, and my shoulders tense. It's way too familiar, and it belongs to only one man I know. Slowly looking up from my phone, I find my ex standing in front of my table.

"Can I have a seat?" he asks in his deep, sensual voice, dipping his head to the side.

"No."

"Well, I'm sure you don't want to cause a scene at your own place." Asher smiles, moving to the chair across from mine and lowering himself onto it. He sets his elbows on the table and puts his chin on his locked hands. "Hey, Evangelina."

"What are you doing here?" I grit my teeth so hard, I'm afraid they're going to break.

"I miss you, and you're not answering your phone. Blocking all of my phone numbers. What else can I do to get your attention?"

"Leave me alone."

"You're not listening," he murmurs. "I miss you, Evangelina, and I want you back."

I blink. The audacity of this man is beyond any normalcy. After everything I've been through with him, how can he even think I would agree to get back together again? The days of me being unreasonable are over.

"What part of 'I'm done' do I need to explain to you?" I cross my arms over my chest, furrowing my brow. "Asher, when I took you to rehab, I said we were over. I meant it."

His gaze softens, and a lopsided grin forms on his face. "You took me to rehab because you wanted to help me get better. Wanted me to get better *for you*, and I did. I'm a new person now, Evangelina. I'm clean, have been for several months."

"That was just me showing you human kindness. You're a talented guy, and you kept wasting your days away on alcohol and drugs. I wanted to help you get back on track," I tell him, coasting my gaze over his face. His deep blue eyes radiate warmth, and there is not even a trace of dark circles on his seemingly flawless skin. His blond hair is slicked back, and the slight stubble on his face adds to his handsome-boy look. Asher does indeed look healthier than ever, but the scars he left on my heart and my body will never let me forget who he really is.

Monsters often hide behind a beautiful mask, and he learned how to do it to perfection.

"You haven't had a boyfriend since we split, and you still don't have one."

"You drained me. Broke my trust so many times I lost count. Are you honestly surprised I'm single?"

"I did you wrong, Evangelina." Asher extends his hand, intending to touch me, but I jerk away, plastering my back to my chair. He grimaces and narrows his eyes, the corners of his mouth dropping. "Let me prove to you I'm not that guy anymore."

Did me wrong? Oh boy, this man is the epitome of a selfish prick who only thinks about himself. It hasn't even occurred to him that I'm really done with him.

"The tattoos on my arm are the best evidence of your cruelty. That's something I'll never forget," I hiss and set my jaw hard. Asher's scowl deepens. The glimmer in his eyes disappears as their color darkens. "I'll never ever get back together with you."

He pushes himself away from the table, flexing his muscles under his tight white T-shirt. "Are you reciting your favorite Taylor Swift song?"

"Goddamnit," I mutter, standing up from my chair. I can't do this anymore. It's like talking to a wall, but in my case the wall talks back and speaks fucking nonsense. "Bye, Asher."

Walking away from my ex is a good idea, but the execution sucks. The swelling of my ankle is getting worse, and all my movements are slowed down. I haven't made it to the kitchen door before the scent of his cologne wafts around me again. He wraps his hand around my elbow, halting me in my tracks.

"I thought we were still talking." Asher pulls me to his side; his hand slides down my hip. He presses his nose into my neck, inhaling my perfume. "I miss you, baby."

"Is there a problem?" Alana steps around the counter, heading in our direction. People's eyes are on us, and it makes my skin crawl. I find the spot on my index finger, wanting nothing more than to get rid of this damaged cuticle. My heartbeat accelerates, and I tap my foot on the floor.

"No." I move away from my ex, and his hands drop to his sides. "Asher was just leaving."

He takes a step back, plastering a smile on his face—the fakest one I know, the one he often uses when his fans want to take a picture of him. "It was nice talking to you, Evangelina. See you soon."

"I hope not," I say loud enough for him to hear without drawing even more attention to us.

My ex looks around my shop. He waves to a couple of teenage girls, who stare at him with awestruck eyes, and trudges to the exit. When he's almost out the door, I call out to him.

"Asher?"

He glances at me over his shoulder, a puzzled look on his face. I saunter over to him, picturing what it'd be like to kick him out of my shop and my life altogether. So satisfying.

Stopping near him, I put my hands on my hips and beam him my cutest smile. "I forgot to mention, you're wrong. I'm seeing someone," I say, mentally slapping myself for my lie.

Asher's expression hardens, and he narrows his eyes to slits, glowering at me. Then he smirks and shakes his head. "As if I'm going to believe you." Inching in, he kisses my cheek and then takes a step back. "Until next time, Evangelina."

With that, he opens the door and edges out of my dessert shop. I stay planted, my mind in total disarray. There's one thing for certain. Out of everything I said, only my words about another man got to him. That hurt his ego and pissed him off quick.

Well, looks like my best friend is right. If I want my ex out of my life, I need to show him that I moved on.

I need a boyfriend.

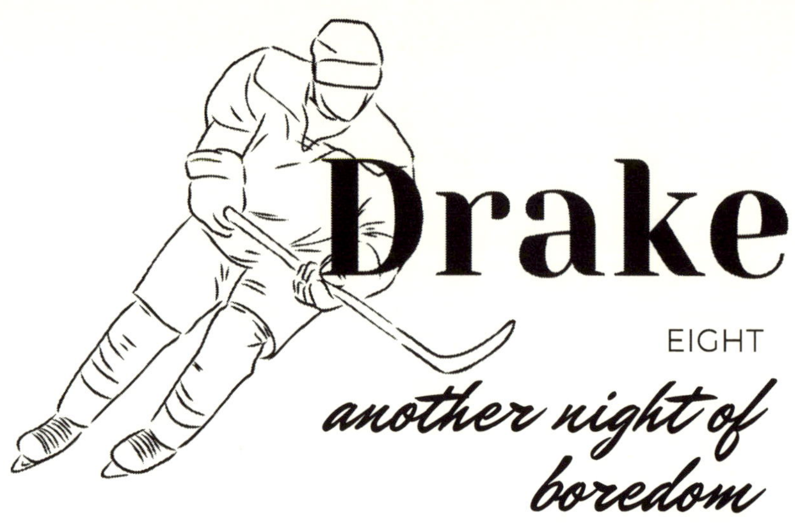

Drake

EIGHT

another night of boredom

I PUT ANOTHER LEGO TOGETHER AND HAND IT TO Michael. He flashes me a smile, excitement bubbling in his eyes. I grin back at him and then look down at the next thing I need to build—a huge red rescue helicopter. Hopefully it'll take me longer to put together than the truck for transporting said helicopter.

"When you said you were going to help him, I thought you were going to *help* him." I swivel my head toward the sound of Ava's voice and arch an eyebrow at her. "You're doing everything on your own."

"Uncle Drake is helping me." Michael frowns, etching his eyebrows together. "Not fair, Mom."

Ava rolls her eyes, absolutely unimpressed by her son's attempt to defend me. She comes closer and lowers herself onto the floor beside him. Her dark brown hair is collected in a high ponytail with a few wild locks framing her face. Ava takes the instructions from Michael's lap. She quickly flips through the pages, then returns it and peers at me.

"And what are you going to do once you're done with this set? In like fifteen minutes?"

"Michael, buddy, do you have other LEGOs for your Uncle Drake to build?"

His small mouth opens as his eyes run between his mom and me.

"I do." He nods slowly, locking his hands in front of him. "But Mommy built them all for me two weeks ago."

I shift my gaze to Ava, smacking my lips together in a tight line. "And you're lecturing me? Are you for real, Mason?"

She pokes her tongue out at me, then a smile blossoms on her face. "There's a difference, Benson. I never promised to help Michael; I just did it on my own *for* him."

"And that makes it better," I utter, snatching the instructions from Michael. "Let me have my fifteen minutes with LEGO in peace, okay? Our truck needs the helicopter."

"Sure," Ava drawls, standing up from the floor. She edges the couch and plops down onto it. "Why did you leave Colton? I thought you liked watching soccer."

"I do," I reply without taking my eyes off the build. "I'm just not a fan of his favorite team, or LaLiga in general. The Italian league is way more interesting to watch."

"Don't say that in front of Colt. He'll annoy you with all the facts and reasons why you're wrong." She beams, lifting a hand and sneaking a glance at her son. Michael's face lights up with a smile, and he stands up from the floor and runs to his mom. A moment later, he's cuddling into her side, looking like the happiest kid in the world. "Though the game is actually over, and now he's watching Los Angeles play Austin. Since Hunter Hale moved back to the US, that team is the only one my husband roots for when it comes to MLS."

"Well, Hale is a legend, so I don't blame Thompson for admiring his game. It's pretty much the same when it comes to European players in the NHL. They are all the GOAT in their home countries."

"Yeah, Roman said it was a big deal when he signed with the Thunders," Ava says, and a comfortable silence fills the room.

It doesn't bother me that she and her son continue to watch me while I finish the helicopter. After years on the ice, having people's attention on me comes as a given. Players learn how to tune it out and focus solely on the game. It also helps in real life a lot.

When I'm done, Michael jumps up from the couch and comes over. I push the helicopter into his hands and stand up, flexing my back muscles and rotating my neck. I'll need a hot shower the instant I'm home. Sitting on the floor for more than an hour is definitely not something my body enjoys.

"Will you stay for dinner?" Ava asks, and I shake my head no. "Why not? It's not a problem. You're always welcome here."

"I know. I'm very grateful to you and Colton for it," I murmur, stretching my hands into the air and then locking them behind my back. "I just don't want to abuse your hospitality. It's only April."

"Oh my God, Benson. I've known you since I was a toddler. Do you think I'll get tired of you now?" she scoffs, her eyebrows reaching her hairline. "You're ridiculous."

"Maybe I am." I laugh, scooping Michael up into my arms and putting him on my shoulders. The kid giggles, winding his hands around my neck. "Let's go join your husband. I'm sure he's lonely."

"I highly doubt it." Ava guffaws, following me. I squint at her, and she presses her head to my forearm for a moment. "I'm really glad you're here with us now."

"Am I your favorite Benson?" I nudge her with my elbow, and she jumps away from me with a squeal.

"Never. But I'm counting on you to bring my best friend to Santa Clara too."

"You know my plan: to settle down, show her that it's my home now, and then convince her to come and stay with me. She needs to know I have my own life. It's the only way she'll even consider joining me."

"Yeah, she's afraid to become a burden. That you'll focus solely on her and Maya and will never find yourself a girlfriend, never give her a sister-in-law, and—"

"Stop." I raise my hand in front of Ava, and she shuts up immediately. The mischievous glint in her eyes indicates how hard it is for her to keep a straight face. She's chewing on the inside of her bottom lip as her whole body starts to shake with silent laughter. For God's sake, she's impossible. I look away and make my way outside.

On the terrace, I put Michael down, and he rushes to his dad. He climbs up onto Colton's lap, wrapping his arms around his neck. My best friend catches his son and presses him to his chest, turning his head toward me and his wife.

"Where did you all go? You missed such a great first half."

Ava and I exchange a look and go join him on the couch. This guy and his love for soccer will never cease to amaze me.

STEPPING OUT OF THE SHOWER, I feel refreshed. My whole body is relaxed and warm; the tension I felt in my muscles is gone. I edge to the mirror and trail my hand over the surface, wiping away the fog. Water drips from my wet hair onto my face, down my neck, and lower, to my chest. I don't move, just stare at my own reflection. The memories rush back at breakneck speed.

The bathroom of my house in Michigan. Janelle and I had just climbed out of the shower after morning sex. I was brushing my teeth, and she was combing her hair, keeping one palm on my chest. The gesture she used any time we went out, showing her possessiveness. I thought we were going somewhere. She'd moved in with me and was talking about our future together almost nonstop. Wedding, babies, vacation plans. I didn't really mind, but...something felt off, as if it was just an agreement, useful for both of us, without even a glimpse of love. With all the conversations we had, she never asked what I wanted, or what my desires or wishes were. As if being a hockey player for an NHL team was the only important thing in my life.

When my phone started ringing that day, I didn't even finish rinsing off my toothpaste. It was still early, and it was the morning after a game. My mind instantly went overboard, imagining all the bad things that could've happened to my family or my friends. The call I got was nothing like that, but it changed my life in the span of a minute.

I leaped to the bedroom, grabbed my phone from the nightstand, and pressed it to my ear without even looking at the caller ID. I expected the worst news ever, but it was just my agent, informing me that I'd been traded to the California Thunders. The spectrum of my emotions went from sadness to disbelief to happiness in a matter of seconds. I absolutely loved my time in Detroit, but playing on the same team as my best friend was something I'd dreamed about since my final year in college. It was finally happening, and I was excited about it despite all the troubles I'd need to deal with—finding a place to stay, buying a house, getting used to a new team so far into the season.

Joke's on me, but I thought my girlfriend would support me. I would've supported her if the roles were reversed. Instead, Janelle threw a tantrum, crying and calling me a selfish jerk for not being sad that I was traded. It came to the point where I was forced to leave the house and go to my sister's place so I could process my move.

When I got home that night, I found it empty. All her belongings were gone, and a breakup note was pinned to my fridge. She said she couldn't see herself in California, and that her future belonged in Michigan. Just like that, my one-year relationship came to an end.

I didn't feel sad or heartbroken that she broke up with me. I was too busy to dwell on my past and analyze where things went wrong between us. The only time I got upset was when I found out how quickly she got herself a new boyfriend. I wasn't even in Santa Clara for two weeks before my friend sent me a picture of Janelle with a center from the AHL team at a bar, a dreamy smile on her face—and her palm glued to the guy's chest. The realization that I'd been thinking about building a future with someone who only cared about me while I was playing hockey was tough. It served as the best evidence of what Layla had been telling me for years: I was choosing the wrong girls, expecting to find happiness.

Well, hopefully next time I decide to give dating a chance, I'll make a better choice. Whenever that will be.

Taking a deep breath, I shoo away all the memories and focus on the present. It's still early, and I have a lot of free time before I go to bed. I quickly dry my body with a towel and head to my bedroom to put on some shorts. I'm not hungry since Colton and Ava made me agree to have dinner with them, so in the kitchen I just open the fridge and take out a bottle of beer.

Back in the living room, I set the bottle on the table, grab the remote, and turn on the TV. Scrolling through Hulu, I start scratching my stubble with my fingers. Nothing catches my attention again, and I feel annoyance spilling into my veins.

God, it's just a TV show. It's not like I'm going to spend my whole life with the characters from whatever show I decide to watch tonight. I huff. An exasperated sound leaves my mouth, and I start the first show from my list. Whatever. I put the remote on the couch and reach for the bottle. The second my fingers wrap around the neck, someone knocks on my door.

No matter who it is, I'm ready to kiss them if they'll save me from another night of boredom. I'm so done with all that.

Angie

NINE

opportunity

Driving home, I keep replaying my talk with Asher in my head. Why can't he move on? He has so many girls lining up to be with him, so his fixation on me doesn't make any sense.

He cheated on me way more times than I actually know about, I'm sure. The last time, I was at his apartment when he brought a girl up for a quickie. They were so high they didn't even notice me as they fucked like rabbits on his living room couch. By that point in our relationship, I didn't feel anything for him, nor did I know why I was staying. Except for the simple fact that I was punishing myself for my past decisions, believing that I deserved it.

Wanting to make a point, I waited for him to wake up before I told him it was over. Everything that happened after is the reason I'll never forgive him. And even if all my cuts have healed, the scars will be with me forever. Scars that I can't erase or hide, no matter how hard I want to. No matter how much ink I inject into my body, no matter how many times I visit my therapist.

My scars are the best reminder of my poor decisions.

Some physical wounds hurt the soul, and unfortunately I've yet to find the cure.

I've had my share of toxic boyfriends, but Asher dethroned all of them one by one, claiming the title of the worst boyfriend in the world. To be fair, though, it's my fault I let him do this to me. It felt like he was pushing my limits, always hitting a new level and watching my reaction. The moment he realized my limits were nonexistent, he knew he could do anything and get away with it. All because I treated this relationship like a self-flagellation practice, replacing the physical pain with a mental one.

Intrusive and distressing thoughts I wasn't able to stop. Gnawing on my skin. Locking the doors and then returning to check if I actually did. Constant worrying about things that hadn't happened and an exceptional need of reassurance. I was closed off from everyone, finding peace only by myself and only for the shortest periods of time. It was exhausting, and I hated myself for that. And, unfortunately for me, Asher used all my weaknesses against me more than once.

It stopped the day I checked him into rehab. I didn't even have time to step inside my house before my best friend dragged me to her car. Nevaeh took me to Dr. Nichols, and, thankfully, talking to him helped me face my obsessive thoughts and find the root cause of all my problems. Perfectionism and overachieving are my Achilles' heels, the two pillars that my whole childhood was built on. The image of myself I created for everyone to see and tried to live up to at my own expense.

Asher's return triggered me. Biting my cuticle is one of the first signs that I need to take care of this situation. He must understand that this time, I'm not going to get back together with him. I not only know my worth, I'm fully acknowledging that I deserve better. There's no point in punishing myself for the mistakes of my youth, especially when no one is blaming me. All that was just my imagination.

The buzzing of my phone diverts my attention from my gloomy thoughts. It's my mom, but I need a moment before I'll be able to answer. I take a few deep breaths, exhaling through my mouth, and my mind clears little by little. I know what I need, and the only thing that matters now is how I'm going to put my plan into action. Partying with Nev is one of the best ways to make it happen, but sadly for me, my ankle doesn't agree.

I park my car, get out, and quickly dial my mom's number. I love both my parents the same, even if I've always been closer to Mom. At least, I used to be. I've told her a lot of lies lately. If she only knew, she'd be extremely disappointed in me. They all would.

Moving to California, I not only created a physical distance, but a mental one too. Even with Ethan—I haven't talked to my brother for several weeks. Not to mention my sister. The last time Emma and I talked was months ago, when she wanted to know the name of my favorite professor at college, and that conversation lasted one minute. There are too many issues between Emma and me, but distance made it worse. My last talk with Dad consisted of only a few words when he called to warn me about the article in *Sports Today*. Which I still managed to forget about.

The award for best daughter or best sister in the world won't be mine.

"Hey, Mom," I say after she picks up. "Sorry, I was parking my car and couldn't answer."

"No worries, sweetheart. I figured you were busy. How have you been?"

"All good." I slowly amble to my house, glancing at Drake's. His car is missing. Looks like he found something to fill his time with. "How are you?"

"Nuh-uh, nope. That's not going to work, Angie." Her voice becomes stern, and I smile. It was so rare for her to scold me for anything when I was small, so I sort of like it when she does it now. "We haven't talked for a week, and 'all good' sounds like bullshit."

"Mom," I scoff, breaking into giggles almost instantly. "Sorry, you're right. I should know better. How about you tell me how you are while I put the leash on Cooper? I need to take him for a walk."

"That I can do," Mom murmurs, as I open the door and step inside. Taking the leash from the little table, I quickly put it on Coop and pull him out of the house. He obeys, following me outside without any resistance. "Your dad is doing great. His team won another game, and to say he was proud would be an understatement. The twins are planning their trip to Europe for the summer. They want to go on a two-month Euro-trip with their friends, and they'll be back just in time for their junior year. Ethan is also planning to come visit you. What do you think?"

"I'll be happy to see him. It's been a while." I'm not lying; my little brother is my favorite out of the twins. More like he's the only sibling that really likes me. "What about you? What have you been up to?"

"My days are filled with work. Not that I'm complaining, because the book I'm editing right now is fabulous. This author's debut is going to rock the publishing world, I can feel it!" Mom exclaims. "It's a fake dating romance, and it's so good. You should read it; I'll send you the link so you can preorder. You won't regret it."

I stop abruptly. My mouth falls open as I stare in front of me, not paying attention to my surroundings. Cooper stops and sits beside me, but I'm too distracted to even glance at him. Mom's words are like a light bulb lighting up the darkness. That's it. The answer I've been looking for.

I need a fake boyfriend. Someone who will pretend to be with me without actually being with me. This way, I can avoid starting a new relationship, and also finally prove to Asher that I've moved on. Oh my God, my mom is my savior.

When the idea settles in, determination fills my veins, and I resume my walk. I talk some more with Mom, telling her about my days, my dessert shop, and my sprained ankle. Hesitating only a moment, I explain to her how my neighbor helped me...and instantly regret it. What is worse, my dad hears her bombarding me with questions and joins the call. They want to know everything about him, and judging by how they both fall silent when I reassure them that he's just a neighbor—they don't believe me. Nothing new, in all honesty.

Before my level of annoyance breaks through the roof, I end the call, promising to call them some other time. Sometimes they can be way too overbearing. Not that it surprises me, considering the rebellious spree I was on in college, but it still kinda sucks they don't trust me.

Slowly making my way back to my house, I let my mind wander to my idea of finding a fake boyfriend. It's the best shot I have, because I'm clearly not ready for a relationship, and leading people on is something I hate more than anything. The most important question is: who could I ask to do this for me? It should be someone Asher doesn't know, someone who will intimidate him with just their look. It should be—

The second my eyes land on the Lexus RX Hybrid now parked near my car, a thrill rushes down my spine. I halt in my tracks, hundreds of ideas swirling in my head. He's the best candidate for the role. Asher will shit his pants if he thinks I'm with a guy like Drake. He's bigger, taller, and also more handsome. It'll be a crushing blow to Asher's ego, and he'll back off. He'll leave me alone, and I'll be able to breathe fully, without worrying about him showing up wherever I go or sending me messages and calling me in the middle of the night. It's exactly what I need.

Cooper growls, and I look down at him. My bubble full of plans and ideas bursts. Shit. I definitely should be more attentive to my dog. "Sorry, Coop. Let's get you home."

It takes me almost an hour to get ready. I feed my dog and refill his water bowl, tend to my sprained ankle with ice and an elastic bandage, and only then am I ready to start Operation Fake Dating.

I'm being overly theatrical, but it's just the mood I'm in. The risk of ruining the little peace we were able to gain yesterday is huge, and there are so many reasons why I should reconsider asking my neighbor to help me. And yet, I ignore them all.

Taking a plate of cupcakes, I straighten my dress and head to the door. After thinking long and hard, I decided not to overdo it, staying in the same dress I wore all day and without any makeup. My goal is to make him agree to pretend to be my boyfriend for a few weeks, not to seduce him.

I knock on his door, and my heart starts beating faster. This is the most ridiculous thing I've done in months. He'll think I'm the weirdest person ever and will probably kick me out. And he'd be totally right to do so. Why would he pretend to have a girlfriend? There's no benefit for him in that.

I'm so delusional. I should just hire someone.

The door swings open, and I'm at loss for words. Drake stands in front of me wearing only shorts that hang low on his hips. My eyes traitorously devour every inch of his toned chest, his muscular arms and six-pack abs. Up close, I notice a delicious-looking V-cut, and that's where my gaze zeroes in.

"Hello to you too, Cupcake." His mocking voice is what finally snaps me out of my thoughts. "What are you doing here?"

"I brought you cupcakes," I blurt, feeling my neck become hot. "I thought you liked them."

"I do," Drake says, snatching the plate I'm holding out to him. "How is your ankle?"

"It started swelling again, but I know what to do now. It's all good." I lick my lips, locking my hands behind my back. "What about you?"

"I'm dying of boredom, and it's only the beginning of my vacation," he huffs.

"How long is your break?" I ask out of curiosity.

"Preseason starts in September, so..." He shrugs, lowering his eyes to the plate of cupcakes.

A familiar song captures my attention, and I frown. No way he's watching this TV show. "Is that what I think it is? Is it..."

Please say no, because this evening has already shocked me into a state of panic.

Drake blinks, and then starts laughing. "Come on in, Cupcake. We can watch *One Tree Hill* together. I don't mind."

He steps back, holding my gaze. It's the reason why I came here in the first place. The opportunity to talk to him. The chance to explain my situation and ask him to help me. Everything's going exactly as I'd hoped.

But why does it feel like I'm making a mistake?

Drake

TEN

fake...what?

Evangelina bounces back and forth on her heels. Her floral summer dress accentuates her round boobs in the most appetizing way, especially with her hands locked behind her back. It takes a lot of self-control to not check her out. She eyes me from under her eyelashes, her eyebrows pinched together. I obviously don't know her well, but she looks like someone who's having second thoughts. It's so abundantly clear that I feel confused. Why is she here?

"It's not my first time watching *One Tree Hill*, but I don't really remember the first episodes," I say, pushing her to decide. Either she stays, or she goes back home. "So, Cupcake, are you in?"

She pauses, tilting her head slightly, her eyes narrowing. Taking a deep breath, she walks inside, throwing a glare my way. "Don't call me that."

"But you brought me cupcakes, Evangelina," I tease her, pushing the door closed. She shakes her head, snorts, and ambles straight into the living room without waiting for me.

Truthfully, I like this bold version of her. Knowing her worth, not being afraid to stand up for herself. And in addition, she's breathtakingly beautiful and unbelievably hot. I've had my share of stunning women, but this one would easily make it to the top of that list. I'm not entirely sure about her character traits though. It's hard to say, considering we've barely talked, but for now I think her personality matches mine like fire matches water. Flawed tandem—and maybe that's why it's so alluring?

I've often been drawn to women who weren't right for me in the long run. Did it ever stop me from trying? Never. I was young and adventurous. Now, I'm nursing my heart in my palm. It's broken so many times I've stopped counting. Fragile, and also cautious, my heart screams, warning me against this girl. Telling me to take a step back and not let her in. Being the fool that I am, I'm not listening.

"Can I have this beer?" Her voice startles me, and I realize I'm still standing in my hallway. I roll my eyes at myself and beeline into the living room.

As I come closer to the couch, I feel her eyes on me. I put the plate of cupcakes on the table and straighten my back, only now meeting her gaze. "Yes."

Evangelina smiles, grabs the beer bottle from the table, and takes a generous sip. I watch her lips move, the drink sliding down her throat, and suddenly, my skin feels warm. The temperature of the room becomes too hot for my liking. I scratch the back of my neck and dash into the kitchen. I need a cold beer to cool down my insides. Watching a TV show will be the only thing I'm going to do tonight.

I return to the living room and plop down on the couch. Avoiding looking at my tempting neighbor is the best shot I have at making it through the night without a massive boner. And it'll be a fucking miracle if I can manage it.

Maybe asking her to join me wasn't the best idea.

The first episode comes to an end, and before I know it, we're already in the middle of the second one. I put my beer on the table and lean against the back of the couch. Evangelina and I don't talk to each other; we just watch the show, but it still feels nice. Having company is nice. This silence is comfortable and doesn't make my skin prickle with distress. I like it. I won't mind even if she doesn't talk—

"I have to ask." I meet Evangelina's gaze. She has a mischievous smile on her face, two adorable dimples on her cheeks. "Lucas or Nathan?"

I snicker, spread my arms, and drape them across the back of the couch. "Nathan."

"Brooke or Peyton?" She wriggles, turning to her left to face me.

"Brooke." Her eyes round a little, and her lips part. "Why?"

"People always have their favorites when it comes to TV shows." Evangelina lifts one shoulder in a tiny shrug. "I was just curious."

"You looked like my answers surprised you."

"Not at all," she says, and then she shifts even more, until she's staring at me. I mirror her, angling my body in her direction. My fingertips are close to her bare shoulder, and a strange energy surges through me. Just one little move, and I could touch her, trace all the tattoos inked on her left arm. "Well, no. Nathan—yes, no surprise there. But I didn't expect Brooke to be your favorite."

"Why was it so obvious I was going to say Nathan?"

"He was an asshole in the beginning, but the more you watch, the more you see what a great guy he is. A loyal friend, a loving husband, a caring father." She ticks the traits off on her fingers. "You helped me with my ankle, even if you weren't obligated to. You went beyond that and made sure I knew what to do, and you brought me your own bandage." Her eyes roam over my face, her features softening. "I think you're a good one too."

I blink. The lyrics from Green Day's "Nice Guys Finish Last" flash in my head on autopilot. What the hell? "Um, and what about Brooke?"

Evangelina is silent, watching me intently. Reaching for her hair, she pulls out her red scrunchie and puts it on her wrist. Her deep brown hair spills down over her shoulders as she rakes her fingers through it.

"Actually, I think I made a mistake," she suddenly mutters. "Brooke is loving and nurturing. She deserves the world, especially after everything she's been through. It makes total sense why you like her."

We lock eyes; neither of us looks away. I clear my throat. "What about you? Who do you like?" My voice is hoarse.

With how she smiles, I know the answer before she even opens her mouth. "Lucas and Peyton. I've been rooting for them since the very first episode."

"I shouldn't have even asked." I laugh, my head tipping back. "I'm not a fan, but I was glad they got their happy ending."

"They deserved it. Lucas and Peyton are the definition of soulmates for me," she says, taking a swig of her beer. "It still feels surreal to know you've watched this."

"My little sister is your age. And we often ended up watching things that only one of us wanted to watch. I didn't care about the show at first, but then I kinda started to enjoy it."

"Oh, I know the feeling. I have a little brother and sister; they're twenty. With them, I was sentenced to watching cartoons as a kid."

"You make it sound as if you don't like cartoons."

"I do, but not when I'm watching the same thing over and over and over because it's their favorite. It was pure torture."

"Dunno, I don't mind. I can watch anything." I run my fingers through my still-wet hair. "I stayed at my friends' house for a few days while I was waiting for my place to be ready, and I watched their son's favorites all the time. So if you're looking for a good cartoon? Try *The Loud House*. I loved it."

Evangelina gawks at me, bursting into laughter a moment later. "Oh my God, you're unbelievable. I didn't think I'd get to know so much about you when I decided to stop by tonight."

I sense the opportunity to ask her about her reasons for knocking on my door, and I go for it. "Why did you decide to come over in the first place? And I'm not buying that shit about cupcakes."

"You needed to ruin everything, didn't you?" She looks at the ceiling, exhaling long and loud. "The thing is, I have a problem. A very annoying and distressing problem. I've been thinking about the options I have for getting rid of it for days, and today I found a solution."

My neighbor clicks her tongue and bores her gaze into mine. Her pupils are dilated, and her cheeks wear a light shade of pink. She's kinda cute when she's nervous.

"What's your problem?" I ask with a nod of my head.

She twirls a long lock of her hair around her finger, watching me. Then she says, "My ex. He's back from rehab and wants me to get back together with him."

I frown, furrowing my brow and pursing my lips into a tight line. That's her problem? "Tell him to fuck off." I shrug.

"I already did, genius." She giggles, covering her eyes with her palm. "He's not listening. That's the problem."

"Do you want me to talk to him?" I suggest, and her laughter instantly dies in her throat. She sighs, puts her hands on her lap, and focuses her attention on me.

"It's not the first time he's come back. We were on and off for months, and I always agreed to get back together with him. Not anymore. Not after what he's done to me."

My frown deepens. Her ex hurt her? I haven't met the guy yet, but I already want to kill him. Without even knowing what happened.

"He won't listen to you; that's how Asher is. But you can help me."

"Okay, what do you want me to do?"

She balls her fists. A curtain of heavy locks falls across her face as she lowers her head. "Asher has a huge ego, like all narcissists, and he believes I'm still in love with him. I need him to understand that it's over. That I've moved on." Evangelina takes a deep breath, and our eyes meet. "I want you to be my fake boyfriend."

"Fake...what?" She just stunned me speechless. I expected anything but this.

"Look, I know it probably sounds crazy. I'm just not ready to go on dates, to meet new people. I don't want to lead anyone on, make them think that something is possible between us and then dump them when they served their purpose." The words pour out of her in one breath. "Asher will back off as soon as he knows I'm taken. Especially if he sees me with you. It'll get rid of him, and I'll be finally free.

Free from his messages, his late-night calls, and his visits to my dessert shop. I'll be able to breathe. I know we don't really know each other, but please, Drake. I'm in desperate need of your help."

I look around my living room. That's a lot to unload, and my mind is ready to explode.

Evangelina has an ex, one who hurt her in the past and now seems to be stalking her. And she wants me to help her...by pretending to be her boyfriend. This has disaster written all over it.

"Let's move on from my initial shock," I utter. "What exactly would you need from me?"

"Go on a few dates with me, to some sort of a public event maybe." The corners of her mouth twitch as she tries to fight a smile. "I was invited to a movie premiere; we could use it as an opportunity to make an appearance."

"To make our fake relationship public," I correct her, still not convinced. Her idea doesn't sit right with me. "And you're asking me...why? Because I'm the safest option?"

Her cheeks go from pink to red in mere seconds, her eyes almost popping out of their sockets. "No, no, no. It's not that. You're handsome and"—she moves her hand up and down, gesturing at me—"hot. I just don't date athletes. And I don't think I'm your type either. But we can be friends. So it should work, right?"

I'm not sure what my type is anymore. Physically speaking, Evangelina doesn't fit the profile, considering all my ex-girlfriends. Personality wise, it's hard to say, but some glimpses remind me of Ava. And I never wanted to date her. My best friend has his hands full with his wife, and that's not what I'm looking for when it comes to relationships. I need calmness and stability, and this girl in front of me is not it.

So maybe she's right, and it will work?

"Don't you have any exes? We can make them regret what they lost."

Janelle's name zips through my brain, and I'm instantly not as opposed to the idea as I was a moment ago. I don't want my ex back, nor do I want to hurt her. But making headlines with a girl like Evangelina will make Janelle think about me, and how quickly she found a substitute for me.

I scratch my stubble, the remains of my doubt disappearing. "Okay, Cupcake. You've got yourself a boyfriend."

Angie

ELEVEN

rules

"Really?" I drawl, my voice shaking. *I can't believe it worked.*

"Really," he says with a broad smile. "I love being the knight in shining armor, helping a damsel in distress."

I narrow my eyes, folding my arms over my chest. "I'm not a damsel in distress. And I'm not Cupcake—remember that."

"Damn, we just started dating, and you're already making the rules? What have I gotten myself into?" Drake taunts, his gaze glowing with mischief. His words echo in my head, settling in and making my jaw drop.

"Oh my God, you're so right," I exclaim, leaning forward. "We need rules."

"Rules? Like what? No kissing, no sex? Are those the kind of rules you want us to have?"

"You're my *fake* boyfriend. Of course there will be no sex," I state, reclining away from him.

Drake shrugs, threading his fingers through his tousled hair. "Your loss."

Hiding my face in my hands, I groan. "You're making me regret this."

A warm palm covers my knee, and suddenly, my chest feels too tight. He's a gorgeous guy, and I'm not entirely immune to his charms. Especially when he's sitting next to me with just shorts on. My skin is scorching hot under his touch, and it takes all my willpower to sit still and not move away. The last thing I need is to lead him on, let him think I'm attracted to him. There's only one word for my reaction, and it's "under-fucked". Good sex is definitely lacking in my life lately.

"I'm just joking. Making fun of this situation," he murmurs in a soothing voice, and I lower my hands. A smile spreads across my lips as our eyes lock, and he grins back. "Let's talk about our rules. I'm all ears."

"Holding hands, hugging, and any other form of tactile contact is only for public eyes."

"Okay, go on." He nods, taking his palm off my knee. "What's next?"

"We'll need to come up with a story about how we met and how it all began between us. Just in case we go to this movie premiere and someone starts asking questions. It should be believable."

"Am I allowed to say your dog played matchmaker? Or should I mention the truth and how Cooper scared me to death?"

"I like the matchmaker story better, thank you very much."

Drake laughs, putting his hand on his belly, and my eyes zero in on it again. His abs flex; the lines of his muscles look impeccable. I feel all tingly, and goosebumps are visible on my skin. "Whatever you say, Cupcake. Just tell me the story, and I'll repeat it if anyone asks."

I want to strangle him, I swear. He's taunting me on purpose with this nickname, knowing damn well I'm not going to say anything because I need his help.

Fuck my life.

"No sex."

"I thought we already discussed that, but okay. You got it. No orgasms for you." He not-so-discreetly rotates his hips, and my gaze drops to the outline of his cock under his shorts. Is he not wearing any underwear? "At least, not from me."

I clench my thighs together, because this man saying the word "orgasm" makes my clit pulsate. *Lovely*. Plastering a smile on my face, I say, "I'll survive. Don't worry."

This time, the silence between us lasts longer, but not because we don't have anything to say. We're just too busy staring each other down as if our lives depend on it. Only the sound of Gavin DeGraw's song interrupts the quiet and brings us back to our senses.

"That's all?"

"No. We'll need to make it *really* official and post on social media. It'll be huge."

"Is that necessary?" he asks, pinching the bridge of his nose.

"I post a lot, and Asher knows it. He'll need to believe we're together, so I'll share some pictures here and there. We can hide your face, you know? Just show your back, or us holding hands. Whatever you're most comfortable with."

"How many followers do you have?"

"It's my new account, where I share my personal life. I have somewhere around five hundred thousand," I blurt, watching his reaction carefully .

He whistles. "Wow. My thirty thousand looks like nothing compared to that."

"I'm a former runway model; most of my followers know me because of that. Some follow me because of my dad. I'm not really interesting just by myself," I tell him, collecting my hair and quickly braiding it. "You have a great following actually. Do you post often?"

"Once or twice every few months. I'm usually too busy playing hockey. This shit doesn't appeal to me at all. I'd prefer to watch a movie or read a book instead of wasting my time on social media. It's not for me."

"You're just like my dad. His agent has been running his profile since forever, and my dad never wants to know what they post or how people react to it. It's just for good publicity, nothing else." I smile involuntarily as my mind drifts to my parents. I'll need to thank Mom for giving me this idea without even knowing that I needed it. "On a positive note, I think we're done."

Drake keeps quiet, but his dark brown eyes unnerve me. "It's kinda funny, but I noticed you never said anything about kissing. Are kisses banned in our fake relationship or not? I want to be safe, you know."

"Well..." I trail off, feeling as if my mind is ready to explode. The simplest answer to his question is no. Kissing and PDA are the best way to show our "love" to the world. On the other hand, kisses might blur some lines, and that's what I'm trying to prevent. "If it's appropriate, then yes. But nothing crazy."

His face lights up with his boyish smile, and two dimples appear on his cheeks. "Duly noted. You'll get the best fake kisses in the world...if it's appropriate."

God, this man is driving me insane. It's impossible to stay serious with him, but I need to voice one more rule. This one is incredibly important—maybe the most important. "Promise me you won't fall in love with me. It's my last rule."

"Excuse me, what?"

"You need to promise me you won't fall in love with me."

"And why is that rule so one-sided?" Drake's face darkens, the corners of his mouth dip down. "Why is it only for me?"

"Because I don't date athletes. My history with guys who play sports isn't good." I trace a fingernail on my right hand, finding a spot I bit yesterday. The skin is broken, and it hurts when I press on it. "I spent a lot of time hating on players of every sport, and it's not something that's easy to forget. You're not my type, Drake."

"And what is your type?" he asks harshly. "Guys who are so high they don't even remember your name? Who have gigs with girls clinging to their side all the time?"

My lips part as I gape at him in shocked silence. Rearing forward, I narrow my eyes and put my elbows on my knees. "And here I thought you told me the truth yesterday. Who knew you're a liar, Drake? My dating life is definitely not something you can find by googling me and reading *only* about my family."

"Sorry, I shouldn't have said anything." He stares at the TV in silence. "It's not my business who you date or what you do with your life in general. I'm sorry, and I promise I won't fall in love with you. You don't have to worry about that."

Drake whips his head toward me, and all his playfulness is gone. I continue to scrutinize him; the emotions he causes me are unfamiliar. The warmth enveloping my body feels like a blanket, keeping me secure from the outside world. He's like a safe haven, all big and bulky with a heart in the right place. The people he calls friends must be immensely happy to have him in their lives. I'll be lucky if he stays my friend after this fake-dating charade.

I hope he will.

"Why did you agree?" The words leave my mouth faster than I think. "Just because you wanted to help me, or was there someone...?"

"I don't want to get back at anyone, but it'd be nice to shove my 'happiness' in my ex's face." It isn't lost on me how he emphasizes the word "happiness". I arch an eyebrow, looking at him quizzically. "I was with Janelle for a year, and I even asked her to move in with me. With my constant traveling for games, it was the best solution for our relationship. I thought we were moving forward, but she broke up with me after I got traded to the Thunders. It would've meant moving here from Michigan, and I wasn't good enough to leave everything behind and come to Santa Clara for."

"I'm sorry—"

"No, no, wait for the best part. Two weeks later, she already had a new boyfriend—another hockey player from the AHL team." He says it with a smirk, but his eyes look shallow. The smile he forces on his face seems fake. "I'm not in love with her, and I don't feel bad we broke up. It just bruised my ego."

"You know what?" I reach for his hand on the back of the couch and put my palm on his. "Your ex-girlfriend sounds like an idiot. We can make her kick herself for leaving you."

"I don't want her back." Drake chuckles under his breath, tipping his chin up. "The past belongs in the past, and I prefer not to look back."

"Wise words," I agree, taking my palm off his. Glancing at the TV screen, I realize we've missed a good part of episode three. "Looks like it wasn't the best idea to watch *One Tree Hill* in my company."

"Nah, it's all good." He grabs the remote and pauses the show. "I don't mind your company; quite the contrary. It feels nice to not be alone once in a while."

"That's why I have Cooper. I never ever feel lonely." I raise my hands, stretching and relaxing my sore muscles.

"With how often I travel, I don't think I'm ready to have a pet," Drake utters, juggling the remote between his palms. "Maybe later, when I settle down."

"Maybe." The vibe he's giving me screams "family man". He has too much love to give, and the thought alone warms my insides. "Well, I'd better go. I have some errands to run tomorrow morning."

"Got what you wanted, and now you're just going to leave me alone? Not cool, Cupcake."

"Stop with the stupid nickname!" I yelp, slapping his chest. He catches my wrist and pulls me closer to him. Placing my palm on his knee for better balance, I give him my best mean look. "I don't like it, I told you that already."

"But that's the whole point, Evangelina," he murmurs pointedly. "The annoyed version of you is my favorite."

I wiggle my hand out of his grip, and he lets go of my wrist. Standing up from the couch, I hover over him. "I thought about inviting you to my place tomorrow so we could continue *One Tree Hill* together, but I changed my mind."

"I'm your boyfriend, baby. I don't need an invitation to show up on your doorstep." He stands up as well, and I take a step back. The smug smile on his face makes my skin itch, irking me to no end. "You're stuck with me till your ex backs off. So you better get used to having me around, Evangelina."

He follows me closely, the heat of his body crowding me. My heart leaps in my chest, and tingles spread all over my skin. It's not fucking fair. What's going on with me? He's just a guy.

"When is our first fake date?" His question halts me in my tracks.

I peek over my shoulder. “Come to my place tomorrow and we’ll decide together. Just like real couples do.”

With that, I walk out of his house, holding my head high and not allowing myself to look back. I know he’s watching me. The intensity of his gaze is definitely something I’ll need to get used to, or it’ll become a problem.

Drake

TWELVE

not metaphorically speaking

SITTING ON THE BENCH IN THE LOCKER ROOM, I TIE MY sneakers. Colton and Xander share a laugh about their kids. I'm barely listening. Way too many thoughts have interfered with my morning. The mess in my head is the reason I agreed to come to the gym with my best friend. Almost two hours later, and I can say it's not working.

This morning, my decision to help Evangelina looks like a recipe for disaster.

What was I thinking?

It's the worst feeling ever, being sure I've made a mistake before anything has even happened. I don't like it.

"Drake?" A heavy hand lands on my shoulder, and I jerk away, looking up and meeting Colton's eyes. "You okay?"

"Yeah." I nod, standing up and pulling on my tee. "Why?"

"I asked you twice about your plans for today, and both times you didn't hear me," Colton says, hiding his hands in his jeans pockets.

"You just continued to scowl at your sneakers with a glassy stare," Xander comments with a sneer, putting on his white T-shirt. Its color is a great contrast to his inked skin, making me wonder again how many hours this guy has spent in tattoo shops. His arms, his chest, his back, and even his fucking neck are covered in so many lines, drawings, and letters that I gave up on trying to figure out what they are and what they mean.

Just like Evangelina's. The tattoos on her left arm intrigue me, causing possibly the worst hangover from just pondering. I'm thinking too much about her in general. It's not normal.

"Drake, you're doing it again." Colt laughs wholeheartedly. "What's on your mind?"

My neighbor. Even if I want her to leave me alone, at least inside my head.

"Nothing." I shrug, reach for my hat, and put it on backward. "I just went to bed past three a.m., and I needed to be here at eight."

"Were you watching something?" Xander asks, shoving his running shoes inside his gym bag.

"Gerard Butler movie marathon."

"You and your movies," Colton teases as we exit the locker room and head outside. "Looks like you decided to break the record for number of movies and shows watched in a row."

"I also read." I let Xander go first. He slows down, glancing at me over his shoulder. "Why is that so surprising?" I ask him.

"My wife loves to read," he says, resuming his walk while I roll my eyes. It's just ridiculous.

"From what I overheard between Ava and Isabella when I met your wife for the first time, they both read mostly romance. I love thrillers and detective novels—the more gruesome, the better."

Xander comes to a stop near his Porsche, and Colton catches up to us. "Your friend is full of surprises."

"I know he is." Thompson peers at me with a coy smile and nudges my forearm with his knuckles. "Let's go grab a coffee."

We both turn to Xander, who only shakes his head. "Sorry, guys. Bella has a meeting with a new client, and I promised to take the kids to the playground. I'm trying to spend as much time as I can with Isla and Ian during the offseason."

"Of course. Totally understandable." He and Colton exchange a knowing look, and I suddenly feel out of place. They are family guys, while I'm...single and don't have any real prospects for anyone I'd want to have a family with. "See you, Xander. Tell Bella and the kids I said hi."

"Sure." Xander opens his car door and slides inside. "Bye, Drake."

"Bye."

Xander drives away from the gym, leaving Colt and me alone. I go to put my gym bag in my backseat, and my friend does the same with his. In silence, we skirt our cars and head in the direction of the coffee shop just around the corner.

After ordering coffee, we return to the parking lot, making small talk. It feels forced, as if Colton is trying to figure out how to make me open up to him. The exasperation climbs up my throat, and my voice cracks. We're friends, for God's sake. Why can't he just ask what he wants to ask?

"Look, I'm sure if there was something serious going on, you'd have already told me," Thompson says, leaning back against his car. "And yet, your behavior today threw me off. Are you okay? Is there something you didn't want to talk to me about in front of Xander?"

I chuckle, taking a sip of my espresso. "Your friend is great, don't worry about it."

"Then what, Benson? You're acting even less like yourself than you did when you first moved here."

I mentally count to ten, preparing to lie to my friend's face. If I'm going to keep the promise I made, Colton and Ava will have to think I'm dating Evangelina. No way am I telling him the truth. He would make fun of me till I was fucking dead. "I'm seeing someone."

"Who?"

"The girl next door."

Colton scrutinizes me without a single detectable emotion. I slide my hands in my pockets, shifting on my heels. My best friend has a perfect poker face, and moments like this drive me nuts. The need to know what he's thinking becomes stronger, and I want to shake him. Anything to make him talk.

He lowers his cup, holding it between his palms. "I have no clue why you're looking at me like you're expecting me to throw up on your shoes, but whatever you're thinking, you're wrong. I'm not going to ask you how it happened or tell you that it's too soon, or any other shit like that. If she's good for you, then that's all that matters. Plus, I saw her when I stopped by the other week. She's very beautiful."

"Yeah, she is." I smile at him. The tiniest feeling of guilt pops up inside my chest. "It's nothing serious, just seeing where things are going. We're very different."

"Maybe different is exactly what you need," he points out. "I'm not one to criticize your girlfriends, but I always had the feeling you were looking in the wrong direction."

"Your wife's words."

"And your sister's," Colton counters with a lift of his shoulder. "You're drawn to fire, but you're choosing water."

"I have no idea what you're talking about." Climbing inside my car, I fasten my seat belt and only then look at my best friend. He's staring at me with a bored expression on his face. "What?"

"Running away from the conversation? How mature of you, Benson." Thompson snorts and shakes his head. "Same time on Thursday?"

"Yeah, sure. See you."

"Bye, Benson." Colton closes my door and steps back, watching me drive away.

He's not wrong. I'm avoiding talking about my dating life because I don't want my friends to realize how bitter I've become. I've learned my lesson, and now I just try to stay afloat.

Do I have a death wish? Probably. It's the only conclusion I can come up with as I get dressed to go to my neighbor's place. She could've gone to a party, or just changed her mind. Anything is possible, and maybe staying home and watching something on my own would be a much better option. Yet I'm already at her door, knocking on it with calculated slowness.

As if hoping she won't hear it.

The dog's paws are the first sound that reaches my ears, and then I hear her voice, telling Cooper to step aside. I run my fingers through my hair just as the door opens, and my eyes find her green ones. The color is vivid and deep, enchanting me every time I see her. It's impossible to look away when she's holding your gaze.

"Hey, Drake. Come on in."

"Hey," I say, walking inside and stopping to pet Cooper. I rub the fur between his ears, and his tail wags. He shifts from one leg to the other, not letting me go further. "Hey, Coop. How have you been? Is this lady treating you right?"

"'This lady' is his owner, and he lives a better life than you and me, trust me." Evangelina chuckles and closes the door. Stepping closer, she bends and gently slaps her dog's butt. "Coop, do me a favor, back off a little. Our guest here came to watch a movie, not stand here and be your hostage."

The dog tilts his head, his eyes focusing on Evangelina. With a huff, he backtracks into the living room. I peek at my neighbor and almost groan in frustration. She's wearing a loose white T-shirt with a red Adidas logo on it and red cotton shorts that highlight her long legs in the most dick-hardening way possible—not metaphorically speaking, because it feels way too tight in my shorts right now.

"I thought you changed your mind," she murmurs, beckoning me to follow her to the living room. "Do you want something to eat? I love having snacks when I watch something."

"Nah, I had dinner already." I beeline to the couch and plop down on it.

Evangelina stops and puts her hands on her hips, eyeing me with a raised eyebrow. "How about something to drink then?"

"Coffee?"

"Sure." She nods and heads to the kitchen. At first I watch her, but then I let my eyes wander around her place.

When I was here helping her with her ankle, I didn't pay attention to my surroundings. The living room is very spacious and light, with bright accents here and there. The cushions on the light gray couch are different shades of pastel blue, just like the chandelier and two floor lamps. White bookshelves are built into the walls, with rows of books arranged by color. There are three beautiful drawings on the wall, and I quickly recognize the theme. It's all Paris—Notre-Dame de Paris, the streets of Montmartre with the cafés and people walking around, and the biggest one: the Eiffel Tower on a rainy day with a girl standing under a red umbrella. The last one is the most detailed one, and I can't stop staring at it.

"Do you like the paintings?" Evangelina's voice rips me out of my thoughts, and I blink, chasing off my trance. "I bought them when I was in Paris last time."

"Did someone draw this one for you?" I point at the painting of the Eiffel Tower, sneaking a glance at my neighbor. Her smile fades away as she puts two mugs on the table. "Evangelina?"

She avoids looking at me as she sits down on the couch. "Yes."

I don't wait for her to continue because I know she's not going to say more. Maybe another time, once she starts trusting me. Right now, we're just two strangers who are forced to spend time together.

I clear my throat. "Are we going to continue watching *One Tree Hill*?"

"Sure. We stopped at episode four, right?"

I nod, and Evangelina takes a remote from the couch, scrolls through some TV shows, and finally finds it. She starts the episode, and we both reach for our mugs. Without asking me how I take my coffee, the girl managed to make it the way I like it: strong and black with no sugar or milk. Its taste is rich, and I enjoy it, relaxing on her couch and fixing my gaze on the TV screen.

We watch an episode, talking here and there about the plot, the characters' actions, and the music. It's easygoing and pleasant. I catch myself thinking that even silence in her company is comfortable. It coats me, warming my insides up and making me feel as if I belong. Not to this place, but with her.

And that's why my fake-dating situation is even more fucked-up than I thought.

Angie

THIRTEEN

game on

"It's almost five a.m.!" I exclaim, dropping my phone back on the couch.

Drake rubs his eyes and then slaps his cheeks, trying to stay awake. "We watched thirteen episodes. Did you think it'd been only an hour?"

"I don't know. I just didn't think it was *that* late." I pull my legs from under my butt and stand up, brushing Drake's knee along the way. Apparently, I didn't notice not only the time, but also our proximity. Somehow, we were almost cuddling. *Dammit.* "Do you have any plans this morning?"

"I was thinking about going for a run, but now I'm planning to sleep. You?" He stands up and takes our empty mugs from the table. Ignoring my extended hand, he proceeds to the kitchen and puts them into the sink. My eyebrows reach my hairline the second he turns on the faucet. Mesmerized, I stay planted near the couch, watching as Drake rinses off our mugs. Once the water stops running, he walks back to me.

"What about you, Cupcake?"

"Nothing. I need to go to my shop at some point," I tell him, hiding my yawn behind my palm. "Thank you for tonight, Drake."

"You're welcome," he says with a smile. "*One Tree Hill* with you is very entertaining."

"Oh yeah? What was the most entertaining part?" I ask, following him to the hallway.

"Dunno, probably the part when you started squealing when Lucas and Peyton kissed in the motel." He throws a wink over his shoulder. "I never expected such sounds from you, Cupcake. I was terrified!"

"Goodness, I take it back." I laugh, not offended in the slightest. "I'm not thanking you for tonight."

Drake opens the door and strolls out of my house. He spins around, facing me, hands hidden in his shorts pockets. "No take-backsies."

Rolling my eyes, I lean against the doorframe. "Whatever you say."

He tilts his head slightly, and his curls fall in his face. "We were so busy watching TV, we totally forgot to talk about our first fake date. You said we were going to decide together."

I gape at Drake and slowly raise my hand. My fingers graze my hoop earring. "You're going to kill me."

"A perfect start," he mutters, scratching his stubble. "Go on, Evangelina. Surprise me."

Biting my bottom lip, I continue toying with my earring. "The movie premiere I mentioned. It's...today."

The silence between us is heavy, just like the weight of his glare on me. His cheeks bulge as he continues to stare at me. Taking a deep breath, he rolls his lips together. "Unbelievable." He pulls his hands out of his pockets and smacks his hips. "What are we seeing?"

"You're not angry with me?" I pinch my eyebrows together.

"What would be the point? Would the movie premiere magically switch to tomorrow?" I shake my head no. "So, what are we seeing?"

"It's a fantasy, something similar to *Game of Thrones*. Dragons, magic, love."

"What? Blood, sex, and war against the living dead—that's what *Game of Thrones* is," he mumbles with a pointed look.

I ignore him. "My friend is starring in the movie, and she got me an invitation. We'll need to be at the venue around six p.m., and I think we'll be done around midnight. Or maybe earlier, if you don't want to go to the after-party."

"Dress code?"

"Black tie optional," I reply with a shrug.

"Well, considering the dress code for games, it's not a problem at all. Anything else?"

"I'll need you at my place at five, so we can run through some ideas about how we first met and what we're going to say if someone asks. Then I'll drive—"

"Not happening. We're going in my car." I open my mouth to disagree with him, but he silences me by saying, "You don't see me complaining about anything else, so please don't try to argue with me about the car. Okay?"

I nod. "Okay. Thank you."

"Uh-huh," he utters and descends the stairs. "See you later, Evangelina."

"Night, Drake," I say and close the door.

With a loud yawn, I drag my feet to my bedroom. After quickly brushing my teeth and changing into my pj's, I crawl under my blanket and fall asleep a minute later. It's been a long day.

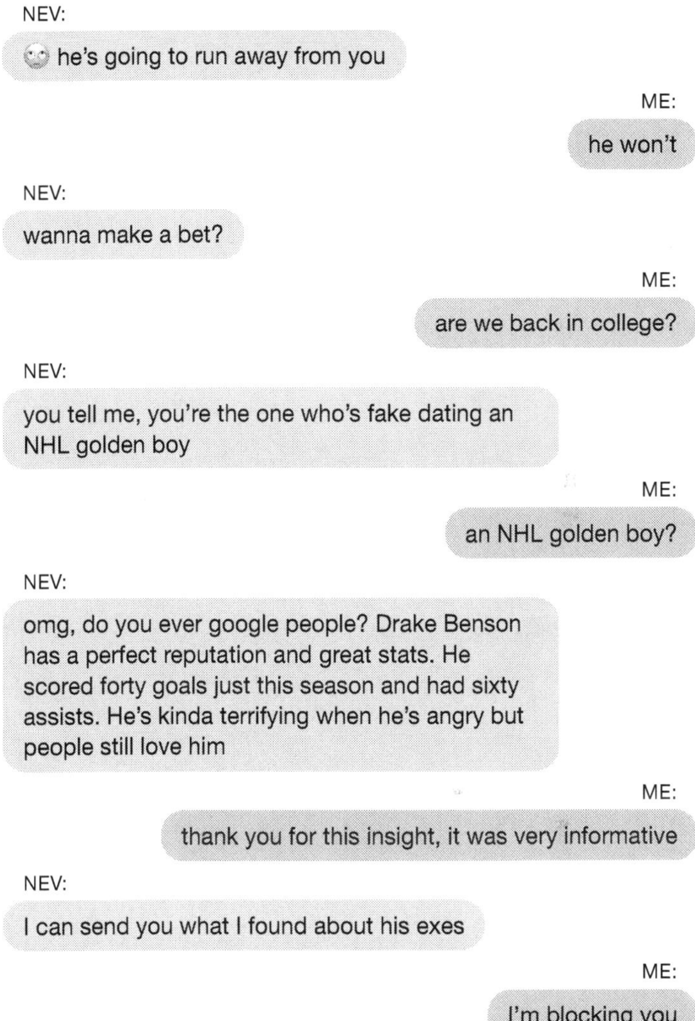

Locking my phone, I put it on my bed and edge back into my closet. Nevaeh chose the worst possible time to annoy me via text. I have no idea what to wear, and it irritates me. Drake is going to be here any minute, and I'm still in my lingerie. And, while I have no doubt I look good in it, I don't think it would be appropriate for a movie premiere.

I sift through the dresses, poking my tongue into my cheek as I do.

It's just utterly ridiculous that even though I have so many clothes, I don't have anything I want to wear. Moving aside another dress, I hear a knock on the door. *Fuck*. I grab a black floral lace overlay fitted sleeveless dress and put it on. Beelining out of the bedroom and to the front door, I try to zip my dress on the way.

Cooper is already by the door, his tail moving at a crazy speed. Why he's always happy to see my neighbor is a mystery to me. My dog has never liked any of my boyfriends the way he likes Drake. I don't get it, except for the most obvious reason: Drake is a good guy, and Coop feels it.

My dog steps aside a little, letting me open the door. The second I do, Cooper is out on the porch, jumping around Drake, trying to get his attention. Not successfully, because my neighbor's eyes are glued to me, and he rubs Coop's fur absentmindedly.

"Hey, Drake."

"Hey, Evangelina." He lets his gaze coast over my form. My skin heats up; the feeling of his eyes on me is like the gentlest caress. Like a cool breeze enveloping my body during the heat of summer, making me crave it more. Like the start of a very strong addiction. "You look absolutely stunning."

"Thank you." I smile, stepping back to let him in. He breezes past me, and the scent of his cologne hits my nostrils. It's woody and fresh at the same time, with notes of lavender, honey, and sandalwood. It suits him to a tee.

I close the door and find him staring at me with a deep frown, his hands balled into fists by his sides. Ignoring the look on his face, my eyes roam over his figure, and I can't help but smile. This man is devilishly handsome, and the suit he's wearing only accentuates it. He's got on a white shirt with a black tie and black trousers, and a buttoned-up black jacket hugs his sculpted body perfectly, letting my imagination run wild. And it's so wrong. *Dammit*.

Sex. Lots of rough and unhinged fucking. That's what I need to stop myself from thinking about it with Drake. It's inappropriate. I asked him to help me with my ex, no more than that.

"I thought you said we needed to be there at six," he deadpans, and I nod. "And yet you're still not ready."

"If you zip my dress, I'll be ready to leave in ten minutes." I walk up to him and give him my back. "Can you please help me?"

Drake's hot breath fanning over my skin is the first thing I feel when he steps closer. His fingers trace my spine, and I shiver. He's not in a rush; all of his movements are slow. The moment he presses his knuckles to the small of my back, I gasp, and my heart rate speeds up. I can only hope he doesn't notice the pulsating vein on my neck.

I need to stop sending him mixed signals. *Do better, Angie.*

"Done." His deep voice sounds soft. "I'll wait in the living room, if that's okay with you?"

"Of course." Without looking at him, I stroll down the hallway to my bedroom. Drake isn't wrong. I need to hurry up.

Ten minutes later, I step into the living room. Cooper is precisely where I expect him to be: in his dog bed, head resting on his paws. Drake, on the other hand, is not where I was picturing him. He's standing in front of my bookshelves with a book in his hands. I saunter over, stand on my tiptoes, and look over his shoulder. It's one of my favorite dark romances.

"Find something interesting?" I ask.

He closes the book and puts it back on the shelf. "You only have romance novels."

"Actually, no. This shelf is full of psychological thrillers," I explain to him, pointing at the shelf to his left. "If that's something you like, you can look through my collection."

"It's one of my favorite genres," he drawls, furrowing his brow. "Maybe next time. I'm sure we'll be late if I start going through your books."

"We have nine seasons to watch; there will definitely be a next time," I say with a lopsided grin. "Should we go? We can talk about our *story* in the car."

"Totally."

Before we leave the house, I check Cooper's water bowl and give him his dinner. When I'm sure he has everything he needs, I walk outside and lock the door. When I have almost reached Drake's car, I wheel around and jog back to the house, turning the handle to make sure I locked it.

The first sign of my anxiety picking up.

Drake helps me climb into his car, makes sure I fasten my seat belt, and only then closes the door and goes around to his side. Starting the engine, he asks for the address, types it into the navigation system, and drives away from our houses.

I sigh, relaxing into my seat and putting my hands on my lap. "Drake, can you please stop calling me Evangelina? I honestly don't really like it, and it's not what my friends and family call me."

"What does your best friend call you?"

"Angie. My family also calls me that."

"And your ex-boyfriends?"

"I was always Evangelina to them," I reply, my fingers tracing the floral lace detail of my dress.

He's driving quietly, eyes on the road. "I like Angie. Can I use that?"

"Absolutely," I confirm. The feeling of a very tight knot unraveling spreads all over my skin, and my muscles relax. I haven't thought about it, but Drake's voice is very soothing. It easily slips right through the walls I've built around myself, affecting me in a way I never anticipated. "Are you going to stop calling me Cupcake now?"

"Not a chance." He guffaws heartily. "I can promise not to call you that at the movie premiere."

"How generous of you." I press my hand to my chest, batting my eyelashes at him. "You're the best fake boyfriend I've ever had."

"And how many fake boyfriends have you had?" Drake stops at a traffic light and rivets his gaze on me.

"You're the only one."

"What an honor." He smirks, resuming our ride when the light changes to green. "Now that it's finally settled, can you tell me what you want me to say if someone asks how we met?"

I fidget in my seat to get a better look at him. Step by step, I explain our meet-cute and how he asked me on a date. It's mostly the true story of how we met, but I leave out the details of our TV nights. It feels too personal, and I want to keep that just for us.

When Drake parks the car, the movie premiere is in full swing. So many moviegoers, reporters, film crew, and paparazzi. Doubts creep into my chest again, and I start fiddling with the hem of my dress. I can't take back what I'm about to do. Once word gets out, there will be no turning back, and we'll need to play our parts to perfection until Asher finally backs off and leaves me alone. I can only hope it won't backfire.

My door opens, and I snap my head to my right, meeting Drake's eyes. "Stop being nervous. Everything is going to be okay."

"Are you sure you wanna do this? We can always go home and pretend—"

"You said your ex is bothering you. The only thing I want is for him to leave you alone. If I need to survive a few fake dates for that, why not? Besides, I like hanging out with you."

"I like hanging out with you too." It rushes out, the words bubbling in my throat.

Drake extends his hand to me, and I take it. "Let's go, Angie. We have a movie premiere to conquer." He pulls me out of his car, entwining our fingers. "Game on."

Drake

FOURTEEN

is this okay?

WALKING SLOWLY TOWARD THE MOVIE THEATER, HAND IN hand with Evangelina, I listen to her inhale and exhale to calm herself down. It makes me wonder how someone can be as confident as she is and also be so vulnerable and timid. The answer is hidden somewhere in her past, and somehow I think it goes even beyond her relationship with her ex. She has anxiety. I saw similar behaviors from my mom when she was grieving my grandmother's death, so it's not something I haven't seen before, but it worries me. Her checking to make sure she locked the door is only one sign. Checking Cooper's bowl several times, rearranging the books on her shelf after I put one back in the same spot I took it from—something triggers that, and hopefully I'll be able to find out the reason.

I want to help her.

We step onto the red carpet, exchanging a look. I sweep my gaze over her face and smile broader. Evangelina is effortlessly beautiful, and she looks incredible without any makeup on, but tonight, with her black eyeliner and her lips painted red, she's simply perfect. Her dark green eyes and her thick black eyelashes are fully capable of making any man lose his mind—especially me, and I'm afraid I'm doing a bad job at hiding it. Her straightened hair shines under the lights; the chocolate highlights catch my attention when she tucks a few locks behind her ears. There are so many people, and cameras flash here and there, but she stands out among them all. It's impossible not to look.

"Ready?" she chirps, and I squeeze her hand instead of answering. Grinning, she takes a step forward, and I follow, smiling from ear to ear. "If you feel uncomfortable or want to leave, just tell me. Okay?"

"I'm a trueborn winner, Angie. Giving up isn't in my nature."

"How many non-sports-related events have you been to?" Evangelina asks, quirking an eyebrow.

"I don't remember." I frown, and she breaks into melodic laughter.

"Then follow my lead, Mr. Benson." She stops walking, and I stop too. Looking up, she winks at me and turns her head toward the horde of photographers. I stare at her for a moment longer, and then I face them too.

Thank God I'm used to taking pictures. Before I started playing in the NHL, I would've freaked out. A few photographers call her name, and a smile blossoms on her lips. She's in her element, not bothered by the attention, and I enjoy the confidence she radiates. It's compelling.

Slowly, Angie moves again, and I follow without a single word. When we stop to take more pictures, I let go of her hand and wrap my arm around her waist.

Leaning to her ear, I whisper, "Giving them a better angle."

She softly chuckles and presses herself closer to me. "You learn faster than I thought."

We pose some more, and I start hearing my name too. I'd hoped to be Mr. Mysterious, but it's not happening. The photographers recognize me, and their murmurs become louder. I'm sure we're not causing the same ruckus the movie cast is, but we'll make the headlines. Evangelina's plan is working.

A girl with a mic blocks our way, her eyes dancing between my date and me. "Evangelina, what a nice surprise," she says with a smile. "Came to see Willow's new movie?"

"Hey, Deb, you're absolutely right. I wouldn't have missed it for the world," Angie replies, angling her body to match mine and pressing her butt to my groin. *Fuck my life.* If I don't get hard, it will be a fucking miracle. "It's Willow's debut as the lead role, and I'm immensely proud of her. She worked so hard, and she deserves all the success."

"Aw, it's so nice to see you supporting your college friend. It's refreshing," the reporter comments sweetly. Then she shifts her gaze to me. "I hope you don't mind, but how did the daughter of Logan Jones end up at this movie premiere with a hockey player? I want some gossip, Evangelina!"

The stiffness of Angie's shoulders makes me drop my eyes to her face. She's still smiling, but the glint in her eyes has turned dark. "Destiny has a very peculiar sense of humor, Deb. Drake and I met not long ago, when he moved to Santa Clara. I can thank my dog for that, because Cooper played matchmaker, running into Drake when I took him for a walk. Now, we're just trying to see where it's all going."

Meticulously, I glide my hand around Angie's waist and cover her belly with my palm. Our bodies are flush against each other, but in this moment it's the last thing I'm worried about. Her shoulders drop, and she leans her back against my chest. A sigh leaves her parted lips, and a satisfied grin forms on my face. *I've got you, Angie.*

"I don't know much about hockey...unfortunately," the reporter says, our eyes meeting. "Drake, I've been told you haven't been in California long, but you have Evangelina Jones as your date. Any chance you've already met her father? Logan Jones is a legend."

"You know, Deb, while I'm sure Evangelina's dad is a great person, his daughter is much more important to me," I state. "So the answer is no, I haven't met her father, and you should think about coming to a hockey game when the season starts again. I'm sure you'll love it."

"Thank you, Drake," she murmurs. A little frown grows on her face, but it fades quickly. "Well, I hope you enjoy the movie. See you later, lovebirds."

"See you," Evangelina utters, taking a step away from me. Without giving it much thought, I grab her palm in mine and earn myself an appreciative smile as we finally enter the movie theater.

We mingle, exchanging a few words with other attendees here and there. I don't expect anyone to recognize me, but I'm wrong. Some men bombard me with questions about last season and my predictions for the next one. It feels nice, not forced, and I relax. I imagined things to be much worse than they are. People here are friendly, with no desire to impress others. I like it.

The moment Evangelina sees her friend, she makes me follow her. I snort in amusement at how she drags me all the way across the hall. This woman is full of energy. She doesn't stay anywhere for too long. How she was able to sit through the thirteen episodes we watched last night is beyond me. She must really like *One Tree Hill*; it's the only explanation I have.

"Willow, you look absolutely fabulous." Evangelina greets her friend, hugging her tightly. She's a redhead with a pretty face and big hazel eyes. Attractive, but not even close to as stunning as my date is... at least in my eyes.

"Look who's talking," Willow replies, taking Angie's hands in hers. "I'm so happy you decided to come."

"I'd never miss this. You're my friend." They hug again, and when Willow leans away, she notices me standing a little behind Evangelina. Her eyes do a round over my body, and then she refocuses on her friend.

"Are you going to introduce me to your date?"

Angie sneaks a glance at me, and a lopsided grin dances across her lips. "Willow, this is Drake."

"It's very nice to meet you, Willow," I say, extending my hand. She shakes it, eyeing me from under her eyelashes.

"You too, Drake." Willow steps back and then averts her gaze to my date. Her teeth are nibbling on her bottom lip. "Angie, can I have a word?"

It takes all my willpower not to laugh. *Try not to be so obvious, girl.*

"Drake?" Angie's eyes roam over my face. She's hesitating, not certain if I'll be okay on my own.

"Find me when you're done," I tell her, dropping my lips to her forehead and quickly pulling away. I hide my hands in my pockets to stop myself from doing anything else. *That's not what fake boyfriends do*. I need to remember that.

I walk away from Angie and her friend, just wandering around the venue and stopping by the table of appetizers. I stare at the food without seeing it; my mind is elsewhere.

"How about these canapes? They look delicious." A woman's deep voice catches me off guard, and I hastily whirl to my right. A woman in a red bodycon dress with dark black hair stands by my side. I've already seen her today, when she approached Angie and me to make some small talk. Is she an actress? I don't remember.

"No, I'm not hungry."

"Your loss then." She bats her eyelashes at me and leans forward, brushing my leg with her hand. She seizes a canape from the table. Holding my gaze, she takes a bite and closes her eyes, moaning at how good it tastes.

I'm not buying the act though. This woman was undressing me with her eyes when she talked to Angie and me, and now she's here again, flirting with me while my date is nowhere near.

"So, you play hockey?" she asks with her mouth full.

"Yes. What about you? What do you do for a living?" I'm not even remotely interested, but if it will keep me from talking about myself, I'm good.

"I'm an actress. This movie is my third one. Not the lead role yet, but I'm working on it." She pushes the last of her canape into her mouth and shakes breadcrumbs off her hands. "I don't believe I've had a chance to introduce myself. I'm Camilla."

"Nice to meet you, Camilla." I don't say my name, just continue to look at her with a smile. She's good-looking, but she gives me the biggest ick.

Two hands snake around my torso from behind; I smell the familiar perfume and have no doubt about who it belongs to. "There you are," Evangelina coos, rounding me and stopping right in front of the girl in the red dress.

Using this opportunity, I wind my hand around Evangelina's

waist and bring my gaze to Camilla's face. "Are you excited to see the movie you worked so hard on?"

Camilla ignores Angie and plasters a toothy smile on her face, softening her eyes. "Absolutely. I hope *you* will like it."

Unbelievable. She's acting like Evangelina isn't even here.

"We'll see about that. I'm a picky audience."

Camilla grimaces, then looks over her shoulder and waves to someone. "I gotta go. It was nice meeting you..." She trails off, expecting me to say my name.

"It was nice meeting you too, Camilla," I say nonchalantly.

She lingers for a moment. Then, without another word, she's gone. Evangelina and I stand still, her back pressed to my chest. Slowly, she turns around, staying in my embrace. Her green eyes are darker than usual as she examines my face.

"You were alone for ten minutes, and you already have girls coming on to you."

"I'm not interested." I shrug, enjoying how incredible she feels in my arms.

"Why not? Camilla is a very beautiful girl," Evangelina insists.

"She saw us together before. She even talked to us, and she still thought it was okay to flirt with me." I drop my head, looking Angie right in the eyes. "I'm not interested in a girl who flirts with a man knowing he has a date. It's disrespectful to you."

The silence between us lasts for what feels like an eternity. As if time is frozen. Neither of us moves. Our gazes stay locked on each other. I slide my hands lower, down her back, and her pupils dilate.

"Is this okay?" I whisper. My voice cracks.

Angie nods, and I find myself leaning down to her face. My nose touches hers, and I inhale. Her scent hits me right in the brain. It's my first sign to break free from her. And yet, I dip my head lower, my competitive side kicking in. When someone is used to winning, it's hard for them to give up...even if sometimes giving up is exactly what needs to be done.

A sudden burst of laughter pierces the air, followed by loud chatter. Evangelina puts her palm on my chest and pushes me away gently, making me take a step back. My hands drop to my sides, and a feeling of emptiness overwhelms me.

"The movie is about to start. We better go inside." She offers me a smile, and I reluctantly return it.

I almost kissed my *fake* girlfriend on our first ever *fake* date. If that's not the best example of me being a complete idiot, I don't know what is.

"Yeah, let's go." I nod, and we follow the crowd inside the theater. Even if it's the last place I want to be.

Angie

FIFTEEN

just my fake boyfriend

"So, what did you think about tonight? You don't regret coming with me?" I ask Drake as we climb out of his car.

The movie ended two hours ago, and we left the after-party as soon as I noticed how miserable my date had become. Something flipped inside him, and instead of a smiling and affectionate guy, I got a broody man who just followed me wherever I went. I'd have to be heartless to not know why it happened. It was all me.

"The movie was good. The battle scenes were stunning, jaw-dropping in some places. But the ending was predictable; I saw it coming a mile away. Though it's a great buildup to the sequel." He hides his hands in his pockets as we stroll in the direction of our houses.

"What about the romance?"

"What about it? It was dead. I didn't see any chemistry between the main characters. I'm glad the guy died," Drake says in a dull voice.

"He'll survive, but his acting needs improvement. Just being handsome is not enough."

"I hope they pick someone else as a love interest for Willow's character. She deserves better," he says matter-of-factly. "Your friend is a very talented actress; I'm not surprised she got the lead role. She carried most of the movie on her own."

"I'm honestly so proud of her. She's been working so hard to get here, and she has real talent. Willow's career is only starting, and I'm excited to see what's going to happen next." My answer earns me a smile from him—the first one since we sat down in the theater.

"You're a good friend."

"I don't have many, so I cherish the relationships I do have," I say, stopping near my porch. Drake stops too, and the look on his face makes my heart ache.

His loneliness is almost palpable, and he's not hiding it this time. He's letting me see him as he is, and it's agonizing. This man seems lost, like a ship without an anchor during a storm. Something is missing; the grounding element is absent. And I'm not sure if he knows how to find it on his own.

"Do you want to come over? We can watch something together," I suggest, locking my hands in front of me to keep myself from reaching out to him. Tactile contact is supposed to be only for the public eye, but after tonight I don't think that's a good idea either.

"No, I better go home," he rasps harshly, instantly pressing a palm to his forehead and dragging it over his face. "Sorry, I'm just tired." And hurt, and he's terrible at hiding it. "Maybe tomorrow? Your place or mine?"

"Yours," I reply, and he looks up. The fervor of his dark brown eyes immobilizes me, and a long-forgotten feeling forms in my belly. *The butterflies.* Something I hoped to never feel again. The graveyard inside me has been silent for a long time...until him. My fingers start to tremble, and I press my palms together tighter, the pain rippling through my bones. "I'll be at my shop for most of the day. How about eight p.m.?"

"Okay." There's a slight movement, and for a second I think he's going to hug me, but instead he starts climbing stairs. "See you tomorrow."

"See you tomorrow," I echo, heading to my front door.

A million thoughts about my evening with Drake whir in my head, disappearing one by one as I go through my bedtime routine. After checking on Cooper in his dog bed, I finally crawl under my blanket. I close my eyes, knowing very well there's only one thought left.

I shouldn't have asked him to be my fake boyfriend. This is a game I'm not going to win.

GOING FOR A RUN WAS A MUST. It cleared my head and helped me sort out my feelings. The exhaustion, the tiredness of my muscles felt like a blessing. The hot shower I took after recharged my batteries and filled me with much-needed energy. I was ready for all the challenges in the world, ready to move mountains.

Until I saw my ex sitting on the hood of my car with two cups of iced coffee in his hands. The day instantly took a turn toward disastrous.

"Go away," I grind out when I reach Asher.

"Good morning, beautiful. You look absolutely breathtaking," he murmurs, extending a cup to me. "It's your favorite, with salted caramel."

"Did you spit in it?"

His eyes round, the corners of his mouth twitching. "Why would I do that, Evangelina?"

"Did you drug it?"

Asher stares at me for a second, then bursts out in laughter. "It's just a coffee, Evangelina. I'm trying to be nice."

I grab the drink out of his hands. My imagination creates a perfect picture of me throwing it all over him, but my car doesn't deserve to be covered in an iced latte with salted caramel. "If you really want to be nice, Asher, leave me alone. This is exhausting."

"I'll never get tired of fighting for you. You are the one, I know it."

Please, if he's my punishment for all the bad I've done, I better fucking die.

"I know I deserve better than your lying and cheating ass." I hover over him, my eyes holding his. "You're a manipulator, a cheater, and an abuser, and I'm a hundred percent better off without you. You're my living nightmare, and I'd do anything to never see you ever again."

His face contorts in anger; a flicker of barely hidden rage passes behind his irises. The monster inside him is still there, lurking in the shadows of his damaged soul. Waiting for a chance to come out and play...with me.

But he quickly recovers. Asher smiles, standing up from the hood of my car and making me take a step back. He invades my personal space, and I freeze on the spot. The mixture of my feelings messes with my head. I want to fight just as much as I want to run away. He scares me and enrages me all at the same time, making my blood boil with anger and my heart rattle in my chest. I'm not the girl he was with anymore, but I'm not my strongest self either. I'm working on it.

"How much did your father pay that guy to go to the movie premiere with you?" Asher hisses. His sudden question throws me off.

"What are you talking about?"

"Your father never liked me, you told me that yourself. The great Logan Jones wanted me out of his little girl's life so he could marry her off to some jock." He steps closer again, just as I take another step back. "Do you think I'm going to believe you and that hockey dude met by accident? It's all your father's doing."

It's so absurd I want to laugh. "My dad was a quarterback. He played for one of the best teams in the NFL," I state, squaring my shoulders, suddenly feeling a rush of energy flow through my whole body. Lifting my chin, I let myself relax and push the latte back into his hands. "He doesn't have friends in the NHL, and he most certainly doesn't know Drake. You're wrong."

"Then you hired him."

I arch an eyebrow at him. "Asher, do you have any idea what an NHL player makes? He doesn't need my money." I have no clue how much Drake makes, and it's not something I'm interested in, but I know what I'm talking about because of my dad. "I didn't hire anyone. Drake is my boyfriend."

"Boyfriend?" Asher asks, narrowing his eyes. "You're more affectionate with your best friend than with your so-called boyfriend. I saw all the pictures and videos from last night. You're lying to my fucking face, Evangelina. It's all pretense. I don't believe you."

Taking a deep breath, I look away. Then I notice the absence of Drake's car and wonder where he is, though deep down I'm happy he's not home. I don't want him to meet Asher. Not now, not ever. He's too good of a guy to deal with someone as rotten as my ex.

"You know, Asher, thankfully, the days when I cared about your opinion are over. I don't give a damn what you think about my relationship with Drake. It's none of your business." I skirt him, unlocking my car. "What matters is that I'm happy with my new guy, and I want you to leave me alone. I'm asking you nicely, for now."

"You're playing games, Evangelina," he growls. "I know you're not over me."

"Bye, Asher. I have more important things to do than listen to your nonsense."

Sliding inside my car, I close the door and start the engine. As I drive away from my house I see him standing in the driveway, his eyes never leaving my car. His fixation on me becomes harder to ignore, taking my anxiety to the next level. If this continues, I'm not sure I'll be able to deal with it without Dr. Nichols's help.

"WHO ARE WE TRYING TO IMPRESS?" Marcy looks over my shoulder at the red velvet cake with cream cheese frosting I just finished. "It looks like a masterpiece, Angie."

"I did it for fun." I shrug, taking the plate in my hands. Smiling at my pastry chef, I open the fridge and put the cake inside. "I love trying my hand at new recipes."

"You do." She grins knowingly, leaning her side against the kitchen counter. Her fiery red hair is collected in a neat bun, adding a colorful element to the black dress she wears at work. "Is there any chance you did it for fun for your hot new boyfriend?"

"My hot new boyfriend?" I ask, raising an eyebrow at Marcy. "What do you know?"

"Well, according to my husband, Drake Benson is the right wing for the California Thunders. A talented player, very skilled and attentive to everything happening around him. He mostly plays nice, but if someone pisses him off or attacks his teammates? Oh boy. The way he threw one player over the board during a game against Toronto was epic. I couldn't stop watching it on repeat." The more she talks, the longer my face becomes. That's not something I expected to hear. "But also he's incredibly handsome, the yummiest thing I've ever seen."

"Is that also according to your husband?" I taunt, and she slaps my hand with a wet towel. "Ouch!"

"You deserve it, young lady, for mocking an old woman."

"Stop. You're not old, Marcy. At forty, life is just starting."

She eyes me for a moment, and then sighs, nodding. "Okay, I'm not old, and you're dating the NHL's golden boy. If we're done stating facts, can we please talk about your boyfriend? Because, holy hotness, I've seen some pictures of him in only his jeans, and I melted. Instantly. Everywhere."

"TMI, Marcy. Remind me to include a no-sharing-personal-information clause in your contract."

"It's not too much information, Angie. I'm telling you the truth. The guy is absolute eye candy, and yet there's something that makes him even more attractive." She winks at me. The smile on her face blooms, and her light blue eyes glimmer with joy.

"Which is?"

"The way he looks at you."

My heart leaps out of my chest as I gawk at my chef. Oblivious to my reaction, she pulls her phone out of her pocket, taps on the screen, and then shoves it in my face. I suck in a breath when I see the picture she's showing me.

I'm cocooned in Drake's arms, our faces an inch apart. The fluttering in my belly grows stronger, and a smile spreads across my lips. *Involuntarily*. But then my good mood suddenly changes when I remember that I pushed him away right after this.

"You look so good together, Angie." Marcy steps closer, winding a hand around my shoulders. "With this man by your side, you were glowing. The brightest smile on your face, the happiest glint in your eyes... It's not something I've seen much of lately."

"Thank you," I mumble under my breath, putting my head on her shoulder. "He's a really good guy."

"Good. You deserve a good one, especially after the assholes you dated before. He's a triple upgrade from that jerk Asher." She kisses the top of my head, presses me harder against her side. "Tell me, how did you meet him?"

Opening my mouth, I'm ready to tell her about our catastrophic meet-cute. About Cooper scaring Drake and me arguing with him because he didn't give me a chance to apologize. But then I remember a little different story I came up with...the one to make Asher back off.

"You'll never believe me if I tell you," I say, plastering on a smile as I lie to Marcy.

He's just my fake boyfriend. I need to focus on that...for his own good.

Drake

SIXTEEN

mine

I'M SITTING AT THE KITCHEN ISLAND, READING A BOOK, nursing a half-empty glass of whiskey. The story is dark and gripping with graphically depictive scenes about an FBI agent trying to catch a serial killer. I have my guess about who the killer is. All the little bread-crumbs point to one guy...and that's why I think I'm wrong. It's too obvious.

The knock on my door makes me close my book and put my glass on the counter. I stand up and unhurriedly saunter to the hallway. With how immersed in the story I've been, I have no idea what time it is. Is it eight p.m. already?

I open my door and see Evangelina in front of me. My eyes travel down her form, assessing every detail of her outfit. She's wearing a short, pastel pink T-shirt dress with red and white sneakers. Her hair is collected into a bun with a braid wrapped around it, a red ribbon securing it. The look is cute, and she's wearing no makeup, a complete difference from her elegant black dress with red stilettos from last night.

"Hey."

"Hey. Come on in." When she passes me, I notice a box in her hands. I close the door and turn around, finding her standing still in the middle of my hallway. "Is something wrong?"

"No. I have something for you." Evangelina speaks softly, extending the box to me. "I've been experimenting with a new recipe, and I thought you'd be interested in trying it."

I take the box from her hands, open it, and look down at a piece of red and white cake. "And what is it? Does this cake have a name?"

"Red velvet, with cream cheese frosting."

"And strawberries," I mutter under my breath, looking up from the cake and closing the box. Her face darkens, and she smooths her hands over her dress.

"You don't like it," Evangelina states. Her index finger circles her thumbnail. It's frantic, and my gaze zeroes in on it. What is she doing? "I should've brought you something else. Marcy made chocolate cupcakes just before I left. I should've—"

"Angie," I say her name, stopping her mumbling. "This cake looks delicious, and I'm sure it tastes incredible. I'll try it tomorrow, I promise." A crooked smile starts playing on my lips. "I had a glass of whiskey already, and I don't want to mix it with the dessert."

"Okay, but you need to put it in the fridge." She points her thumb in the direction of my living room. "Are you ready to go back to *One Tree Hill*?"

Smirking, I stroll past Evangelina and head to the kitchen. Once the cake is safe in the fridge, I notice her watching me. "Do you want something to drink? I'm thinking about pouring myself another glass of whiskey."

"Same as you." Angie shrugs, and I nod.

A few minutes later, Evangelina and I are sitting on the couch. I start the next episode, but when I feel her gaze on me, I instantly pause it. Turning to my right, I meet her eyes. A few ice cubes clink together as I watch her sip her drink. Matching her, I take a sip of my own whiskey, enjoying how the liquid slides down my throat and sets my skin on fire.

"How was your day?" she asks.

"It was fine. I went to the gym, then met my friend for a bit and then came home. When you knocked, I was actually reading."

"What book? Maybe I've heard about it, or read it already."

"And that's the reason I won't tell you. I'm very close to finally discovering who the serial killer is, and I don't want you to spoil it for me if you know."

"You're unbelievable." Evangelina presses her glass to her mouth, rolling it over her lips. "I love spoilers, but I never ever talk about plot twists with anyone. It steals all the fun."

"Speaking of fun." I set my glass aside and take my phone from the table. Unlocking it, I quickly find what I want to show her and toss it onto her lap. "Look what I got this morning."

Angie takes my phone in her hand and reads the message. "Janelle? Is this from your ex?"

"Yeah, she saw our photos from the movie premiere, and it made her think about me."

"According to her, you moved on real fast." Evangelina teases me, and I grab my phone from her hand. "She's funny. Why didn't you answer her though? She's trying to blame you for her own behavior. She's the one who found herself a boyfriend as soon as she broke up with you."

"Janelle isn't aware that I know that."

Her mouth drops open, and her eyes round. "Are you joking? Why didn't you confront her? Your life was in Michigan, and it suddenly changed without you having any control over it, and she left you despite how stressful it was."

"Haven't I told you I don't want anything from her?" I put my phone on the table and pick up my glass instead. "Janelle knows I'm not miserable or heartbroken, and that's enough for me. I'm good."

"What if she wants you back?"

"I'm not looking to step into the same river twice." I gulp a good amount of my drink, noticing how silent she's suddenly become. "What about you? Did you hear from your ex?"

"Unfortunately," Angie confirms, wiggling on my couch. The skirt of her dress rides up as she tucks her legs under her butt. She keeps her gaze glued to the floor, not noticing how slowly my eyes devour her exposed skin. I need to stop doing that...one of these days.

"He didn't send a message, or call. Asher was waiting for me by my car this morning."

Looking up, I stare at her with my eyebrows furrowed and my jaw set hard. "What?"

"Nothing really new. Aside from the theory he had about us."

"Which is?"

"There are two, actually. One: my dad set me up with you because he always hated Asher. Two: I hired you to fool him into believing that I'm taken."

I snicker, laughing loud. "Too bad he didn't come up with the third one: how you begged me to be your fake boyfriend."

"In your dreams," Evangelina says snidely.

"In my dreams?" I repeat, and she nods, a smile still playing on her lips. "Sure, I can easily imagine you on your knees for me."

The hand holding her drink freezes midair. She narrows her eyes, and a hidden fire reflects in her pupils. "I should've made a rule for that too."

"A rule about jokes?"

"A rule about sex jokes," Evangelina corrects me, then chokes on a sip of her drink. Tears form in her eyes, but she refuses to look away. She coughs, pressing her palm to her mouth. "You jinxed me."

"It was your ex," I counter with a broad smile on my face. She holds my gaze for a moment longer, and then she shakes her head.

"He cursed me, Drake. Jinxing is amateur level. And Asher is a real pro at ruining my life."

"What did he do?" I try, dipping my head lower so our eyes are on the same level.

Angie scrutinizes me, her glass pressed to her cheek. "I'm not drunk yet, so I won't spill my secrets."

"I need to get you drunk so I can learn all your secrets? Good to know," I tell her over the rim of my glass. She rolls her eyes and grabs the remote from the table.

Restarting the episode, she says, "Let's start watching."

I GROAN, banging the nape of my neck against the back of my couch. "This show is so fucking dramatic sometimes."

"It's also about the decisions we all make, and how our words can affect others, especially when we say them without thinking. It's about how we follow our hearts despite knowing how wrong it is. About life, love, and friendship. Is it exaggeration? Yes, but it's still good."

The living room is dark; the only light comes from the TV. It's around one a.m., and the first episode of season two is just starting. I'm having my fourth glass of whiskey, and my emotions are on high alert, sensing every change of the atmosphere in the room. Evangelina is on her third drink, and she's definitely more playful.

"I don't believe in coincidence, and in this show most things are too far-fetched."

She laughs heartily. The sound reverberates through my whole body. "Thank God you play hockey and don't write for TV."

"Cheers to that." I raise my glass before taking a sip. "Have you ever been to a hockey game?"

"I watched a few, mostly the Olympics and the Stanley Cup playoffs. But I've never been to an actual game."

"Then the first thing I'll do when the season starts in October is invite you to one of my games. You'll get the best seats."

"Will you give me your jersey to wear?" she asks, moving to her left to get a better look at me.

I study her, sipping my drink in silence. The image of her in just my jersey makes my dick twitch in my shorts. Even in my imagination, she looks divine in it. "If you are still my girlfriend."

"Your *fake* girlfriend." She eyeballs the floor. "I hope Asher will be long gone by October. I'm so tired of him and his nonsense."

"What else did he say to you?"

"That I'm lying to his face, that I still want to be with him. Not with anyone else, and especially not with you. He said he saw the pictures from the premiere, insinuating that we don't have any chemistry."

"That's because you chickened out," I say, putting my arm across the back of the couch. I was upset with her last night, so making her uncomfortable today seems like good payback. It's innocent.

"What?" Evangelina asks. She sets her empty glass on the table.

"You didn't let me kiss you, and now your ex isn't convinced we're together." Gulping down the rest of my drink, I watch her over the rim of my glass. I wish the room were brighter so I could see all the emotions on her face.

"I didn't chicken out."

"You did. I asked if it was okay, and you said yes, but then you pushed me away."

"The movie was about to start, and we were standing in the middle of the fucking hall. We were in everyone's way," she grits through her teeth.

"If that makes you feel better. But I prefer the truth." I lean forward and put my glass on the table next to hers. "You started a game, but I don't think you know how to play it. So your ex showing up again is totally on you."

Her lips twist into a scowl, and she glares at me. "I better go home," Evangelina says, standing up from the couch. "I'll talk to you later, when you stop being a dick."

"Sure, Cupcake." Our gazes lock on each other as I remain seated.

Evangelina towers over me, her chest heaving from her erratic breathing. She's pissed, and I suddenly want to fucking smile. Even furious, she's stunning, and I can't take my eyes off her. Raising her hand, she opens her mouth, intending to say something, but no sound follows.

"Is there something else?" I kid her, arching an eyebrow with a slight tilt of my head. Instead of an answer, Evangelina dashes out of the room. A moment later, my front door slams shut.

Well, the girl definitely has a temper.

I take the remote from the couch, debating if I should keep watching or just go to bed. The episode starts as I hit play and put the remote aside. Spreading my arms, I stretch them across the back of my couch and mindlessly stare at the TV. My mind is too far gone to follow what's happening on the screen.

Not sure that's what I wanted to happen when I started teasing her. Maybe I should have—

My thoughts halt abruptly when the sound of the door closing reaches my ears. I turn my head just in time to see Evangelina in the doorframe. Her eyes are narrowed, glued to my face. She scurries to the couch, stopping right in front of me with her hands on her hips. Taking a deep breath, she clicks her tongue and climbs onto my lap, her arms wrapping around my shoulders.

And I'm suddenly so full of her. With the scent of her perfume, with the warmth of her skin, her hot breath fanning over my face. I want it all, savoring, drinking her till the last drop. Winding my hands around her waist, I keep her in place.

Evangelina bends toward my face; our noses touch. Her lips are an inch from mine, and I try to kiss her, but she pulls away. Just slightly, only to bring her lips back to mine a second later. This time, she's done playing, because her mouth covers mine, and nothing else matters to me anymore.

Her lips are full and soft, moving with mine in a perfect tempo. It's slow, and so damn arousing, so my cock grows harder underneath her. Her tongue brushes my bottom lip, and I open up for her, letting her dive in.

Our tongues swirl around each other, the kiss turning wild and hungry. My grip on her waist tightens when I haul her closer to me. Her breasts are pressed to my chest, the hard points of her nipples chafing against my skin. Her hands roam over my shoulders and up my neck, until her fingers dig into my skull. Twisting my hair, she tilts my head and pulls away.

The glint in her eyes makes my heartbeat gallop. It's heated, fully capable of setting my whole house on fire, not just me. Her parted lips look puffy, and I smile, noticing a tint of pink on her cheeks.

"Pull something like that again..." she whispers, still sitting on my lap with my hard-on pressed to her pussy. There is no way she can't feel it, but it doesn't seem to bother her. "...and I'll find myself another fake boyfriend."

"You won't." I grin, my hands slowly sliding down her hips.

Hopping off my lap, she straightens her dress. Then, without another word, she ambles out of the living room. She pauses in the doorframe and glances at the TV over her shoulder. Then she looks at me. "Don't you dare watch without me."

A second later, she's out of the room, and I shout after her, "Your place or mine tomorrow?"

And before Evangelina bolts out of my house, I hear her voice again: "Mine."

Mine, indeed. That's what I want to call her.

Angie

SEVENTEEN

a full-blown disaster

Living with regrets isn't like me. No matter what I do, I've learned how to embrace the consequences. How to fix things if something is broken. Anything instead of regretting my decisions. What's done is done, and thinking about the what-ifs is never good.

Kissing Drake last night wasn't a mistake—rather, a complication. One I should've counted on when planning this whole fake-dating charade, but instead I chose to ignore it. Guarding my heart for years, building walls around myself and not letting a single guy get too close to me...all those years of hard work, undone. All it took was my new neighbor and his loneliness.

Well, and my stalker ex, but he's the last person I want to think about. Drake, on the other hand...

The clink of glasses brings me back to reality. I blink and focus on my best friend, who's sitting in front of me in a packed restaurant. Nevaeh's blue eyes are examining me.

"What are you thinking about?" she asks.

"Nothing," I reply with a slight jerk of my head.

Nevaeh frowns and puts her glass down. Setting her elbows on the table, she lowers her chin onto her hands and observes me. "Angie, you're only this quiet when you have a lot on your mind. What's going on?"

"I kissed Drake last night," I blurt out, lifting my shoulder in a shrug.

Nevaeh's pupils dilate, her blues opening wider. "No way," she whispers. Then her lips ease into a broad smile. "Is he, like, your *boyfriend* boyfriend now, or are you still fake dating, but with kisses?"

I cover my face with my palms, silent giggles wracking my body. This reaction is so her; I shouldn't be surprised at all.

"The kiss didn't mean anything. He's my...friend," I say when my laughter finally subsides. "And he's still just my fake boyfriend. That's not going to change."

"Well, I know you have a tendency to kiss your friends." Nev waggles her eyebrows suggestively. "And even sleep with them."

An eye roll is all I give her. "We have a no-sex rule."

"Correct me if I'm wrong, but kisses were supposed to be for the public eye, and only if it was appropriate." I nod, confirming her words. "And where were you last night when you kissed your hot fake boyfriend? I thought you were watching *One Tree Hill* with him...at his place."

"He wanted to kiss me at the movie premiere, but I pushed him away. He was all broody after that—"

"So you kissed him last night out of pity?"

"Of course not. He said I chickened out at the premiere, and I kinda wanted to prove him wrong," I mutter, tucking a lock of hair behind my ear.

"Wow, he's smart. I like the guy even more now." She chuckles, leaning toward me. "He dared you to kiss him without actually daring you."

I know he did, and I know I didn't have anything against it by how quickly I returned to his house and climbed onto his lap. His hard dick poking into my pussy through our clothes was the cherry on top—a little problem I had to deal with when I got back home and my panties were drenched. But that's something I definitely don't plan on telling Nev.

"It doesn't change the fact that it meant nothing."

"Keep telling yourself that, baby." Nevaeh taps on my nose and leans back, picking up her glass from the table.

"Nev, I don't need a relationship. Especially a relationship with a professional athlete," I argue, grabbing my glass and taking a sip of my wine.

"The guys you dated in school were pigs. Jocks who wanted to use you to get close to your dad so he could help them with their college stipends and future careers," she states, pointing her finger at me. "Drake is already a professional hockey player with a successful career, and maybe he has zero interest in football. He might not even know who your dad is. Why are you comparing him to them?"

"I'm not. He's different, I know that," I reassure her and down the rest of my drink. Setting my empty glass on the table, I meet my best friend's gaze. "I like him, but he's just a friend."

Nevaeh narrows her eyes to slits, scowling at me. After a short silence, she says, "Let's go to the club after dinner."

I knit my brows together, gaping at her. "I can't. I promised Drake we'd watch—"

"That's what I'm talking about. You *want* to spend time with him."

"Nev, he's lonely. He didn't ask to be traded. It just happened, and he moved here all alone. I think he could use a friend," I tell her with a smile. "Besides, I don't have his phone number, so I can't call or text him to reschedule."

My best friend stares at me for a moment, and then bursts out laughing. "Leave it to Evangelina Jones to always find an excuse." When she finally settles down, she takes a deep breath, and a lopsided grin plays on her lips. "Speaking of excuses. Are we going to the music festival on Saturday, or have you come up with a reason to skip it?"

"We're going. I want to see Sabotage play. They're all I've listened to this week."

"Me too." Nev sips her drink, her eyes glimmering mischievously. "Road trip with my best friend, and then dancing and singing at the top of our lungs at the festival. What could be better?"

I nod. "It's the best."

Suddenly, Nevaeh's eyebrows go up, and her jaw drops.

"What brilliant idea just popped into your head this time?" I ask.

"Let's invite your fake boyfriend. There will be a lot of people; it's a good chance for you to be photographed with him. Plus, Asher and some of his friends might be there too. What a great way to flaunt your fake relationship in your ex's face."

I open my mouth and close it again, looking at my best friend as if I'm seeing her for the first time. "He won't come."

"You said he's lonely. I bet going to a music festival with two hot girls would be way more fun than staying home alone. Ask him."

"I don't even know what kind of music he likes."

"Ask him," Nev repeats, smiling at me from ear to ear. "If he says yes, I'll book another room for him. It will be fun, Angie."

It might be fun, and it might be good for my situation with Asher —she's not wrong. I continue watching my best friend, my fingers rapping on the table. With a sigh, I nod and start smiling. "Okay, I'll ask him tonight."

Nevaeh clasps her hands together with a squeal. "It will be a fucking blast, I can feel it."

Shaking my head, I say nothing, just listen to her ramble about the festival and what she wants to do while we're there. Her enthusiasm is contagious, and when I leave the restaurant to go home, I feel excited too. This road trip with my best friend and my neighbor might be a once-in-a-lifetime experience.

"You're late," I say, letting Drake in. He passes me with two pizza boxes and a six-pack of beer in his hands.

"My sister FaceTimed me, and my mom was there," he tells me as we enter the living room.

Cooper follows us, patiently waiting for Drake to put his things on the table so he can pet him. After a few minutes of belly rubs, I shoo Coop away and give him a big bone so he won't try to guilt-trip us into giving him pizza. Returning to the couch, I sit beside Drake, and he turns to look at me.

"I thought about sending you a quick text to let you know I'd be late, but then I realized I don't have your phone number." He shrugs and then raises an eyebrow. "Any chance my fake girlfriend would give me her phone number?"

He takes his cell out of his pocket and stares at me expectantly. I smile, telling him my phone number. He saves it and calls me so I can save his too.

"What name did you save my number under?" I ask, putting my phone on the table.

Drake opens one of the pizza boxes, takes a slice, and only then glances at me. "Cupcake, obviously."

I roll my eyes, scooting closer to him so I can take a slice of pizza too. One is Margherita, and the other one is pepperoni. Hovering over the pizza box, I grab a slice of the first one and take a bite.

"It's delicious." I shoot my eyes to look at Drake, only now fully acknowledging how close I am to him. My bare leg is pressed to his, and the second I realize it, my neck feels hotter. I grab a beer from the table and move away from him, trying to act nonchalant. "Thank you."

"Don't mention it." He gives me a crooked smile and takes a beer too. Then I move to the kitchen and put them in the fridge. "How was your day?" he calls.

"It was nice. I spent most of it at my dessert shop, and then I had dinner with Nevaeh." I come back to the couch and sit down.

"How is your best friend doing?" Drake asks around a bite of pizza.

"She's great, in her usual Nevaeh fashion." I snort. "She gave me an idea, actually. Do you have any plans for this weekend?" He shakes his head no. "Do you want to go to a music festival with me and Nevaeh?"

"Music festival?"

"There will be a lot of incredible bands, and there's this new one, Sabotage—Nev and I love their music," I explain. "We're planning to drive there early Saturday morning, check into our hotel, then go to the festival. If everything goes as planned, we'll be home around four p.m. on Sunday."

Drake chews his pizza, eyeing me with a blank expression. I have no idea what he's thinking. Yet I'm grateful to him for acting as if nothing happened last night. It would be terrible if our kiss changed things between us. I like his company...way more than I'm willing to admit.

"What about Cooper? Do you have someone who can take care of him?" His question throws me off, and I just gawk at him for a minute.

"Yeah, I always leave him with Marcy. She's my chef, and her family adores Coop." My belly warms up at the thought that he's worried about my dog.

"Can we take my car? Yours won't fit us all, and Nevaeh's convertible is too small for me."

"Of course. We can even switch drivers if you get tired."

"Cool," he says, winking at me. "It'll be a good opportunity to show off our *relationship*, to make it social media official, like you wanted."

I watch him as he reaches over to the pizza box and takes another slice. Tilting my head, I smile and murmur, "Are you looking forward to getting your hands on me in public?"

Well, I've officially lost my mind. Why am I flirting with him? It goes against everything I've tried to convince Nevaeh of.

"Maybe a little," he coos, inching toward my ear. "I always look forward to getting my hands on you. Not just in public, Cupcake."

Drake leans away with a satisfied grin. The resurrected butterflies somersault in my stomach as I take a swig of my beer, trying to act calm. I grab the remote and turn on the first episode of the second season. It's my only hope to divert his attention from me...and mine from him.

Kissing Drake isn't even a complication anymore. It's a full-blown disaster.

Drake

EIGHTEEN

crushing

My legs hurt like hell. I've spent an hour exercising with the focus on them and my balance. Sitting on the bench, I rotate my ankle with a bumper plate fixed to my sneaker. I'm sweaty, and I need a fucking shower, but I refuse to cut my exercise short.

"One hundred," I mutter under my breath. I reach over my foot, unclasp the plate, and put it down. Groaning, I stretch my legs and wipe the sweat from my forehead, my curls falling into my face. More and more, it looks like I need a haircut. I need to remember to ask Colton about his barber. It always slips my mind.

Lowering onto the mat, I prop myself on my right elbow and position my left knee on the bench. I lift my right leg in front of me, bend it, and press my left arm to my hip. Taking a deep breath, I close my eyes and start counting. I hate this one, just like I hate holding a plank, and yet it's super effective for my groin area.

I repeat the exercise on both sides, and then I add the last one for my hips. I keep myself propped on my right elbow. My right knee is resting on the bench, and my left bent knee is lifted in the air. Not the most pleasant move, but it's easier this time.

When I'm done, I plop onto my back and just lie here with my eyes closed. The only thing on my mind is an ice bath. *Hell, I should take it easier next time.* I just need to keep myself in shape, not kill myself practicing during the offseason.

"Did you decide to break a record today?" Colt's voice rings in my ear, and I open my eyes as he sits beside me on the mat.

"Just thought it'd be a good idea to focus on my legs."

He snickers, shaking his head. His breathing is heavy, his hair soaked with sweat. It's just the two of us here, because Xander's daughter, Isla, got sick, and he needed to stay home with her while his wife helped another client with their interior design. Isabella's ideas for my house were a pleasant surprise, and I'd never regret hiring her. She's a real professional.

"I'm thinking about going to the rink next week. Are you in?" Colton asks and smiles at me. "I miss the ice."

"Me too." I smile back, sitting up and looking around the half-empty gym. There is another gym closer to my house, but I prefer this one because my friends come here. "I'll go with you. Just let me know when."

My best friend nods and stretches his arms in the air, grumbling, "I'm so ready to go home. You?"

Without answering, I slowly stand up and extend my hand to him, helping him to his feet. "How are things at home? How is Michael?"

"Everything is great. Michael goes to school, Ava has work, and I just chill."

I squint at Colton as we make our way to the locker room. "You're bored to death?"

"Bingo." He laughs and nudges me in my ribs with his elbow. "What about you? How are things with Evangelina?"

My days are a thousand times better now, all thanks to Angie. Watching TV together, talking, laughing, bantering, and even texting, everything I do with her makes me smile harder, makes my mood lighter. She's like my most treasured possession, one I want to keep to myself for as long as possible. Or, even better, forever—but we're only at the beginning of our journey.

Convincing my fake girlfriend to give me a real chance is a challenge I plan to win. She's worth fighting for.

"All good. I'm going to a music festival with her this weekend."

"That's awesome, dude. I'm happy for you." Colton opens the door, and I follow him into the locker room. "My wife and your sister like your girl. I heard them talking about the pictures from the movie premiere. It won't take long for Ava to make up some excuse to invite you two to our place. You know how she is."

"Always gets what she wants and has her husband wrapped around her little finger?" I taunt him, and he flips me off.

"Get yourself a wife, and we'll check in a year after marriage," he tells me, approaching his locker.

"*If* I get myself a wife."

Colton pulls out a towel from his locker and then whips his head to look at me. "*When*, not if," he insists. Then he locks his locker and edges toward the showers. "Who knows, maybe the right girl is already with you, Drake."

I stay stiff, fiddling with the towel in my hands. Sometimes I see similarities between Evangelina and me, but other days we are complete opposites. Black and white. Sweet and sour. Funny and sad. Not synonyms, but antonyms. Though the truth is, our differences are something that pulls us closer. They pique my curiosity, making me want to know more about her, to see more of her...to feel more of her. The feeling turns me into someone I don't even recognize, but I like it. I like myself more when I'm with her.

Hearing the sound of running water, I shake my head and close my locker. I better hurry up; the locker room isn't the best place to daydream about the girl I've started crushing on.

MY PHONE DINGS with an incoming message, and I look up from my book. I grab my cell from the table and unlock it, staring at the text I just received. She's gotta be kidding me. It's just absolutely naive, and it reeks of desperation. Does she really think I want to talk to her?

JANELLE:

Made myself espresso, and now I'm thinking about you. I miss you, Drake.

My thumbs are hovering over the screen, ready to reply. A ton of crazy ideas come to mind, but I sweep them all away. Instead, I just delete her message and put my phone aside. I was done with her the minute she walked out of my house without a goodbye. If all it took was some pictures from a fancy event to remind her about me and show her what the life she could've had looks like, then my only regret is wasting a year of my time on someone like her.

It's better to be alone than with someone who doesn't appreciate me for who I am, who wants me only because of the number of zeros in my bank account. Those days are gone, and I'll stop at nothing to never repeat them again.

I pick up my book and continue reading, enjoying the plot to the point of not being able to put it down. The culmination is close, and it becomes harder and harder for me not to check the ending. An intensifying need to know who the serial killer is makes me impatient. It's one of the best books I've read in a while, and I've already ordered the next books in the series. Hopefully they will be delivered soon.

The buzzing of my phone rips me out of the story again, making me grimace. *Can't I fucking read in peace?* But the second I see it's Layla, my scowl transforms into a smile.

"Hey." I press the phone to my ear. "How is my favorite sister doing?"

"I'm your only sister." Layla breaks into giggles. "Honestly, everything is fine. Even with Maya. She's been doing great; she has three teeth already. You won't recognize her when you come to visit."

I put my book down and stand up from the couch, edging to the window. "That hurt, little one," I mumble, eyes focused on my backyard. The water in the pool is still and reflects the sunrays. "I miss you two so much."

"Sorry, Drake." My sister sighs. "We miss you too. Every day."

"How about *you* visit *me*? Just to see if you like Santa Clara?"

Layla laughs. Maya's babbling is loud and cheerful in the distance. "Maybe later. I want Maya to be a bit older." I raise my fist in the air, screaming *yes!* in my head. Her answer is the tiniest victory, and I'm happy she's no longer as hostile about the idea. "But we're waiting for you to come visit. You're on vacation, brother, and your little niece misses her favorite uncle."

"I'm her only uncle," I snort, stepping out of the house. The warm air hits my face, and I inhale, closing my eyes. A little breeze caresses my skin; I smile, enjoying the feeling. It's so calm and wholesome. "I'm going to a music festival this weekend, and next week I promised we'd go to the ice rink to practice together. Other than that, I have no plans, and I think coming back home to see my precious niece and my annoying little sister sounds like a good plan."

"Your annoying little sister has a question for you, big brother. What's the deal with you and your neighbor? First I hear you hate her, and then suddenly you show up at a movie premiere with her, acting all lovey-dovey."

"I didn't hate her. It was just that her dog scared me, and we said some shit to each other when we first met. I apologized, and so did she." I shrug, glancing at Angie's house. "I like her."

"Are you two dating?" Layla asks.

"We're seeing each other," I explain, and my sister whistles. "It's nothing serious."

"Whatever you say, Drake," she gushes. "Who knows, maybe I'll come visit earlier so I can meet your girl. I like her way more than Janelle, or any of your other girlfriends."

"You don't even know her." I furrow my brow.

"So? I saw pictures from the movie premiere, and I watched your interview with the reporter. You look good together, such a beautiful couple."

"It was a public event. Everyone is pretending to be someone they're not."

The silence on the other end lasts too long for my liking. "Drake, what exactly are you and Evangelina doing together? Is it some PR stunt?"

Fuck. I have no idea how to lie. Honest people definitely live longer, because my heart rate suddenly broke through the roof.

I clear my throat as I walk back inside the house and close the door. "It's not a PR stunt or anything. We're just spending time together. She comes to my place; I go to hers," I explain, and my heartbeat gradually calms down. "We're watching *One Tree Hill*."

"Oh my God, are you serious?" Layla shrieks in my ear, and I roll my eyes, mentally applauding myself for handling my slipup so well. "I want to know *everything* about your time with this girl."

Sitting on the couch, I nestle more comfortably and start telling Layla about the time I've spent with Evangelina. The more I talk, the more I smile, and the warmer my insides become. When the memories of our kiss resurface in my brain, my whole body hums. The softness of her lips and the heat of her skin make my breath hitch, and I pause, keeping all the details to myself. She's my secret...the sweetest and naughtiest little secret I've ever had.

When Layla and I hang up, I decide to go for a little walk and get something to eat. The book I was reading is now in the back of my mind, as the whole space is occupied with Evangelina. I grab my wallet and my phone, push them into my pockets, and go outside, locking the door behind me.

Just as I go down the stairs, the sound of a door closing catches my attention. Turning my head to my right, I see Evangelina standing on her porch with Cooper on his leash. She's wearing a white top and light blue denim overall shorts, looking incredible. A smile forms on my lips as I stop in my tracks, waiting for her to notice me. The second she does, she smiles too.

"Hey, Drake." She comes over, stopping beside me.

"Hey, Cupcake," I tease, and she pokes her tongue out at me. "Hey, Coop."

"What are you doing?" Evangelina asks as I pet her dog.

"I was just going out to get something to eat."

"What if we join you? I didn't have lunch either."

"I'll never say no to your company," I confess. My eyes are locked on hers. Her pupils dilate slightly, and her gaze darkens. "Let's go. It's a good opportunity for you to tell me more about our trip on Saturday. Did you book the extra room?"

"Nevaeh did," Angie replies as we stroll away from our houses. Listening to her talk about our road trip and the plans for the festival, I find myself mesmerized with her. Her voice, the animated movements of her hands, her perfume.

Crushing on the girl next door is one thing. Being obsessed with my fake girlfriend is a totally different story, and I'm heading in that direction at Formula 1 racing speed.

Angie

NINETEEN

truth or truth

I CHECK THE TIME AND SMILE DESPITE HOW ANGRY I AM. It's 12:12, so I close my eyes and wish for today to turn out amazing. Even if my best friend is risking ruining it.

What's taking her so long?

"Stop pacing." His soothing, velvety voice surrounds me, and I look at Drake. He's sitting on the stairs of my house, his phone in his hands. "If we leave in the next thirty minutes, we'll still be on time."

"And if not?" I bite out, throwing my hands in the air in frustration. I take a step forward, but he catches my wrist.

"Sit," he commands as he pulls me down to sit beside him. Once I'm level with him, I peel my eyes to his face. Drake quirks a smile and nudges me with his shoulder. "Everything is going to be fine."

My stomach coils; the butterflies slowly flutter their wings. His presence is like the best cure for my stress. The warmth of his deep brown eyes, the scent of his cologne mixed with the rich aroma of the strong black coffee he's been drinking. I don't feel trapped with him. He feels like freedom.

"I'm sorry about this, Drake. She was supposed to be here twenty minutes ago. I called her, sent her more than ten messages already, and still nothing."

"Nevaeh is on her way, I'm sure of it," he murmurs, and his eyes turn piercing. "I listened to that new band you mentioned, Sabotage. I liked their songs, especially 'Believe In Me'."

"Love that one!" I exclaim. Suddenly, I yawn, trying to hide it behind my palm. "Sorry, I slept terribly. Without Cooper in the house, it felt so empty."

"You could've stayed at my place; you didn't have to leave at three a.m."

"Agree to disagree." I smile, remembering how he tried to convince me to stay. He said I could sleep in his guest room. The thing is, lines are blurring between us, and spending the night in the same house is definitely something I should avoid. For both of us. "I can't believe we finished the second season already."

"I can't believe you were yelling at my TV when Lucas was confessing his feelings. It was hilarious, but you kinda ruined the dramatic effect."

Hiding my face in my hands, I laugh. "Why do you always need to remind me about my embarrassing moments?"

The world around me bursts with the scent of his cologne, diving under my skin and flowing through my veins. It's like a direct injection of Drake Benson into my system. He drapes his big arm around my shoulder, pressing me to his side. His hot breath warms up my skin, his lips almost touching the shell of my ear.

"There is nothing embarrassing about you, Angie. Your reactions are genuine, and that's why I like watching the show with you," he whispers sweetly. Tingles spread over my skin, blanketing me in the heat of his body. "And I'm happy you knocked on my door that night, even if your reasons were pretty selfish."

I take my hands off my face and turn my head to him. He's a handsome man, with sun-kissed skin and the most exquisite eye color I've ever seen. The sun reflects in his deep brown eyes, reminding me of his favorite: espresso with a dash of milk. They're beautifully deep, and they only become richer under the golden rays of sunshine. His slightly crooked nose makes me wonder if it's been broken before. Just like his lips make me wonder: How many women get to know how he tastes? The question awakens a strange feeling inside my chest.

The sound of a car coming breaks the moment between us. I look away, watching as Nevaeh parks her vehicle beside mine. She jumps out of her BMW, grabs a backpack from her backseat, locks the door, and heads in our direction. Her eyes coast over Drake, still sitting on the stairs with his arm around me, and she starts smiling.

"Traffic was awful." She stops in front of us.

I ask, "Did you oversleep?"

"I did," she confirms. Her gaze darts between Drake and me. "I'm sorry for making you wait. It's not something I wanted to happen."

Sighing, I wiggle out of his embrace and stand up. "Let's go. It's time for us to hit the road."

Drake descends the stairs and takes Nevaeh's backpack out of her hands. *Always the gentleman*. I hide a smile, chewing on the inside of my cheek as I walk to his car. While he puts my best friend's things in his trunk, I stand still, not even looking in Nev's direction. She deserves my silent treatment for being late, and for not picking up her phone, but I know that in the car I won't have an escape from her.

"Fine, I'll take the backseat," she mutters, opening the door and climbing inside.

Drake comes closer and opens the door for me. I shoot my eyes up to his, and my legs become weak as I get into his car. The way he looks at me affects my body in more ways than I ever thought possible. If this continues, it will become painfully obvious to everyone else... including him.

A few minutes later, Drake is driving away from our houses. Quiet music swims around us as he keeps his eyes glued to the road. I glance at my best friend, and she pokes her tongue out at me. Snorting, I flip her the bird, a smile playing on my lips. The next thing I know, Nevaeh cracks, and hysterical giggling comes out of her throat. Drake and I exchange a look, and he arches an eyebrow at me.

"If you expected someone more mature, then think again. This is what we're going to deal with tonight," I tell him, and he smiles, shaking his head.

Nevaeh's head pops up between our seats. "Aw, are you two pairing up to babysit me?"

I press my palm to her forehead and push her back. “No, we’re planning an escape from you.” I wheel around in my seat to get a better look at Nevaeh. She holds my gaze for a moment, then reclines in her seat. Mischief flickers in her eyes. Pulling her phone out of her purse, she focuses on it, and I look away.

I spend two hours of our ride chatting with Drake. He’s not a big football fan, but he knows who my dad is. He said he always had a huge amount of respect for Logan Jones, but he never rooted for his team. Drake loves and supports his home state’s team, the Red Lions, and I find it admirable. Just like I’m absolutely in love with the fact that he’s not trying to get to know more about my father. It’s like that detail doesn’t interest him in the slightest, and it’s definitely something I’m not used to.

“It’s a three-hour ride,” Nevaeh suddenly states, her head appearing between our seats. “We have one more hour, right?”

“Yeah.” My eyebrows etch together. “Why?”

“I’m bored!” she exclaims, making Drake snort beside me. “And I’m tired of the two of you talking about sports.”

“You want us to entertain you?” he asks sarcastically, and her face lights up with a smile.

“I knew I was right for liking you,” Nev chirps. Then she taps her index finger against her lips. “Let’s play Truth or Dare.”

“We’re in a car on the highway; no one is going to choose Dare,” I mumble.

“Let’s play Truth or Truth then. It’s just semantics, sweetheart.” Nevaeh dismisses me, and her smile only grows wider. “Drake, Truth or Truth.”

“I don’t remember agreeing—” I say, but his voice cuts me short.

“Truth.”

“When did your last relationship end?” I chuckle at her question, utterly surprised she started with that one. It’s not how she usually plays.

“Around two months ago,” he deadpans, sneaking a glance at me. “Truth or Truth, Angie.”

Oh God, this is ridiculous. “Truth.”

"What does your tattoo mean?" I lower my gaze to my left arm and keep silent for a moment, collecting my thoughts. He doesn't know that it's not about what it means, but what it hides.

"At first I thought about a few small tattoos, connected together by some lines and drawings, maybe some flowers or ivy. But then I saw a girl with a lace tattoo, and I knew I wanted one. It's feminine and very sensual; it makes me feel more graceful than I am," I say casually, feeling his eyes on me. "I still have a few words woven here and there, but mostly it's just lace."

"What words?" he blurts out, instantly getting a slap on the shoulder from Nev.

"Nope, Mr. Hockey Pants, that's not how Truth or Truth works. Wait for your turn," she scolds him, and then peers at me. "Truth, Angie."

I nod, grateful for the intervention, knowing she's not going to like my question. "If Travis asked you to be his girlfriend, what would you say?"

Nevaeh's face becomes blank, and she narrows her eyes. "I'd say I don't have a best friend anymore, and he can take her place instead." She switches her gaze to Drake; the glint in her eyes has darkened. "Have you ever slept with someone you weren't supposed to? And sex with exes doesn't count."

Drake contemplates her for a moment, and then answers with a shrug, "My sister's best friend."

My mouth hangs open, and I gawk at him. "You slept with your best friend's wife? With Ava?"

His laughter erupts in the car, rolling right through me. "Good to know you're listening to what I tell you," he manages to say between fits of laughter. "But yes, and it was before Ava and Colton got together. He wasn't even my best friend at the time, just a teammate."

I shake my head with a smile. "You're full of surprises."

"Yeah?" He tilts his head, his tongue clicking. "Have you ever slept with someone you weren't supposed to?"

I don't even have time to answer before Nevaeh decides to lend me a hand. "Me." Just fucking great.

Drake seizes me with his eyes, then glances at Nev through the rearview mirror. "Were you two dating?"

"No. It was just one drunken night, and it never happened again," I tell him, thinking about the most torturous death for my best friend once we get to our room. I snap my head in Nev's direction. "When are you going to tell Travis you want more than just hooking up?"

"Never, because that's a lie." She grimaces and turns away from me, looking out the window. "This was supposed to be fun, and you're ruining it with your serious questions."

I shrink in my seat. The tiniest feeling of guilt finds its way to my heart. "I'm sorry, Nev. I shouldn't have pressured you. How about you ask me something instead?"

I know I'm going to regret suggesting it, but I still do. She's my best friend, and I hate seeing her upset. Even if all my questions have one purpose only: to help her see something I noticed a long time ago. She likes this guy...and he genuinely likes her. They're just both confused and reluctant to open up and admit their feelings.

A smile creeps onto Nevaeh's lips as she continues to study me. "When was the last time you had sex, Angie? With someone—not your toys or your fingers."

"Almost five months ago," I reply, holding her gaze, even if she's not the one whose reaction I want to see. "And I think we're done with this game."

"Whatever you say." Nev winks at me and takes her phone in her hand again.

We spend the rest of the ride just listening to music, with Nevaeh typing on her phone. The silence doesn't bother me—quite the contrary. It helps to lull my nerves and relax my tightened muscles. A feeling of something good happening vibrates through my body, filling me with hope.

STANDING in the middle of the hotel lobby, I watch the people around us. This festival is very popular in California, and the place is packed. It's a miracle Nev was able to change our booking at the last minute.

"Okay, I've got our keys." Nevaeh comes closer to us and stops. "This one's mine." She pushes a white card into her back pocket and then looks up, extending the other to Drake and me. "And this one is yours."

"What do you mean?" I ask. A realization dawns on me, even if I don't want to accept it.

She can't do this.

"All the hotels are fully booked. It was pure luck I got to change our booking," my best friend says pointedly. "I got myself a room, and I got another one for you two. It shouldn't be a problem, right?"

And to think I was sure spending the night in his guest room would be a problem. *God, I hope we at least have two beds.*

Drake

TWENTY

let them watch

A BROAD SMILE ILLUMINATES NEVAEH'S FACE AS SHE stands in front of us with a card in her outstretched hand. She doesn't feel bad about the situation she's putting her best friend in; she's enjoying Evangelina's shocked expression. I want to smile—even the idea of spending the night in the same room as my fake girlfriend is exhilarating. Yet, I try to keep my face even...for my own good. As long as I play it cool, she won't run away from me.

Angie snatches the card out of Nevaeh's hand. "See you in an hour," she says through gritted teeth. Without waiting for any reaction from her best friend or me, she turns on her heel and heads to the elevator.

My gaze instantly locks on Nevaeh, and she winks, mouthing, *You're welcome.*

Damn, I need to learn to be more discreet. She has me all figured out after just one car ride.

I nod and adjust the strap of my backpack on my shoulder, then I follow Evangelina. The elevator doors open just as I stop beside her. We step inside, and she punches the button for the eleventh floor. Her foot taps the ground, her arms folded across her chest as she stares in front of her. I stay silent, bottling up my laughter. The angry version of her is quickly becoming my favorite.

"I still can make her switch rooms," Angie mutters. "You don't have to—"

"I don't mind," I tell her with a slight dip of my chin. "It's just one night."

She gives me a half smile, tucking a strand of hair behind her ear. "There might be two beds."

"Do you believe that?"

She shakes her head no.

"Me neither."

The elevator comes to a stop, and we saunter out of it, my shoulder brushing hers as we go. Her gaze darts to my face, and the moment she realizes I'm watching her, she looks away. A tinge of pink spreading across her cheeks makes my body warmer. I like how she reacts to me, and even more, I like how she thinks I'm not aware of it.

I'm alarmingly conscious of anything Evangelina does. She's always on my mind, and when she's around, she's all I want to look at. Watching *One Tree Hill* with her has become troublesome, because I have a hard time focusing on the TV. The time I spend with her is like a barn burner—an exciting and intense game from start to finish. A game I'm eager to win.

We stop at door number 1101, and Angie puts the card into the lock. "Well, welcome to our room."

I hold the door open for her and walk inside a second later. It closes behind us with a light thud. Ambling farther, Evangelina and I stop at a king-size bed. We glance at each other, and everything in her look screams "I told you so". With a deep breath, she puts her back-pack on the floor and lowers herself onto the bed. I sit beside her and gradually lie back on the covers.

"It's pretty soft," I say, and she chuckles, lying down and turning her head to look at me. "And it's pretty big; you won't even notice me."

"It's impossible not to notice you, especially when we're sleeping in the same bed," Evangelina murmurs. A lock of her hair falls in her face, and she sweeps it away with her hand. "At least the room is nice; I love it when a space is decorated minimally."

Propping myself up on my elbows, I look around and nod in agreement. A TV hangs above a little table with a chair, and the bed takes up most of the space. Two bedside tables with lamps on them are the only other pieces of furniture. They're cozy and comfortable in white and light brown colors, helping to make the room look more spacious.

"I think we got the better room," I say.

"Oh, I'm pretty sure you're wrong. My best friend never deprives herself." Angie stands up from the bed, glancing at me. "Do you need to take a shower?"

"Just to freshen up."

"Great. Um, how about I go first, and while I get dressed, you can take your shower?" Evangelina asks, and I shrug instead of answering her. She raises her eyes to the ceiling and then looks down at me again. "Words, Mr. Benson. I need your words."

I push myself to sit up straight. "You can go first."

"Thank you," she teases, doing a small curtsy.

Kneeling by her backpack, she opens it and rummages through her stuff. I continue watching her, wondering about her outfit for the festival. Angie can wear absolutely anything and still look like the best-dressed woman in the whole world. And tonight, she's going to this festival with me, as my date. The curiosity I feel mixes with something I haven't experienced in a long time—possessiveness. It's not a good sign.

"See you in a few." Angie looks up from her backpack and finds me staring at her. She presses her clothes to her chest, stands up, and beelines into the bathroom, leaving me alone.

With a yawn, I plop onto my back, staring at the ceiling. I close my eyes and listen to the shower running. I let my mind wander, creating naughtier and naughtier pictures in my head, all featuring Evangelina. The swelling in my jeans intensifies, and I no longer think it's a good idea to share a room—much less a bed—with her.

When the bathroom door opens, I'm sitting on the bed with a book in my hands, my back pressed to the headboard. It's a new one, and I'm trying hard to remember all the characters. But the only distraction I came up with to help me not think about Evangelina isn't really working. As soon as she steps into the room, my eyes fly to her without any self-control.

Evangelina is wearing a red crop top and light blue jeans. Her feet are bare, and her long dark brown hair is still wet. Her round tits look perfect in that top, and her toned midriff is something my gaze focuses on, and I'm having a hard time looking away.

"Shower is all yours." She comes closer and steals my book from me. The smell of strawberries wafts around her, lulling me, and I watch her read the book's title. "This is one of my favorites."

"No spoilers." I take the clothes I laid out from the bed and head into the bathroom. Keeping my distance is the only way for me to survive this without the biggest hard-on. One I won't be able to get rid of with her around.

In the shower, I turn on the cold water and stand still, chasing off the arousal I felt a moment ago. If I want to enjoy the festival, I better focus solely on myself. Her presence is already the biggest temptation I've ever needed to resist. I need to do better.

"Okay, Sabotage is playing next!" Evangelina shouts in my ear. Powerful bass thumps in my body; loud music swims around us. We've been at the festival for five hours straight, and it's already close to eleven p.m. It's been a blast, and I'm enjoying my time to the fullest.

"Do you want to try getting closer?" I ask, raising my voice as I lean to her ear.

She shakes her head. "No. I have another plan."

"Which is?" Nevaeh asks.

"I want to meet their lead singer!" she exclaims, a big, radiant smile playing on her lips. A pang of jealousy worms its way under my skin, and I scowl. That's definitely not what I expected her to say. "Hopefully, he'll agree to sign a picture. I brought one with me."

"Hayden Hale can sign whatever he wants as long as he does it on my body." Nevaeh laughs heartily, taking Evangelina's hand and entwining their fingers. "Let's go find them; our VIP tickets should help get us through."

I don't even have a moment to grasp the situation before Angie grabs my hand and makes me follow them. My frown only deepens as I watch Nevaeh quickly make her way past all the security guards. It takes her no longer than a minute to convince security to let us in. Is she a fucking magician or something? How is it possible that they are letting us through without any complications?

My mood is all over the place when we stop near some guy with drumsticks in his hands. He stands with his eyes closed, his head bouncing back and forth to the rhythm. The music is quieter here. I can even hear him counting under his breath.

"Hey, Bo," Nevaeh murmurs, and the guy snaps his head in our direction, only now noticing us. "Sorry for the interruption, but we're looking for Hayden. Any chance you know where he is?"

"It's almost time to go on stage..." he mumbles, his brows pinched together.

Evangelina frees her hand from her best friend's grip and takes a step forward, letting go of my hand too. "I absolutely love your music, and I was just hoping Hayden could sign this for me?" She pulls the picture out of her belt bag and shoves it toward the guy. "Pretty please?"

He takes a step back, his eyes traveling up and down her form. A sly smile forms on his face, and my knuckles suddenly start to itch. He's checking her out right in front of me, and I fucking hate it.

"One minute." The guy beckons Evangelina to follow him inside the trailer. Nevaeh stands still beside me, her mouth hanging open. We both watch as Angie disappears from view.

"What the hell?" Nevaeh shrieks. Her short white dress barely hides her ass when she raises on her tiptoes to see what's going on inside the trailer—not successfully, and that plays on my nerves as well. "Why did Bo only take Angie to see Hayden? It's not fair. She already has you. Why does she need my favorite singer too?"

I fold my arms over my chest, my stare locked on the door of the trailer. Men have been watching Evangelina and Nevaeh the whole festival. It didn't bother me. Quite the contrary; it made me feel proud to be with such gorgeous girls. We've been dancing, singing, and laughing together. It's been probably one of the best days I've had in months...until now.

She's not my real girlfriend. I have no right to be jealous. And yet I am. The fact that I've had a few drinks isn't helping either.

The door of the trailer finally opens, and Evangelina strolls outside, followed by a guy in a white T-shirt I haven't seen before. His platinum blond hair is short, and the tattoos covering his neck and arms draw my attention. Though I don't have time to figure out who he is on my own, because Nevaeh squeals by my side and rushes to the guy. He catches her with ease, a broad smile quirking his lips. He reminds me of someone, but I can't put my finger on who.

"Apparently, Hayden loves hockey," Evangelina says with a quiet chuckle when she stops by my side. "He agreed to sign my picture, but only if you take a photo with him."

"Hey, Drake." The blond guy stops in front of me, extending his palm for a handshake. Nevaeh stands by his side, grinning from ear to ear. "I'm Hayden, the lead singer of Sabotage."

"Nice to meet you." I shake his hand, and it becomes easier to breathe. Evangelina is with me; her arm is casually wrapped around my torso. "I love 'Believe In Me'; it's one of my favorites on the album."

"Cool. It's a dedication to my family—to my brother, to be exact."

The second he says it, I knit my brows together, watching him closely. "Any chance Hunter Hale is your brother?" The words rush out, and a burst of laughter from Hayden and Angie follows my question.

"He is," he confirms, pulling his phone out of his pocket. "I'd love to talk more, but we have to be on stage in less than three minutes."

Evangelina takes a few pictures, and then we part ways. I promise to come to another Sabotage concert, and Hayden promises to come to the first game of the season. He's carefree and calm, and when the members of his band spill out of the trailer, his expression doesn't change. Hayden smiles, waves at us, and whisks off toward the stage with his band members in tow.

In the blink of an eye, Nevaeh is already pulling us back to the main floor so we can hear Sabotage play. Too bad I can't share her excitement. All I can think about is my hand gently cradling Angie's palm, how she doesn't leave my side the entire way back to the stage and even after the music starts playing.

Turning my head to my right, I notice that we stopped just in front of the Ferris wheel. Nevaeh is dancing a bit farther away from us, yelling the lyrics at the top of her lungs. When I gather the courage to look at Evangelina again, our eyes lock. She's a bit tense, and it makes me furrow my brow.

"People are taking pictures of us. Several already," she mutters when I lean down to her lips.

I straighten my back. Sure enough, I see two girls with their phones pointed at us. They aren't even trying to hide what they are doing. One of them catches my gaze, and I wink at her, seeing her eyebrows go up to her hairline.

Looking down, I take Angie's chin between my fingers and lift her face to mine. "You said this would be a good opportunity to show off our *relationship*. You said some of your ex's friends are here, and they'd seen us together." She nods, her lips parting. "I'm going to kiss you right now...and as for them, let them watch."

Angie

TWENTY-ONE

say yes

I DON'T KNOW HOW MANY PEOPLE ARE AT THIS FESTIVAL. I'm barely paying any attention to my surroundings, or even the music—all I see is him. It's much more than just invading my personal space. Little by little, he breaks through my defenses, sliding under my skin and refueling my veins with his presence. He's like a storm on a very hot sunny day, showing up out of nowhere, not giving me even a single opportunity to escape, until there's nothing but him.

I've always loved rainy days more than sunny ones. Rain keeps my secrets, hides even the most unbearable ones from the light. Rain gives me solace and refuge, and it's very similar to how I feel around this guy. He's like a safe place...one I don't want to leave because I can be myself here.

Drake holds my chin between his thumb and index finger, gently tilting my head to him. He bends down, his lips hover over my mouth, his nose brushing mine. My knees give out, and I clutch his tee in my hands, fisting it roughly. His hot breath fans over my face as he smiles, happy with the effect he has on me.

Blame it on the alcohol, but it's the first time in days I don't want to hide. I want to be myself, at least while we're here and Drake lets me. Even if it's just an act, an opportunity to help me with my Asher situation. He's playing the role of fake boyfriend to a tee.

Running his tongue over my bottom lip, he finally presses his mouth to mine. His hands wind around my waist, and he pulls me flush against his body. A breathless moan slips past my parted lips when he pushes his hips into me, his mouth never leaving mine. Our kiss becomes more heated and passionate with each stroke of our tongues. It takes my breath away and makes me dizzy; I can barely stand still.

Sliding his hands down to my ass, he hoists me up, and I wrap my legs around his hips. Letting go of his T-shirt, I snake my hands around his shoulders and lock them behind the back of his neck. This moment is everything and much more than I ever expected. The emotions I feel are running so high, I'm losing my mind.

My fake boyfriend kisses me better than any of my real boyfriends ever did. It's pure ecstasy, all I've ever hoped to feel from a guy's mouth on mine. My whole body hums; a tingling sensation spreads over my skin. The feeling is overwhelming and wholesome, and I let myself get carried away—until the wetness between my thighs and the feeling of his hard cock through his clothes sober me up.

Oh my God, what the hell am I doing?

I break our kiss and lean away, my eyes still hooked on his. My breathing is ragged, and my heart beats fast, ready to jump out of my chest. *Something fake shouldn't feel this good.* And I definitely shouldn't be so turned on after making out with my fake boyfriend.

Drake's gaze is dark, the golden flames of his irises burning like the wildest fires. Slowly, he lowers me to my feet, his arms still circling me. He dips his head, so our eyes are level.

"Is everything okay?" he asks in his deep voice.

I nod. "I think we were more than convincing." The corners of his mouth instantly drop, and I inwardly curse myself. *Fix it, Angie.* He doesn't deserve to feel bad just because I can't control myself. "My head is spinning a little, because of the alcohol..." I pause for a second, and then I whisper, "And you."

A lopsided grin forms on his handsome face. "Anything for you, Cupcake," he says, and I start smiling too. He goes easy on me, again.

Slowly, he twirls me around. My back is pressed to his solid chest.

His big arms are wrapped around me from behind, warming me up and making me feel secure. I stop caring about the girls who were taking pictures, about Asher's friends who saw me with Drake and the fact that I already got another message from my ex. Nothing matters anymore. Only the steady beating of Drake's heart, echoing mine, means something to me.

"I SAW YOU TWO KISSING," Nevaeh blurts, trying to keep her voice even. Her hand is draped around my shoulder as we make our way back to our hotel. "First, it was unbelievably hot. Second, you should've never asked him to play this game with you. Guys like him are rare diamonds, ones you find and keep secret from everyone, cherishing every fucking moment with him."

"He's a great friend." I mutter the first thing that comes to my mind. Drake is a bit farther away from us, talking on the phone with his sister.

"Angie, do you really see him as a friend?" My steps falter, and I twist my ankle again. The pain isn't as strong as it was the first time, but it still hurts. I close my eyes, my eyebrows pinching together. "Hey, what's wrong?"

"I sprained my ankle a little. Nothing serious."

Nevaeh gazes at me with a serious expression on her face. Then she glances at Drake and leans into my ear. "Interesting reaction to my question. I think the answer is no, and you're mentally freaking out." She pulls back, a triumphant smile on her lips. "You like your neighbor...or should I say your fake boyfriend."

Instead of an answer, I wiggle out of her embrace and limp toward our hotel. My best friend follows me; her silvery laughter behind my back makes me squirm. She doesn't need my answer. She already knows it. Nev reads me like an open book, and that's why she doesn't push the issue. I'm not ready for a relationship, and she knows it.

A guy like Drake doesn't deserve a girl with as many unresolved issues as me.

I feel his presence even before I see him. His arm slips around my waist, and he pulls me to his side. "I left you for twenty minutes, and you already sprained your ankle."

"It's all because of me." Nev sidles up to us, hurrying to open the door, and we walk inside the hotel. "She doesn't like my questions."

A smile ghosts over Drake's lips. "The last time she sprained her ankle was when I was asking questions too."

"Looks like my best friend doesn't like interrogations." Nevaeh giggles, proceeding to the elevator, and Drake makes us follow her. As the three of us step inside, she hits the number seven and then number eleven. "You've got the best room, by the way. I thought it would be fair."

"Really?" I frown, eyeing her with doubt.

"Really, Angie," Nev states, her gaze dancing between Drake and me, lingering on his hand on my waist. "I hope you make the most of it." The door opens, and she sashays out, throwing a wink over her shoulder. "See you in the morning for breakfast. Don't be late."

"We will try," I mumble, and the door closes again. The elevator moves higher. "How is your sister?"

Drake chuckles. "Layla is great. She got my niece in bed, poured herself some wine, and decided to call me...to ask a gazillion of questions."

"Wow." I exhale, hearing the door open. "You have a niece.... How old is she? And what about your sister? What did she want to know?"

"Maya is ten months old, and she's the most adorable kid I've ever seen," Drake says as we stroll down the hallway to our room. "Pictures of our kiss are everywhere. My sister wanted to know if she'd meet you if she decided to visit in a few months."

"I'd love to meet your sister and your niece." I stop in front of our door, reach for my belt bag, and pull the key card out. "No matter what happens with our fake relationship, we're still neighbors. And friends."

Drake's gaze hardens, and his hand drops from my side. *Great.* My foot is so deep in my mouth, I'm ready to throw up. He doesn't say anything, just pushes the door open and lets me into the room. Sighing, I trudge inside, wobbling a little.

"Will you show me your ankle?"

"No, I'll handle it myself, don't worry." I move past him and enter the bathroom. "I'm gonna take a quick shower," I say, and I close the door behind me, leaning my back against it.

Right, because running away from him is exactly what I should do.

STANDING in front of the fogged mirror, I shift from one leg to the other with the towel wrapped tightly around my body. I forgot the tiniest detail while rushing into the bathroom to avoid Drake...my clothes. I pull my hair into a bun, secure it with my red scrunchie, and take a deep breath. *Make it or break it, Angie.*

I straighten my back and open the door, stepping out of the bathroom. Taking two tentative steps, I stop beside my backpack and kneel, hoping Drake will stay put and pretend he doesn't notice me. Quickly, I grab my pj's and rise to my feet, only to find my fake boyfriend standing on my left, his shoulder propped against the wall —his very naked shoulder, may I add, as the only clothes he's still wearing are his jeans.

"Is the bathroom free?" He arches an eyebrow, and I nod, unable to say a word. "Good."

Drake rounds me and strolls into the bathroom, closing the door in my face. He has every right to be angry with me. I'm not my biggest fan at the moment either. I keep ruining things with my careless words. His patience definitely has its limit, and it looks like it's on a very tight rope already. All because of me.

I drop the towel and put on my white cotton shorts and loose red T-shirt. Putting my phone on the charger, I swipe away Asher's message without reading it. His words lost their appeal a long time ago. All I want is for him to finally leave me alone.

When I'm tucked under the blanket, the bathroom door opens,

and Drake comes into view. I avert my gaze, not allowing myself even a peek. Staying in the same room as him after our kiss is already an enticement I'm not sure I know how to bear. Sleeping in one bed might easily turn into the toughest challenge I've ever faced.

"Can I turn off the lights?" he asks.

"Sure." My response is husky, so I clear my throat, feeling my cheeks warm up. *Well, at least in the darkness he won't be able to see how embarrassed I am.*

The lights go off, and the room is plunged into total darkness. I close my eyes, but I can still feel him moving around. The moment the mattress creaks, I know he's on the bed. A shuffling noise fills the room, and then comes deafening silence. I quietly lie on my right side with my eyes closed, wishing for sleep to overtake me. No luck. After a few minutes of lying still, I start tossing and turning, kicking my blanket aside. When I finally settle, my right leg is bent in front of me as I turn onto my left, my hands locked together and hidden under the pillow.

"How long was your relationship with your ex? With Asher?" His voice comes so suddenly that my eyes instantly fly open. He's been so quiet; I was sure he fell asleep a long time ago.

"A year," I whisper, staring at Drake's silhouette in front of me. "We met when I was still in Philadelphia."

"Did you move to California for him?"

"No, it was just a coincidence. Nev landed a job at a fashion magazine, and I got an offer to walk in a few fashion shows. We decided a change of scenery would do us a lot of good. Asher was supposed to go to Miami, but he freaked out and ended up here in Santa Clara with me."

"Do you miss anything about your relationship?"

"Absolutely not." I shake my head, feeling my heartbeat calm down.

"Not even your sex?" he asks, and I burst out laughing.

"Thanks to Asher, I forgot what it's like to have an orgasm with a partner. He's always been extremely selfish, so trust me, my sex life is definitely better off without him. At least I know how to make myself come; otherwise it would've been a disaster," I mutter. "What about you? What do you miss?"

"If I say sex it would be a cliché, but it's the truth. It's probably the only thing Janelle and I were good at as a couple."

I keep silent, thinking about his words. Mind-blowing sex and can't-walk-after orgasms are great, but after a while I stopped caring about them. Toys and my knowledge of my own body help me bring myself to orgasm, and if a guy makes me at least feel good—it's already enough. I'm not going to be with someone just because they are a good fuck. I need more. A lot more.

"I miss holding someone." His voice cracks when he whispers it. "Just cuddling, nothing crazy."

"Oh, I hadn't even thought about that, but you're right. I always loved cuddling," I murmur, smiling. "It helps me fall asleep faster."

"Considering you were just tossing and turning, I think maybe that's what you need," he states matter-of-factly. "Fancy some cuddles, Cupcake?"

Say yes.

What? My inner voice has surely lost its mind. I should say no.

"Why not?" *Oh my fucking God. Consistency, Angie. Have you ever heard of it?*

I don't know what I expected, but when his arm slips between my thighs I gasp. Drake ignores the sound and just pulls me to him. My right leg is on his left hip, while my left one is tucked between his thighs. He's wearing sweatpants, and I'm grateful for that. He wraps me in his arms. His left hand slides to my ass, keeping me in place. I wind my hands around his shoulders and hide my face in the crook of his neck.

"Is this comfortable for you?" Drake asks, and I nod, afraid to move even a muscle. "Then sleep. Night, Angie."

"Night, Drake." I close my eyes, inhaling his scent. Warm and spicy, familiar, and so intimate. He smells like sandalwood and coffee. And it's slowly becoming my favorite scent...because it's his.

Drake

TWENTY-TWO

are you a swiftie?

SUGGESTING CUDDLES WAS THE MOST IRRATIONAL THING I could've done. Angie is still deep asleep with her pretty round ass pressed against my groin, her head resting on my right arm, and her body aligned with mine. My cock is hard, and I'm afraid to fucking move because I don't want to wake her up.

It's going to be the most awkward morning ever.

Though I'm sure it's not going to be worse than how our night ended. I got upset over something I shouldn't be upset about. She just stated facts. We're neighbors, we're probably becoming friends, and we most definitely don't know what's going to happen with our fake dating and her ex. The last thing I want is for my sister or any of my friends to find out that my relationship with Evangelina is fake, so it's all good. And yet, it feels kinda wrong.

There was nothing fake about our kiss at the festival. At least, not for me.

I blow out a deep breath, and Angie stirs, her ass grinding over my dick. *Jesus fucking Christ, I need to get out of this bed before she opens her eyes.* As slowly as possible, I start to detach myself from her, pulling my hand out from under her head. I almost stop breathing when her eyes pop open.

"Are you running away?" she whispers.

"Just to the bathroom," I say on an exhale.

"Okay."

Angie closes her eyes again, her eyelashes fluttering. Swallowing my nerves, I move away from her and get up from the bed. I head straight to the bathroom and quietly shut the door behind me. Running a hand over my face, I stop in front of the mirror and stare at my reflection. I have some serious stubble, and my hair is a mess, but I feel good being with this girl. Despite all the shit, I had an absolutely amazing time at the festival...all because of her.

Evangelina is funny and has a smart mouth. It's never a dull moment with her. She's stunning, with an absolutely perfect body—one I crave to touch when she's around. Her jade-colored eyes look right into my soul any time our gazes lock. Her deep brown hair feels like silk when I thread my fingers through it, her full lips and those cute little dimples... Kissing her feels like winning. Like my mind just blows up and all I'm left with is happiness and joy. And I smile any time she looks at me.

Layla's words from last night come back, and I brace my hands on either side of the sink. She said I never looked happier with a girl in my arms than I look with Evangelina. The saddest thing is, I guess she's right. My fake girlfriend makes me feel a thousand times better than any of my actual ones ever did.

The question is, can I ever make her mine for real?

"I THOUGHT you flushed yourself down the toilet," Angie says when I finally exit the bathroom. She's sitting on the bed in her pj's. Her bun is messy after a night of sleep.

"Why would I do that?" I ask, coming closer and sitting on the edge of the bed.

"I don't know." She smiles with a lift of her shoulder. "Maybe you didn't want it to be awkward after your hard dick was poking my ass when I woke up."

I chuckle. "That's not something I can control, you know."

"Yeah, morning wood." Evangelina stretches her arms in the air. Her tee sticks to her body, and all I can look at are her nipples, which are directed right at me. "It's not awkward unless you make it awkward. You let me cuddle with you all night, holding me close to your body. It's no surprise you got hard."

Definitely no surprise. This woman is my most delicious and forbidden sex fantasy. I've never wanted a girl as much as I want her.

"I thought you didn't like sex jokes."

"I learned from the best." She winks at me and stands up from the bed. "I'm going to go wash my face, and then we can meet Nev for breakfast. What do you think?"

"Sounds good. I'll change while you're in the bathroom."

"Do it quick, or I might take a peek." Angie walks past me and enters the bathroom.

When the door is closed, I whisper down at my hard dick, which is visible in my pants, "Please don't."

On the ride back home, we listen to music nonstop. Nevaeh finds some random playlists, making us guess the song and the singer. Angie guesses every one way faster than I do, and she sings along, dancing in her seat. I can't stop watching her be so carefree and so cheerful. It's like she allowed herself to forget about all her problems and just enjoy her time, laughing and joking to the point of tears in her eyes. She's flawless, and it's harder and harder for me to take my eyes off her.

When we near our houses, a song starts playing, and Nevaeh and Evangelina go off. They both sing so loud, I can barely hear the music. And yet, I know the song. Smiling, I start humming along, tapping my fingers on the steering wheel to the rhythm.

The sudden silence makes me shut my mouth. Angie's watching me, slack-jawed. I glance in my rearview mirror and notice Nevaeh wearing the exact same expression. The song is still playing, so I have no clue what made them speechless.

"You know the lyrics," Evangelina mutters, leaning toward me from her seat.

"How on Earth do you know the lyrics?" her best friend demands. Her head pops up between me and Evangelina's seats. "Are you a Swiftie?"

"What? No." I shake my head. Taylor Swift's "Cruel Summer" is still playing. "I know a few damn songs. It's all because of my sister. She used to sing this one a lot because she loved this TV show called *The Summer I Turned Pretty* or something."

They both continue staring at me in silence, while I prefer to focus on the road. Knowing lyrics is not a crime. It's not like I suddenly turned into Captain America without realizing it. These two are being overly dramatic about something incredibly simple.

"You know what?" Nevaeh says, leaning away. "I think you should keep him. He's the best guy you've ever had." She looks around her and then knocks on her forehead three times. "Knock on wood. I don't want to jinx it."

The light shade of pink creeping up Angie's cheeks is the most divine thing I've ever seen. I smile from ear to ear, and just look at the road. There is no reason for me to feel smug, but I do. I think I just got her best friend's blessing, and in the long run, I believe that's a good thing.

"How was the festival?" Colton asks as I skate over to him with three pucks in one hand and my hockey stick in the other.

"It was packed; so were the hotels." I shrug, shoving the pucks into the puck bag. "The lineup was awesome. I had lots of fun with Angie and her best friend."

"Her best friend was there?"

"I just tagged along on their trip. I was lucky there were still tickets."

"What did you think about your girlfriend's friend? Did she like you? For Ava, it was always a big deal that Layla and I got along. Especially after Clay, you know."

I nod, remembering how rocky things were after my sister broke up with our friend right after graduation. Clay was heartbroken, and Colton had nothing nice to say to Layla for months. If it weren't for Ava, I have no clue if we would still be friends.

"Nevaeh likes me. She thinks I'm good...for her friend." I grab my water bottle and take a sip.

Colton watches me quietly, and then tips his head to the side. "You said it was their trip, and you weren't supposed to go. And the hotels were full. Does that mean you spent the night with both girls in the same room, Drake?"

"A very interesting conclusion, Thompson. I just love how your brain works," I mumble, heading to the locker room with my friend following me. "Angie and I shared a room, and Nev was in another one."

"Looks like things are moving steadily with you and your new girl. I like it." He claps me on the back as we enter the locker room. "Do you remember when I said Ava would figure out a way to invite you two over?"

"Yeah, why?"

"Well, she doesn't need to come up with a reason now. We have news to share, and we'd love to have you and Evangelina over to our place." Colton sits down on the bench, untying his skates. "Do you think next weekend will work for you? It'll just be us, Xander and Bella with their kids, Roman, you, and Evangelina. Maybe Clay too, but only if the Hawks lose their final game this week."

"I actually planned to fly home on Friday. I promised to visit Layla and Maya. I'll be there for a week."

Thompson nods, a smile on his face. "When you get back then. There's no way we're doing this without you. Your sister already told Ava she couldn't come because she's waiting for your niece to turn one before she comes to visit. We can't do this without the two Bensons."

I slump down onto the bench near my open locker and eye my

best friend. My hunch seems logical, but I've never heard them talking about it. They're happy with the little family they have. I highly doubt it's going to be another kid. But what if I'm wrong?

"Can I ask what the news is now?"

"No, it's too soon. We're still dealing with something. We'll tell you after we know more."

"Okay, cool." I smile and start untying my skates. The feeling in the pit of my stomach feels heavy, as if I just swallowed a bunch of rocks. I hate the way I'm reacting. No matter what the news is, I should be happy for my friends. There is no reason to throw myself a pity party.

I have no one to blame except me for my poor choices. For all the girls I've dated, only to be disappointed, over and over again. For all the decisions I've made that led me to this moment, when the only girl in my life is not interested in me as a boyfriend, but as a friend she can count on...a dude to help her get rid of her ex. Definitely not someone she can see herself with. Agreeing to be a fake boyfriend when the only thing I want is to have someone who will love me for me? It's a terrible mistake.

ME:

Sorry, Cupcake, I need to bail on you. Our OTH marathon is on pause

CUPCAKE:

Why? Hey, by the way

ME:

Hey, sorry, my mind is a mess. I'm going to visit my sister. I'll be back in a week

CUPCAKE:

Is everything okay? Is your niece alright?

ME:

Yeah, don't worry about it. I've been planning to go visit them, just forgot to mention it

CUPCAKE:

Have a good time then. I think I'm gonna miss you

ME:

I think I'm gonna miss you too

I TURN ON AIRPLANE MODE, lock my phone, and hide it in my pocket as I follow the signs to my gate. Getting back to my roots is exactly what I need.

Angie

TWENTY-THREE

texting or sexting

"We're going out tonight," Nevaeh states, crouching to pet Cooper.

"Hello to you too, my dear best friend," I mutter under my breath, closing the door. "How are you? Good? Me too. Thank you so much for asking."

When I turn around, I find Nev still on the floor near Cooper, but her blue eyes are focused on me under her furrowed brows.

"What?" I ask.

"Don't 'what' me. You're talking to yourself, Angie. That's what happens to workaholics like you."

Rolling my eyes, I stomp past her and head to the couch in my living room. I grab my laptop from the table, unlock it, and start reading Amelie's marketing plan from the very beginning to make sure I'm one hundred percent on board with her strategy for my shop.

"What are you doing?" My best friend walks up to me and plops herself down on the couch.

"Working."

"It's seven p.m. on Friday," she counters, moving closer to me. "Your workday is over."

"My workday is over when I say it's over, Nev. I want to finish checking out the second draft of the marketing plan. Amelie worked hard on it, and she's waiting for my feedback. It's important."

"When will she get back to you?"

"On Monday."

"Nothing is going to change if you finish reading this on Monday morning, Angie." Nevaeh presses her palm to my laptop's cover. "Stop working. Let's go have some fun. Please."

I hesitate. She might have a point. I've been trying to read through this document for the last hour, and I can't focus.

"Okay," I say, nodding, and Nev closes my laptop. She takes it from my hands and puts it back on the table. "What now?"

"Now, we're going to get you dressed up, and then I'm going to do your hair and makeup." She pinches my cheek, and I push her away, rubbing my skin and glaring at my best friend. "Keep up this attitude, sweetheart. You'll need it at the club."

"I don't remember saying yes to the club," I mumble, letting Nevaeh drag me to my bedroom. She pushes me onto the bed and then goes to my closet, determination written all over her face. Without saying anything, I just continue to watch her, curious to see what she has in mind.

Nev sifts through my dresses. I have no idea what she's looking for, but I'm not going to ask. I better use this time to send a quick message to Drake. Just to know how he is. This week without him sucked a lot.

ME:

Hey, stranger, how are you?

DRAKE:

Hey, Cupcake, I'm good. Been playing with my niece since early this morning. You? Any fun plans for tonight?

ME:

My fun plans included watching more OTH with you, but since you left me...I'm going out with Nevaeh. She's planning some secret mission

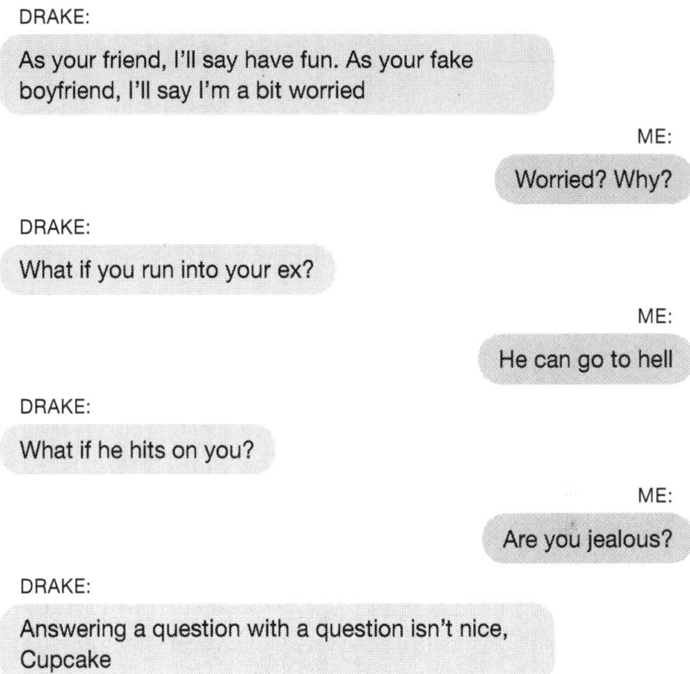

I smile, reading his answer and watching three dots appear then disappear on the screen. We've been texting since the day he flew home. Just fun stuff, mostly memes and YouTube videos. A lot of bantering and laughing my ass off.

DRAKE:

I am

I start sweating, and my skin turns scorching hot.

Tracing my bottom lip with my index finger, I stare at the screen. Flirting started naturally, probably the day after he left. A little bit of teasing, some sex jokes here and there, as if we were trying to see where the other would draw the line. Considering I sent him a picture of my new lingerie after he asked what I bought shopping one day, we're getting close to a line we shouldn't cross.

ME:

Good to know. And don't worry about him. D-bags don't get to touch me

DRAKE:

But nice guys do?

My heart gallops, and my fingers tremble as I type my answer. I'm raising the stakes, and I can only hope he'll get on board. Because one of my fake-dating rules isn't all that appealing to me anymore. If it ever was.

ME:

Come home and find out for yourself

"This is perfect for you." Nevaeh's voice brings me back to reality, just as a pile of clothes lands on my lap. My phone is buried under it. "What were you doing?"

"Nothing, just texting with Drake," I deadpan, pushing the clothes and my phone onto my bed. Standing up, I hover over the pile and take out a black sleeveless crop top with slashes in front. "Where are we going, exactly, if *this* is perfect for me? My boobs will literally be exposed for everyone to see."

"Sexting or texting?"

"What?" I frown.

"Were you texting with Drake, or sexting?"

"Texting."

Nevaeh's eyes roam over my face. Her eyebrow is arched, her lips curled into a small smile. "Uh-huh, let's pretend I believe you." She bends down, fishes some light blue jeans out of the pile of clothes, and pushes them into my hands. "Go change."

I hold the crop top and jeans to my chest. Obviously, I can choose something else, but at the same time, this outfit is sexy and casual all at once. It's great for dancing or just sitting at the bar. It should be fine.

With a sigh, I head to the bathroom. Before I close the door, I peek out and say, "Can you please take Cooper out? I always take him for an afternoon walk if I'm going to be late. I'll take a shower in the meantime. Please?"

Nev clicks her tongue and pivots to the door. "You're *really* lucky I love you."

"Love you too!" I shout and close the door. Well, I just earned myself thirty or forty minutes of quiet. There is no way Coop lets her come back home quicker. My boy is my best partner in crime.

THE BLASTING SOUNDS of music swim around me as I sip my Cosmopolitan. My gaze is glued to Nevaeh as she dances with Travis nearby. The sequins on her little black dress shimmer with different colors, drawing the attention of people around her. She smiles and points her finger at me, urging me to join them. I shake my head no and salute her with my drink. It's been almost five hours since we got to the club, and I'm immensely tired, especially after the long week I've had.

"Hey, doll. Can I buy you a drink?"

Arching an eyebrow, I turn my head toward a guy in a white shirt. I look him up and down, keeping silent and making him shift uncomfortably.

"Um, what about a drink?" he asks again.

I raise my glass in front of me. "Already have one."

He exhales, stepping closer and setting his elbow on the bar to have a better look at me. Okay, apparently talking back is an invitation to continue. "How about another one?"

"No, thank you." I catch Nevaeh's gaze over this guy's shoulder, and she lifts her chin, as if asking if I need her help. I jerk my head no and she nods, shifting her attention back to Travis.

"You know, you look very familiar," the shirt guy mutters, and I bring my eyes back to his face.

"I'm sure we haven't met before."

"Oh my God, I know you. You were in *Sports Today* with your parents. Girl, your father is a fucking legend. I grew up watching him play, dreaming about meeting him one day just to say thank you for everything he has done for the Beavers. His interview was fire. I loved it."

I suck in a breath, then gulp down my drink in one go. "My dad would be flattered," I grit, setting the empty glass on the bartop.

"I'm from Philly, actually. Just like you."

"Nice." I jump to my feet. "I gotta go."

"Wait, wait, is there any chance—"

"No. Bye." I barrel through the dancing crowd to Nevaeh. I'll say bye and go home.

"Angie?" my friend says as soon as our eyes meet. She moves away from Travis and takes my hand in hers. "What's wrong?"

"I'm going home."

"Was that guy bothering you?" Nevaeh winds her hand around my waist, pulling me to her.

"No. Just another NFL fan."

She lifts her hand and presses it to my cheek, caressing it tenderly. "I'm so sorry."

"That's okay. I've had a very busy week, working from home and from the shop. I'm honestly just tired." I hug her tightly and take a step back. "It was a lot of fun, thanks to you and Travis. But now I want to go home."

Nevaeh gives me a sympathetic smile and kisses my cheek. "Bye, Angie. See you on Monday for our lunch date."

"Bye, Nev," I tell her. Then I look at Travis. His blond hair falls in his eyes, and he pushes it away, winking at me. "Bye, Travis. It was nice seeing you. Keep an eye on my best friend for me, will you?"

"Always." He wraps his arm around Nevaeh's waist, and waves at me. "Bye, Angie."

Slowly, I stroll away from my friends, pushing through the crowd. I stop short when a guy blocks my way. As soon as I see it's Asher, I'm ready to scream in frustration. What the hell is he doing here?

"Wow, this outfit is just perfection, Evangelina. You look amazing." A sly grin forms on his lips as his eyes travel up and down my body, lingering on my boobs.

"Bye." I move to my left, but he does the same. I curse inwardly and level him with a stare. "What do you want, Asher?"

"You. It's always only you." He steps closer to me.

"Oh my God, you're unbelievable," I grunt, running my fingers through my hair. "I'm not single anymore. I have a boyfriend, and he—"

"That kiss at the festival was pretty hot, I must admit. But you were there with Nevaeh too. Did you share a bed with both of them?"

"Leave me alone." I skirt him, but he halts me in my tracks, grabbing my hand roughly.

"You know you're mine. It's not something you can escape," Asher hisses, his eyes darkening.

"You sound like a broken record; you're disgusting." I pull my hand out of his grip. "Bye, Asher."

I zip to the exit, and thankfully, he doesn't follow me. It doesn't take long for me to climb inside my Uber and ride away from the club. I'm angry and tired at the same time. All I want now is to crash in my bed and fall asleep with Cooper near me. It does seem like a perfect ending for a very long day.

When the car stops in front of my house, it's past two a.m. The whole ride, I've been texting about Europe with my little brother in the group chat we have for me and the twins. It's morning in Spain, and Ethan mentioned he and Emma went to breakfast. He said my sister has been busy hanging out with their friends, but I know the truth. If Emma can avoid talking to me, she will. I'm her least favorite person in our family. It doesn't surprise me in the slightest, considering our past.

ME:

don't forget to send me some pictures from Madrid. Chao, cariño

ETHAN:

anything for you 😘 Chao

Smiling, I pocket my phone and climb out of the car. I'm ready to go home, but something catches my attention. I stare at Drake's Lexus parked beside my Aventador.

I bite my bottom lip, twirling a lock of my hair around my index finger. He might be asleep already, but he might also still be up. I don't think he's been home for long, and the second option sounds more appealing to me. Or do I just want to see him?

"Screw it." I start climbing the stairs of his house. I'm going to knock once, and if he's already asleep, I'll just go home. The last thing I need is for him to think I'm some kind of stalker.

Stopping at his door, I knock on it and take a step back. My pulse jackhammers. If he was coming home, why didn't he tell me? This thought sinks deeper, and I'm ready to lose my shit.

Oh my God, I'm knocking on my fake boyfriend's door at two a.m. after telling him to come home and find out if I'll let him touch me. I'm so fucked-up. I hope he's already sound asleep, because if not—

The door swings open, and my eyes lock on Drake's. He smiles and props his shoulder against the doorframe, crossing his arms over his bare chest. "Hey, Angie. Couldn't wait to see me?"

Drake

TWENTY-FOUR

good girl

EVANGELINA STARES AT ME WITH ROUND EYES. NOT A single sound escapes her parted lips. Her long hair cascades down her shoulders, and her chest rises and falls with her rapid breathing. It takes titanic effort not to let my gaze fix on her tits...because Jesus fucking Christ, what on Earth is that top supposed to hide?

"Where were you when we were texting?" she asks, finally breaking her silence.

"At the airport," I tell her, stepping aside. "Come on in. I got home twenty minutes ago."

"It's late."

"You didn't think it was late when you knocked on my door."

She shrugs and walks inside my house. The scent of her perfume hits my nostrils, and I'm full of memories of her. This week without Angie proved I'm not ready to give up on the idea of her being my girl. Just like her texts have also shown one tiny detail I hadn't realized before—she likes me. Not because I'm an NHL hockey player with a great paycheck. She likes me for me.

"I just don't get it. You didn't tell me you were leaving, and you didn't tell me you were coming back. What's wrong with sharing your plans? I thought we were friends."

"About my plans," I mutter, strolling past her to the living room and turning on the lights. "Any chance you're free on Sunday?"

"Think so. Where do you want to go?" Evangelina takes off her heels and joins me on the couch a second later. "Somewhere fun?"

I swivel to my left and glue my gaze onto her face. In addition to a very sexy outfit, she has on immaculate makeup, highlighting her deep green eyes and her plump lips. Her hair is pinned to one side, where it freely streams down her shoulders. She's so devastatingly beautiful, I find it hard to believe I'll ever look at anyone else. I just need her.

"My friends invited me to their place for lunch, and they want to meet my girlfriend." I watch her reaction with curiosity. I don't know what I expect, but all I get is a radiant smile. "Are you okay with that?"

"Why not? You've already met Nev and Willow, and I'd love to meet your friends," she murmurs, pulling her legs under her butt.

It doesn't sound like fake dating. Or a PR stunt, as Layla suggested when she was trying to figure out how I ended up getting together with Evangelina in such a short time. It feels normal, and it's exactly how it should be.

"Awesome." I run my fingers through my hair, not knowing what else I can say.

Evangelina tilts her head, her eyes narrowing. She leans forward and touches my hair with her hand. "Did you get a cut?"

"I did." I nod, suddenly aware of how close she is to me. "Do you like it?"

She threads her fingers through my locks, whispering, "I do."

If I don't kiss her now, I'll be the biggest loser on this planet.

I close the distance between us. Putting my hand on the back of her neck, I pull her to me, and our mouths slam against each other. I drape my hand around her waist and haul her to my lap, my lips ravishing hers. She tastes like alcohol and something sweet, and her tongue playing with mine makes me lose my mind. *She's perfect.*

Her hands slowly roam over my chest, as if she's trying to memorize every line of my body. Leaning away, Angie brushes her nose over mine, her lips an inch away from my mouth. Her gaze is feverish when I allow myself to meet her eyes again. I smile and move closer; my teeth graze her bottom lip. The sweetest moan I've ever heard fills my ears, and my dick hardens in my jeans.

"I want you so bad," I whisper. My hands circle around her waist and slide to her hips. She wiggles on my lap, and a smile blooms on her lips once she feels how hard I am for her.

"Then what are you waiting for?" she taunts, brushing her nose over mine again, her tongue tracing my bottom lip.

Moving my hands up, I grab the bottom of her top, and she helps me slide it over her head. Her hair spills down over her naked tits when I toss her top aside. The hard points of her nipples make my mouth water, and I don't waste even a goddamn minute palming her round breasts and feeling her up. Angie closes her eyes the second I rub her nipples between my fingers. A breathless moan slips out of her mouth.

Gently, I close my lips around her nipple, my tongue curling around it. I suck and tease, making her arch her back for me, her moans becoming louder. She grinds her pussy over my dick, and I have a feeling I'm going to fucking explode right now.

Lowering Angie onto her back, I pull away. My breathing is ragged, as if I just completed a marathon. My cock strains against my jeans, and the only thing I want is to feel her walls squeezing around me. Rising to my feet, I tower over her, admiring how stunning she is. It's a fucking crime to hide breasts like hers under all those clothes. I'll be craving to touch her even more now, because there is no going back. Evangelina is ruining me for all other women with such ease that I truly doubt I ever had a chance to resist her.

"Drake?" Her voice saying my name snaps me back to reality, and I quickly turn around, rushing out of the living room to snatch a condom from my wallet. When I return, I find Angie propped up on her elbows. "You almost ruined the moment."

Instead of answering her, I bend down, unzip her jeans, and slowly drag them down until they are on the floor. Lacy red panties draw my attention, and my fingers tremble when I unzip my fly, pushing down my jeans and stepping out of them.

"Would you rather I fucked you bare?" I ask, clearing my throat and tearing the wrapper open. Taking off my briefs, I roll the condom down my cock and give myself a single stroke.

Angie's eyes zero in on my dick, and she licks her lips. "I'm clean, and I'm on the pill." Her breathing quickens as I step closer. "You?"

I nudge her legs apart, my knee sinking between her thighs on the couch. "Me too. I can show you all the tests—"

She pulls me down, her lips in desperate need of mine. Our mouths collide; the kiss is languorous and intense. My skin becomes scorching. For the first time in years, I'm choosing fire, and I'm not afraid to get burned.

Her hands move frantically over my back. My lips travel down her throat, and I nibble on her skin. She moans and presses herself closer to me, molding us together, and there's no escape for me anymore. Reaching between us, I push her panties aside and slowly slide inside her. Inch by inch, moving in and out without any rush. Savoring this moment, engraving it in my brain so I can always remember it. Letting her adjust to my length and girth, I fuck her slow and gentle.

Angie seeks my lips, whimpering quietly any time I sink deeper. It's pure pleasure, and my mind fogs, happiness overwhelming me. I kiss her, our tongues dancing together, hands caressing each other's skin. She's soft and warm, her curves have perfect lines and shapes. Touching her feels like scoring the most important penalty shot during a shootout, one that makes me hold my breath waiting to see if I made it. And I want to see it all.

I hover over her, my hands gripping her ass. Moving my palms up her skin, I guide her legs to my shoulders. Angie gasps when I'm inside her to the hilt. Her eyes fall closed, and her hand cups her breast, her fingers playing with her nipple. I lower my gaze to her pussy, mesmerized by how perfectly we fit.

"Look at you, Angie," I whisper, and her eyes fly open. "You take me so good, pulling me deeper and deeper with each thrust. Do you like it?"

"Yes," she sighs softly. "I'm so close, Drake.... Make me come, please...I'm begging you...."

My lips fall on hers, devouring her mouth, sucking her tongue inside. I move my hips faster, fucking her long and hard. Her words from the night of the festival come back to me, and I want her to come first. And she does, falling apart right in front of me...and it's the most beautiful sight I've ever seen.

Her walls squeeze around me, her whole body trembles. "Oh my God...you feel so good...."

Evangelina tries to cover her face, but I grab her wrists and hold them over her head, driving myself faster and rougher to my orgasm. It builds within me as her pussy continues to pulse on the waves of her own pleasure.

"Such a good girl you are.... Such a good fucking girl, Angie," I grunt, spilling my cum inside the condom. God, fucking her is like nothing else. My veins burst with fire, sparks flying everywhere, and I want more. This feeling is like an obsession. She makes me lose control.

Pressing my forehead to hers, I close my eyes, slowing my breathing. I'm still inside her, and my hand is curled around her wrists, which are locked together over her head. My fingers tenderly skim down her skin, and suddenly I halt my caresses, my eyes snapping open.

Her left arm is covered in scars, some longer than others. The longest one crosses her wrist, and I swallow a lump in my throat, feeling uneasy. "Your tattoos...they are meant to hide your scars," I say, barely breathing, releasing her wrists.

Angie presses a hand to my chest, and I awkwardly move away, sitting beside her. She bends to pick up her clothes, but I stop her, hauling her to me and holding her close. "Talk to me."

She keeps silent. Her breathing is shallow, but she's not pushing me away. When I start to think she's not going to say anything, she whispers, "Can I stay the night? I'll go home first thing in the morning. Coop will be waiting."

"Of course." I kiss her temple, dropping my hands off her sides.

Ten minutes later, Angie is already in bed with me, tucked safely under the blanket with my body wrapped around hers. She used my toothpaste when she went to the bathroom, and now the minty scent wafts around her. Her hair is collected into a long braid, which rests on her right shoulder. She looks comfortable and relaxed, like she belongs with me in this room and in my bed. Like she's found a refuge, and there is no need to run away anymore because she knows she's safe with me.

"Did you do this to yourself?" The question has been burning a hole in my tongue since the second I discovered her scars.

"No."

It takes me a moment to collect myself; anger rises inside my chest. "Who did this to you, Angie?" I lower my voice and hold her closer.

"It's not what you're probably imagining." She takes a deep breath. "Asher brought a girl back to his place for a quickie when I was there. Any sensible person would've left, but I stayed. I wanted to make a point. To make sure he knew it was the last time he saw me. Well, things definitely didn't go as I planned when she left. He was out of it because of the drugs and had no idea what was going on or who I was. He cut me... That horrible experience knocked me off my feet for a long time."

"Did you call the police?"

"No. As soon as he passed out, I patched myself up, dragged him to my car, and drove him to rehab. It'd been my backup plan for months. To help him get better and help him quit our codependent relationship. To help him move on."

"Nothing really worked, from what I know," I tell her, splaying my palm over her belly as she snuggles into me.

"He's doing better now, but he refuses to understand that I no longer want to be in his life. Even at the club tonight, he kept saying the same thing." Evangelina breathes a long sigh, followed by a loud yawn.

I tighten my grip around her and kiss her shoulder. "You need to sleep; we can talk more in the morning. Night, Angie."

"Night, Drake."

Listening to her even breathing when she finally falls asleep, I close my eyes too. Her revelations change everything for me, just like us having sex in my living room. Making her mine isn't the only goal I have in mind. I still don't know the whole story, but I refuse to believe that sudden burst of anger was the only time Asher hurt her. Protecting her from this asshole is something I should focus on too.

She has easily become someone I can't imagine myself without.

Angie

TWENTY-FIVE

my destruction

Sneaking out of Drake's bed isn't the simplest task. Not only because he's holding me close, his solid body caging mine, but also because I don't want to leave. I've been lying with my eyes open, trying to convince myself to go—not successfully, since I haven't moved an inch.

Cooper is going to hate me if I don't go home soon.

I count to ten and slowly move away from Drake, little by little, until I'm standing. Bending down to get my clothes, I put on my crop top and tiptoe to the door with my jeans pressed to my chest. When I'm out of his bedroom, I exhale loudly, relieved he's still asleep. In the hallway, I pull on my jeans, almost falling in the process. It's not a walk of shame, but it will be equally humiliating if I land on my face in his hallway. He'd never forget me then, for sure. I saunter to the living room, grab my phone from my purse, and check the time. It's just past eight a.m., and there is nothing I want more than to go back to his bed. But I can't. My little boy is waiting for me.

Walking out of Drake's house, I close the door and rush to my own place. If everything goes as I plan, I'll be able to catch a few hours of sleep once I get Coop back home. Let's hope I'll manage, because I'm spent. Making a good impression on Drake's friends won't be possible tomorrow if I don't get a chance to relax and recharge my batteries today. And I want them to like me.

The first thing I see when I open the door is Cooper. He's sitting in the middle of the hallway, wearing the most condemning look I've ever seen from him. I edge closer to him and kneel, so our eyes are level.

"I'm sorry for leaving you alone. For not coming home when you were waiting for me." I rub his fur, gently caressing it. "I promise I'll do better next time. Do you want to go for a walk?"

Coop stands up, his tail wagging. I stand too, smiling broadly. *Phew, this has been pretty easy.* Turning around, I snatch his leash from the table and quickly put it on him. As I head out of the house, my mood is cheerful and my steps are light.

I have a few things to be happy about. First, my dog doesn't hate me, and he doesn't hold any grudges, which is important, considering how he can be sometimes. The other one makes my smile brighter and my panties wetter. Last night, I had my first orgasm with a guy in over a year. And what an orgasm it was. Drake made my toes curl and my body tremble like no one ever did. Our sex was passionate, raw, and insanely good, and if there is anything I know for certain...it's the fact that I want him again.

SHOULD I INVITE HIM OVER? I can always use *One Tree Hill* as an excuse, because we're still on season three and have a lot of episodes to watch. And yet I don't want him to think I'm clingy and dependent, or that sex with him is the only thing that's been on my mind since I woke up two hours ago.

I'm acting like a schoolgirl, and it's confusing. Being so out of character is unusual for me, and it's not something I'm proud of. I need to act, not just wait and see how things will turn out. There is nothing wrong with taking risks.

Grabbing my phone from the couch, I unlock it and launch the

Messages app. I don't have time to even start typing before I get a text from Drake.

DRAKE:

Yours or mine?

My heart goes berserk, and the butterflies in my stomach flutter their wings fast. A smile stretches across my lips, and I instantly feel happy and content. It's a coincidence that he sent me a message just as I was ready to text him, a little reminder that if I want something good to happen, I need to take matters into my own hands. Just like Drake does.

ME:

Mine

Not even fifteen minutes later, I hear the knock on my door. Jumping to my feet, I stroll to the hallway and let Drake in. He saunters past me, grinning. He's wearing only shorts again, and I have a slight guess that I might be the reason. The guy is perfectly aware of how much I like watching his impeccable body, all those defined lines and sculpted abs, flexing whenever he moves and making my mouth water in the process.

"You have some serious skills, Cupcake," he says, plopping onto the couch. "You snuck out of my house without me even noticing."

"That was the whole point," I comment, sitting down beside him. "It was early, and I didn't want to wake you up. You look so cute when you sleep, I felt like an intruder climbing out of your bed."

"And yet you still did." Drake reaches over to Cooper, who's standing in front of him, and starts rubbing his fur.

Our eyes lock, and warmth unfurls under my skin. It's like the world around me stops existing, and all that remains is this man. He wasn't meant to be anything more than a pretense. Maybe a friend. But the emotions he causes me and how easily his words and his touch tug at the strings of my heart show me that he's already so much more than that. The connection I share with my fake boyfriend urges me to unravel the layers of my own feelings, little by little, discovering my true self behind all the walls I surround myself with.

He's the key to my undoing, and I'm no longer afraid of it.

"You're petting the reason I needed to leave. He was waiting for me, sitting by the door, and let me tell you, he wasn't happy." I grab the remote from the table. "Last time I stayed out all night, he ate my favorite sneakers."

Drake arches an eyebrow at me and turns to look at Cooper. "I never thought you'd be such a menace. Should I be afraid of you?" My dog tilts his head, listening attentively, and then just licks Drake's hand and wags his tail faster. "I'll take that as a no. You're a good boy, Coop."

I suck in a breath, my skin suddenly burning hot. His praise from last night replays in my head, and I'm a puddle already. It's like this man doesn't have a single less-than-perfect bone in his body. His striking looks and kind, caring personality go hand in hand with how his cock fills me, how he fucks me long and hard, and how he kisses me, leaving me breathless and yearning for more. I clench my thighs together, shifting to scoot away from Drake. It's not going to end well if I continue sitting so close to him.

"Cooper." I raise my voice, and my dog snaps his head in my direction. "Go to your bed. Now."

With a sigh, Coop steps back and leaves the living room. A tinge of guilt flashes in my heart, but I quickly ignore it.

"What was that?"

I sneak a glance in Drake's direction and shrug in response.

"Why did you send him away?" he asks again.

"I plan to go to bed early tonight since we're going to visit your friends tomorrow. So it's time for us to start watching again," I mutter. Then I quickly launch the third episode of season three. "Welcome back to *One Tree Hill*, Mr. Benson."

"I love it when you're so official, Ms. Jones. The difference between you last night and you now is insane." My jaw drops, and he winks at me, spreading his arms across the back of the couch. "Welcome back, indeed."

WITH A SOFT GROAN, I slump down on the couch and close my eyes. It's a bit past eight p.m., and Drake and I just returned from our walk with Cooper, which we took right after dinner. We spent the whole day together. The only time I was alone was when Drake dashed to his house to put on a T-shirt. Watching TV, dinner, going for a walk... They're things couples do, and I have no idea what he thinks about our Saturday. The only feeling I have is happiness.

"What's up with you and Paris?"

My eyes open, and I sit up straighter, placing my hands on my lap as I watch Drake standing in front of the drawings on my wall. His tee is already nowhere to be seen, but fortunately his question helps me to focus on something else—my past, to be precise.

"It's boring," I mumble.

Drake spins around, smiling gently. He edges toward me and sits on the couch. "I'm still curious. Why Paris?"

"A long time ago, my dad took Mom to Paris, a city of love and dreams. He wanted to propose to her in a very expensive restaurant with a perfect view of the Eiffel Tower. Dad planned everything, but Mom blew it up. She ruined his proposal, and they got into a little argument." I hesitate, biting my bottom lip. "I'm the result of that argument."

"No way. Really?" he laughs, his head dropping back. Calming down, he peers at me. "Where did your dad propose to your mom then?"

"After a game. When he won the Super Bowl."

Watching me in silence, Drake leans closer, his fingers brushing locks of hair from my face. "Your parents have a great history, Cupcake. Proposing to someone you love right after you win a very important game? A classic that never gets old." His finger slides along my jaw, caressing it slightly. "Do you go to Paris often?"

"Once every few months. I love the city, and France in general. The old, beautiful buildings, the cobblestone streets, the delicious food and drinks. It feels like magic. No other place in the world affects me the way Paris does," I confess, glancing at my drawings on the wall. "Seven months ago, when I was in Paris for a fashion show, I decided to go for a walk to Montmartre, to look for some art to decorate my house. That's when I met Louis, a very talented artist. That girl under the red umbrella is me; you were right. He saw me like that, and when he gave me this drawing, he wished for me to find someone to share the umbrella with."

I fall silent, a flurry of different emotions dancing within me. It's hard to breathe, and my heart feels like it weighs a ton. Drake cups my cheek with his palm, outlining my cheekbones and my bottom lip with his thumb. The uncertainty of what's going to happen next worries me just as much as it excites me.

"What if I told you I couldn't stop thinking about you since the moment I opened my eyes this morning?" he whispers, his voice husky.

"Then I'd tell you that leaving your bed was one of the hardest things I've done in a very long time."

My words linger on my lips when Drake pulls me to him and smashes his mouth on mine. It's passion in its purest form, untamed and overpowering. He devours me, his tongue playing with mine and making me squeeze my legs together, the heat in my lower abdomen spreading across my veins. His palm slides down my throat, circling it and taking control of my body. Drake makes my body hum, and a myriad of tingles scatters over my skin.

"Do you want me to fuck you?" he asks, his lips just an inch away from mine. I nod, trying to close the distance between us to feel his mouth again. "Use your words, Angie. Tell me what you want me to do."

I place my hand on his lap and glide it up until my fingers stumble over his hard-on. Feeling him up through his shorts, I watch his eyes turn almost black with how wide his pupils become.

"I want you to take me to my bedroom, bend me over my bed, and fuck me so hard until my legs no longer hold my weight," I coo hoarsely. His hand on my throat makes it hard to breathe.

He watches me intently, and I start smiling, feeling my nipples poking through my tee. Drawing me to him, he covers my lips with his. His hands coast to my waist and haul me onto his lap. I moan into his mouth, feeling his dick under his shorts. The level of my arousal goes through the roof and right into space. I've never been more turned on than I am now. He's perfect.

Standing up from the couch, Drake makes me wrap my legs around his hips as he carries me to my bedroom, his hands firmly holding my ass. He enters my room and pushes the door closed with his leg. Stopping by my bed, he lowers me to my feet, and his fingers skim down my body until he digs them into my skin, yanking my hips to his.

We kiss, our noses brushing, his tongue teasing mine. He pulls away, his hand on my throat, tilting my face slightly. The silence fills the room, but we don't need words. It's a moment of surrender. All my senses ignite, and indefinite pleasure ripples through my body from just his touch.

"Take off your clothes," he commands. I obey, pulling my loose T-shirt over my head and hastily casting it onto the floor. Without any bra, only shorts still cover my body. Drake takes my chin between his fingers, and a smile crosses his features. "I want you naked, Angie."

I push down my shorts and panties, step out of them, and look up at him. His eyes flicker to my lips as he grips my hips, his hands sliding down and splaying possessively on my butt. Drake bends his head down, his nose nudging mine, his lips grazing my bottom lip and sending an electric current through my veins. Our breaths mingle, and I close my eyes, enjoying the caress of his tongue and the softness of his lips. I'm dripping wet, and a moan escapes my throat when I press my hands to his chest.

The moment ends abruptly. My eyes fly open when he steps back from me. A wicked grin lights up his face as he takes off his shorts. His well-defined body, honed from years of playing hockey, exudes strength and power, drawing me in and making it impossible to resist him. My gaze falls on his long, thick cock, and my mind empties of all other thoughts. He becomes the center of my attention, turning the rest of the world into nothingness.

"What my girl wants..." Drake whispers, encircling his arm around my waist. He turns me around and pushes me facedown onto my bed. "She gets."

He aligns his body with mine, his hard dick pressed against my butt. My heart hammers against my chest, intoxicating my veins and making me feel high. He teases my opening with the tip of his cock, and I push my hips back to take more of him.

"Can I fuck you bare, baby?" he coos, his fingers gently curling around my hair. "I have a condom with me."

"Bare, please," I reply quietly. A second later, I whimper when he slides into me. My eyes roll back, and I fist the sheets, enjoying how full he makes me feel.

His thrusts are deep and slow, pumping into me and making me moan as our bodies slam together. The feeling evokes something inside me, blending together broken parts of my soul and making me whole. Unspoken words mixed with the sounds we make create a language of our own, laced with understanding and fervent desire. I've never felt more alive than when I'm with him.

"Your pussy takes me so well, baby." He glides his hands up my back. "I love making you take me deeper." Drake puts both of his hands on my lower back, adding more pressure. "Lift your ass higher for me, and put your hands behind your back."

I do as he says, barely understanding what's going on around me. Drake seizes my hands, pressing them against my lower back. His other hand is on the back of my neck. He's all I feel. All I think about. His cock slides so deep inside me, my legs are shaking.

"Baby, your pussy is so warm...so fucking perfect. You gonna come for me like the good girl you are?"

"Oh God, Drake..." I moan loudly as his movements become rougher. "Oh my God... You feel so good, I'm gonna come...so fucking hard. Drake, please..."

"That's it, baby... Who's my beautiful girl? You're my beautiful girl." He praises me, and I burst with pleasure, hiding my face in my sheets, my pussy throbbing around his cock. Screaming his name and feeling euphoric, I'm riding the waves of the strongest orgasm I've ever felt. Even the one he gave me yesterday wasn't as powerful as this one. This man is a fucking pussy whisperer. It's like he knows my body and how to make me feel good without even asking what I want.

"Drake..." I moan breathlessly, closing my eyes and giving all of myself to him.

A few more deep and hard thrusts, and a groan of pleasure leaves his mouth. He comes and comes, spilling inside me. Letting go of my wrists, he hovers over me, his hands caging me. I lie with my lips parted, trying to catch my breath. Drake pulls his dick out of me, wraps his arms around my waist, and turns me to face him. Our gazes are feverish; our emotions entwine, blending not only our bodies, but our souls.

He dips his head down, his sweaty forehead pressed to mine. His hot breath warms up my skin as he exhales loudly. "Did your legs give out?"

I chuckle softly, circling my arms around his shoulders and pulling him to me. "Almost," I whisper against his mouth, a happy smile curving my lips.

"Well, if you don't mind, I want to stay and make it up to you," Drake murmurs, sliding his hands under my ass. "You're my girl, Angie. I'll do anything to give you what you want."

The butterflies in my stomach erupt, blazing every nerve in my body. I know this feeling all too well. If I don't stop it now, I'm going to fall in love with him...and I don't think the broken version of me is worthy of someone like him. Drake is the brightest light of sunshine to ever cross my path, and he deserves so much more than I can give him.

"Stop it." I blink, refocusing on him. His deep brown eyes emit warmth as he keeps staring at me. "Whatever is going on in your head —stop. Don't overthink it, okay?" he says.

"But, Drake—"

He presses his finger to my mouth, making me fall silent. "Shh, baby, everything is fine. You're with me." He tenderly pecks my lips, then leans away. "Let's take a shower together."

"Okay," I whisper, and he hauls me to him, making me wrap my legs around his hips once more. Winding my hands around his shoulders, I look him in the eyes, and my heart goes pitter-patter. The huffing sound on the other side of the door makes me snort. "He'll want to come in at some point."

"Sure." Drake nods as he proceeds into my bathroom. "After I make you come a few more times, I'll let your dog in."

"A few more times, huh?" I ask playfully.

He steps into my shower and lowers me to my feet. Turning on the water, he starts adjusting the temperature until it's perfect—not hot, just warm. Then he invades my personal space, and I back away a little, my ass hitting the glass.

"And I'm going to start in the shower," he croons. His hand wraps around my knee, lifting my leg and spreading me open. "I hope you don't mind."

"Never," I sigh as he slides his cock inside me.

Well, no matter how selfish it is, Cooper will definitely have to wait. I'm heading at full speed into being enamored with my fake boyfriend, my neighbor...the most perfect guy I've ever known. Drake Benson is my weakness...and most probably my destruction, one I can't help but marvel at.

Drake

TWENTY-SIX

just on time

I SIT ON ANGIE'S PORCH, WAITING FOR HER TO COME OUT. She's taking forever, and I check my phone again. This is just lunch, probably a barbecue at my friends' house, with a bunch of kids running around since Xander and Bella are also invited. I remember telling her all of that, so there is no way she doesn't know what to expect from today's visit to Colton and Ava's.

Unlocking my phone, I open the last text I received and sigh in exasperation. My ex-girlfriend continues to send me messages a few times a week. I never reply, so it's starting to remind me of a circus. Especially after my friend called to warn me that she's been asking around, trying to get my home address here in Santa Clara. If she's going to show up at my place, I'm afraid she's going to get a very unwelcome greeting. Janelle is my past, and that's where I want her to stay.

The door opens behind me, and I lock my phone again, standing up to look at Evangelina. I prepared a smart remark about her being late, but my words die in my throat. Her dress is white with little red flowers, a cut-out waist, and puffy sleeves. It ends above her knees, emphasizing her long legs and highlighting her tanned skin, and her red high-heeled sandals only complement her look. She has two little braids framing her face and collected into one at the back, and the rest of her hair cascades down her shoulders in little waves. Angie looks absolutely breathtaking, and I can't take my eyes off her.

"Sorry it took me so long. I was waiting for the frosting on my cupcakes to be ready." She approaches me with a plastic box in her hands. "I hope your friends like them...." She falls silent, finally noticing me staring at her. "Is everything okay?"

A smile spreads across my lips when I wrap my arm around her waist and pull her to me for a kiss. It's sweet, and not just because of how she feels, but also how she tastes.

"Did you try your frosting?" I ask, leaning away and examining her face. There is just a little makeup on her eyes and lips.

"Maybe."

"Can I have one?"

"Nope, they are for your friends and their kids," she states, taking a step back and heading to my car. "We better hurry, or we're going to be late."

"You don't say," I mutter, following her closely and fighting the urge to touch her. Her body is just as delicious as her cupcakes, making me want to devour her. Again and again, just like I did last night.

I found my new favorite pastime—making Angie come. Listening to her scream my name as her pussy grips my cock so hard I come too. Seeing my cum dripping out of her makes me go feral. My possessive side kicks in, and she's all I can think about. Her in my bed, on my couch, in my car, and in my fucking life. She's everything I want.

I help her climb into my car, then I quickly round it and join her inside, starting the engine. As I drive away from our houses, my usual playlist starts playing, and "House of Memories" by Panic! at the Disco fills the space. Glancing at Angie, I can't help but smile.

"How are your legs?" I ask, failing to conceal the humor in my voice. "Still shaking?"

Angie whips her head in my direction, rolling her lips together. "My legs are fine, but I'm going to be sore for days. Good thing I'm leaving for my grandma's surprise birthday party on Monday."

I cock my head, frowning.

"I thought about not telling you, just like you left me hanging when you went to visit your sister, but I'm not like you. So I'm giving you a heads-up that I won't be back till next Friday."

My smile grows broader when I say, "Well, looks like I gave you something to remember me by while you're gone."

She points at her neck, an eyebrow arched. "I spent ten minutes trying to cover up this hickey, and that's just one. I counted like seven of them."

"I got carried away." Shrugging, I throw her a wink. "You make it way too easy to be obsessed with you."

This time, Angie doesn't say anything, just gives me a smile and reaches for my hand. The second our fingers entwine, I'm ready to purr like a cat. When I agreed to be her fake boyfriend, I didn't expect much. I planned to help her deal with her ex and prove to mine that I don't feel bad after our breakup. What I gained instead is so much more, and I'd be a fool to let her go.

"Hey, come on in!" Ava exclaims, letting Angie and me into the house. I step aside, letting my girl go first, and only then do I follow her inside, my hand securely on her lower back. "I know we've met before, but—"

"Hey, Ava. I remember you." Angie extends the plastic container of cupcakes to my friend. "These are for you; I made them myself. Hope you like them."

"I'm sure we will, Evangelina," Ava says, taking them from her. "Drake said you have a dessert shop."

"Yeah, it's my little project. Something I'm very proud of." She smiles, leaning her back against my chest. I wind my hand around her waist from behind, holding her close to me. I notice how Ava's eyes zero in on my palm, which is plastered to Angie's belly, and her lips curl into a big, lopsided grin. "We also take orders, so if you have an occasion, I'll be more than happy to help with it—cakes, cupcakes, shortbreads. Just name it," Angie says.

"Oh, we'll definitely have an occasion soon," Ava chirps, glancing at me and then back at my girl. "Do you mind if I steal you? Bella and I are in the kitchen; she's helping me with snacks. Girl talk, you know."

"Sure." Angie nods and turns to look at me. Her eyes are sparkling with joy, and I smile. "I'll find you later."

"Have fun," I tell her and lean in to kiss her forehead. Then I shift my attention to Ava. "Where is your husband?"

"Colt's in the backyard with Xander and Roman. They're waiting for you," she replies. Then she peers at Angie. "Let's go; I want to introduce you to my son. Once he knows you brought us cupcakes, you'll be his favorite person ever."

"After me," I add, to the sound of their loud laughter.

"I THOUGHT YOU FLEW BACK HOME," I say, sipping my beer as Roman sits beside me. "It's the middle of June."

"My mom is flying out here next week," he answers, taking a sip of his drink. His accent is stronger now, because he's in a relaxed atmosphere and doesn't try to control himself. "Except for her, I don't have any reason to go to Belarus. This is my home now."

"Unless the team decides to trade you, and suddenly you're moving to a totally new state—or even a new country, if the Canadians want you."

"Wow, thanks for the vote of confidence. You know how to cheer people up." Pashkevich laughs, shaking his head. The door opens, and Bella walks outside, followed by Angie, who's holding hands with Ian, Xander and Bella's son. "Your girl is gorgeous."

"She is," I admit, admiring how effortlessly she moves, how light her steps are.

Evangelina is smiling and winning over everyone around her. Bending, she takes the little boy in her arms, and he lets her. His face lights up with a big, toothy smile. I watch how she talks to him, making him giggle. Images of my niece flash in my head, and the only thing I want is to introduce Angie to my sister and Maya. They'll love her.

WE'RE in the middle of a delicious meal. Angie sits beside me, my hand draped over the back of her chair. We talk, joking and laughing. The kids barely join us, playing tag. Their nonstop chatter fills the air, making us speak louder from time to time. When Colton raises his glass, we all follow him, turning our heads to hear what he has to say.

"Once again, I wanted to say thank you for agreeing to come. What I'm about to tell you means everything to our family, and we wanted to share this special news with our closest friends." He looks at all of us in turn, a mischievous smile plastered to his face. "Ava and I are expecting. My wife is pregnant with our second child, and we honestly couldn't be happier. This time, we actually planned to get pregnant, so it's also a new experience for us."

Everyone around me bursts out laughing, clapping, and congratulating Colton and Ava. I do too, but my mind is elsewhere. Happiness for my friends mixes with sadness, overwhelming me and making me feel lost. This feeling is all-consuming, and when it's time for me to say something, I barely find the right words. What's happening to me is wrong, and I never in my life thought I'd be in a situation like this... envious of what my friends have. What a fucking joke.

The ringing of my phone saves me, giving me a little moment to compose myself. I edge away from the table, sit by the pool, and listen to my mom talk. She goes on and on, telling me about the time she spent with Layla and Maya yesterday. I smile despite a pang in my chest.

Bathed in warm, fading evening light, the water shimmers under the sunrays, and I stare at my reflection. My mind drifts, envisioning the future I want for myself as I watch Michael running after Isla, their infectious laughter reverberating through my body. An ache in my heart takes hold, and I finish the call quickly, unable to continue conversation.

I don't even know how to explain how I feel without feeling like an intruder at this party celebrating life.

"A penny for your thoughts?" Angie's soft voice takes me aback, and I hurriedly whirl to my right as she lowers beside me. She presses a coin to my palm, and I close my fingers around it.

"It's nothing."

"Try me." She rests her head on my shoulder, and I wrap my arm around her, hauling her to my side.

"I grew up watching Layla and Ava, being a protective older brother to them both. I was the captain of my high school team, and later of my college's one. I've always been there for others, always cared about my friends and my family. You know, I never tried to plan my life, but I want to have a family one day." I shrug, hanging my head low. "My little sister has a daughter, my friends are expecting their second child. And I'm twenty-seven with no wife and no kids."

"Drake." She puts her hand on my knee.

"I'm so happy for them, Angie, but I'm sad for myself. And I hate this feeling, as if I'm fucking late for life. People are getting married, having kids. One of my college teammates, Hudson Moore, is already a divorced, single dad. Back in college, he was an arrogant asshole, but..."

"Your feelings are valid, Drake. Trust me. There's nothing wrong with how you feel." I turn my head toward her. "You're *just* twenty-seven, and you're right on time for your journey. Because your destiny is yours, and everything happens at the right time for *you*—not for your friends or the norms of society. Your timeline is just different. I'm sure you'll find the girl you want to marry, and she'll give you a dozen very beautiful babies."

"I don't want a dozen kids," I protest, frowning.

Bursting into giggles, she leans forward. "No matter how many kids you want, you'll be an amazing dad. And I'm sure the right girl will come along. Whenever you meet her, you'll know that she's the one. And from that moment on, everything that happens will lead to your happy ending. I believe that."

I hold her gaze, marveling at how irresistibly stunning she is in the warm light of the setting sun. Her words went right through me, finding a place in my heart and giving me hope. "Maybe you're right," I say slowly. "What about you? Do you want to have a family?"

"One day," she answers, smiling gently at me. "I'm not in the best mental state to even think about a family right now."

The weight burdening my soul dissipates. A newfound lightness makes me relax, and a smile crosses my lips. It's all her. She brightens everything around me with vibrant colors. A gentle breeze carries the laughter and voices of my friends to us, but we're enveloped in our own world. A place where we're alone, even if we're surrounded by people.

"I'm gonna miss you, Cupcake," I whisper, inching toward her face, my lips hovering over hers.

"I'm gonna miss you too," Angie murmurs. She closes the distance between us, and our lips collide in a slow and gentle kiss.

The longer I sit with her by the pool, the more clearly I see it. She was right. I'm not behind. I'm right on time, and she's exactly what I've been looking for.

Angie

TWENTY-SEVEN

a good one

I LOUNGE ON THE PORCH OUTSIDE MY PARENTS' HOUSE, reading a book. The air is thick and humid, almost suffocating, and I'm debating whether I should go inside and sit in the air conditioning. Dark clouds are gathering on the horizon, casting fleeting shadows over the grass. They're the reason I'm staying where I am. The distant rumble of thunder serves as a reminder of impending rain.

My phone rings, and I close my book, putting it beside me. When I answer the FaceTime, my lips stretch into a big smile. After my plane landed in Philadelphia on Monday, Drake and I texted nonstop—then we quickly realized texting wasn't enough. Switching to phone calls and then FaceTime happened naturally, and when I finished one call, I was already waiting for another one.

Drake Benson bulldozed his way inside my heart, not leaving me a single chance for resistance. Our fake relationship turned into something I'd never experienced. And that's why, in addition to the happiness I feel, I'm also scared. What if we're just so good at pretending I see something that isn't there?

"Hey, Cupcake. What are you up to?" he asks, grinning from ear to ear. His deep brown eyes have a mischievous twinkle, a boyish look that makes him even more handsome than he usually is. A backwards hat hides his curls. He holds his phone in one hand and a green apple in his other as he sits on his back porch.

"Hey, Drake. Nothing really. I've been reading." I pick up my book and show it to him. He narrows his eyes, reads the title, and then chuckles knowingly. "What?"

"*Dating Mr. Right*?"

"It's the last book my mom worked on. She was sure I was going to love it."

"Do you love it?"

"A tad too cheesy for me, but overall I think it's an amazing read. Especially since it's the author's debut novel," I tell him, lowering the book onto my lap. "What about you? Have you been doing anything fun?"

"Let me think…." Drake presses his apple to his cheek and stares wistfully at something above his phone. Bringing his gaze back to me, he shrugs. "I can't remember anything fun. Without you, all my days have turned into one big Groundhog Day."

I push strands of my hair behind my ear. The butterflies in my stomach flutter their wings, as if they are preparing for a gymnastics competition. "Do you think we can watch *One Tree Hill* tonight?"

"Sure, but just for the record, I love watching it with you when you're here with me. Sitting on my couch, your long legs hidden under your butt, your melodic laughter breaking the atmosphere at the most ridiculous scenes, and the whole space filled with your perfume and the best vanilla scent I've ever smelled after you spent the day at your shop, baking and making those delicious cupcakes," he murmurs, and I'm instantly regretting not coming home sooner. Tomorrow can't come fast enough. "Watching it with you on FaceTime is also cool, but it doesn't feel the same."

"I'll be home tomorrow evening, so we can plan something nice."

"Something nice sounds great. I'm all ears. What do you want to do? Other than me doing you." His gaze darkens; it's noticeable even through my phone screen.

"Aren't you bold?" I ask. My lower abdomen warms up, and my legs become weaker. The way my body ignites just from his words is madness. I'm going crazy over this man, and it's probably the most reckless thing I've ever done.

"No. I know you want me just as much as I want you, and it's...a lot."

I lick my lips, studying him intently. "Do you take orders?"

"You, naked, on your knees for me, will get you anything," Drake coos, and I can barely keep myself from moaning. A wave of heat ripples through my veins, reminding me of a hurricane. One that sweeps me off my feet, not letting me realize what's going on until I'm totally at his mercy.

I feign offense. "Excuse me, you want me to beg you?"

He tilts his head, his lips parting as he studies me. "You're my girl, Angie. You don't need to beg me to get what you want."

Him calling me his girl echoes in my mind. It's the most beautiful melody I've ever heard, and I don't want to ever forget it. The uncharted territory inside my heart grows bigger, filling to the brim with him.

I finally find my voice. "I think—"

"Wait...someone is here."

I frown, watching as he stands up and goes inside, holding his phone up to his face. Someone is knocking on his front door, and he stops to open it. I don't see who it is, but the change in his features worries me.

"Hey, Drake." A sugary-sweet woman's voice reaches my ears. I bite my bottom lip, unsure what to think.

"Janelle? What are you doing here?"

Janelle? As in his ex, Janelle? I hold my breath, listening to every word. Bile climbs my throat. The excitement I felt quickly ebbs, replaced by...jealousy.

"You weren't answering my messages, so I thought coming to visit you would be my only chance to make things right," she says. Her voice quavers, as if she's on the verge of tears. "I miss you, Drake. Every day without you feels like torture. I was a fool to think my home is in Michigan, because my home is wherever you are. Can you forgive me? We were so happy together, and I believe our love deserves a second chance."

Second chance? What's wrong with this woman? She broke up with him without even making an effort to understand his situation. Dumped him and instantly got with another man. Does she really think he would be interested?

"Erm..." Drake's face appears on the screen. Anxiety knots in the pit of my stomach, intertwining with the tinge of jealousy I feel. It takes a lot of effort not to show it. "Do you mind if I call you later?"

Mustering a smile, I nod. "Sure. Bye." As I end the call, a pang in my chest makes me feel uneasy.

The sudden change in the atmosphere startles me. The first droplets of rain fall on the grass and on the pavement, the rhythmic melody of raindrops filling the air. The intensity of the rain grows with each passing moment. As I close my eyes, the freshness of the air overwhelms my senses, drawing me deeper into the moment. A million thoughts appear in my head. Janelle is his ex, and from what I know about Drake, he's not going to get back together with her. She's in his past, like a book he's finished and doesn't plan to reread.

If he takes her back, then he's a masterful liar, and I failed to notice it.

I reach out my hand. Goosebumps arise as the raindrops caress my skin. The rain washes away my secrets, carrying away my worries and my scars, helping me to feel better. The longer I stay on the porch, the more my determination grows. Taking my phone from my lap, I quickly type a message and click send, then I stand up. It's time for me to go inside.

ME:

Something came up, and I'll need to reschedule OTH. See you tomorrow.

Without waiting for his reply, I open the front door and head straight to my bedroom on the second floor. I have no idea what I'm going to do tonight, but I'm definitely not staying home alone. Over-thinking while he's talking to his ex will drive me insane. I need company.

"What are you reading?"

I look up from my book, meeting my dad's eyes. His gaze quickly drops to my teeth, which are sunk into the skin around my index finger. I lower my hand and swallow my nerves. I haven't done that in a few weeks, not since things between Drake and me started to change. The slightest sidestep, and I'm gnawing off my cuticle again.

"Mom's latest work," I tell him, closing the book and smoothing my hand over the cover. "Is something wrong?"

"Me coming to talk to my daughter means something is wrong?" Dad asks, sitting beside me on my bed. "You're leaving again tomorrow, and I wanted to spend time with you. Just the two of us, like the good old days."

"It's raining," I counter, and he snorts, snagging the book out of my hands. "Why did you do that?"

Dad stands up and extends his hand to me. "Let's go for a ride."

Rolling my eyes, I give him my hand and let him pull me to my feet. I trail him down the steps and right to the front door. As he opens it and steps outside, the scent of rain hits my nostrils, and I can't help but smile. My love for rainy days will never change.

"Whoever gets to my car first chooses where we're going and what we're going to eat for dinner," Dad states. He unlocks his car with the remote, and the next thing I know he's running into the pouring rain and straight to his Land Rover, which is parked in the driveway. He's something else.

I shake my head and start off, knowing perfectly well I'm not going to beat him. He was one of the fastest guys in the league back in the day, and I'm just an amateur in comparison.

The second we are both in the car, it fills with our laughter. My hair is a mess and my jean shorts and hoodie are sticking to my body, but it doesn't matter. The biggest smile is plastered onto my face, and

I have tears in my eyes. I feel like a little girl, just because my dad is with me.

Dad's chocolate brown eyes sparkle with playfulness. An open, toothy smile lights up his face, and an adorable dimple appears on his cheek. The strands of gray in his brown hair add something exquisite to his look. Dad is all big and muscular, but the wrinkles bracketing the contour of his mouth are the best testament to the countless smiles that have graced his lips.

I chuckle to myself, suddenly realizing how much Drake has in common with my dad when it comes to looks—the color of their eyes, their cute dimples, and their builds. Even their personalities are similar—family guys to the core, men who will do absolutely anything for their loved ones.

"So, where are we going?" I ask Dad, arching an eyebrow.

"It's a surprise." He bumps his fist lightly against my shoulder, winking. "Just wait and see, baby."

With a deep breath, I let my body relax and look out the window. My dad is exactly who I needed to help me take my mind off my worries...or should I say my fake boyfriend and his ex.

"How are you?" Dad asks. He takes a bite of his sandwich, looking at me expectantly.

"Fine." I shrug, taking a sip of my milkshake. The patter of the raindrops on the car's roof is steady and cadenced, like a heartbeat. "I've been home for a week, and—"

"I'm not asking how you are now. I want to know how your life is in California. What about your shop? Your friends? Your boyfriend? Since you moved to another state, I feel like there's been a huge void between us. Sometimes, in order to know what you've been up to, we've needed to check the news, because you weren't answering your phone. And even if you did, you still weren't telling us everything...." He hesitates, carefully choosing what he has to say. "I just want to know what I did to make you feel uncomfortable talking to me."

Putting my milkshake in the cupholder, I focus on my dad. An avalanche of regret makes my heart constrict. I owe him and my mom an explanation, but it's so hard to find the right words. "It's not you, or Mom. I'm the problem. There are a lot of things to unload, and I'm not sure you'll understand."

Dad sighs, sets down his sandwich, and turns to his right, mirroring me. "Some days, I had no idea what was going on with you or how I could help. But I wanted to, so damn much. You're my daughter, my beautiful baby, and all I ever want is for you to be happy."

I keep silent, my index fingers moving in circles around my thumbnails. My foot taps on the floor, accompanying the sound of rain. Dad is watching me. I don't dare look at him; my eyes are focused on my hands. I can continue to hide everything from my family, but is it worth it? My brother is the only person who knows some of the truth behind my actions. Don't my parents deserve to know too?

"Since I was a very little girl, I wanted to be perfect. How could I not? My dad is a talented football player—famous, handsome, and rich. My mom is a successful editor, authors are dying to hire. She's smart and beautiful. I wanted to be like you two. A normal desire for any child, but not in my case," I mutter, not looking up.

"I was the best in my class, always striving for perfection. If I got an A, I could do better, right? So next time my goal was an A+, and that mindset quickly spread to all areas of my life. If it had just been about my grades, it would've been so much easier. Swim team, choir, theater, and chess—I wanted to be the best of the best, and I was, and for some time I was happy with that, surrounded by kids who wanted to be my friend."

Closing my eyes, I take a deep breath in through my nose and then release it through my mouth. I do it again and again, calming my erratic heartbeat. Dad is quiet, and I'm grateful to him for that. I won't have it in me to continue if he interrupts me.

"As I got older, I started noticing that my friends weren't as eager to spend time with me. I was more like a burden. Their parents were forcing them to call me, to invite me over, and they'd praise me for my perfect grades and my success in extracurriculars. Telling me I was setting an example for their kids. It was a tiny wake-up call, but I ignored it and continued to work harder. Until one day I realized there was a party at my friend's house, and I wasn't invited. No one wanted me to come."

I lick my lips. My throat has become dry, but I don't reach for my milkshake. "I was the most unpopular popular kid in school, and it was gnawing at me. I wanted to change that. I tried to not care about my grades, to show my classmates I was cool. My image, though? The image I'd created was working against me. Seeing my teachers' disappointment was bad, and hearing my classmates' parents say that my family must be having problems because they couldn't think of any other reason for my downward spiral was the worst. I sucked it up and decided to try to be both—a perfect student and the life of the party. Day by day, meticulously, without trying to take a step back or a break, I kept going until I succeeded...and started hating my life."

"Angie..." Dad breathes. His voice cracks, but I raise my hand, making him fall silent again.

"There was something I didn't see coming. Becoming Miss Popular, I got on people's radar—or more like boys' radar. They all wanted to get in my pants, but more than that, they wanted to meet you. I was their free ticket to Logan Jones's closest circle. Some of them thought that dating me would help their career, like you'd magically decide to help them get noticed." Brushing away tears from the corners of my eyes, I take a deep breath.

"At eighteen, I ended up hating my entire existence. I was exhausted to the point of mental breakdown, but I was also the top student in all of my classes. I had no real friends, and I'd had my heart broken so many times, I truly started doubting my worth and began to despise all those jocks. They were getting in my bed only to sneak out of my room in hopes of meeting you. The cherry on top? My little sister hated me so much, she stopped talking to me for a year, just as I was about to go to college."

"Emma didn't talk to you? For a year?" Dad asks, and I meet his eyes for the first time since I opened my mouth. "Why?"

"The same reason my classmates hated me. People were constantly comparing us. And I always was better, according to them." I tuck my hair behind my ear, my fingers circling my earring. "It was hard for Ethan. He loves me, but he loves her too, and she's his twin. He was between two fires—one wrong step, and he was done."

"I had no idea.... What about Mom? Did she know?"

"Of course not. We didn't want to trouble you." I shrug. "I was so excited to go to college. It was a place where no one knew I was your daughter. Just Evangelina Jones." My foot starts tapping faster, as I'm getting to the part of the story where my life turned into a mess. "Old habits die hard, and... It wasn't easy for me to stop caring about my grades, about not being first in my class, but I was trying to get better.

"Ethan's call changed everything...for the worse. He went on and on about the trip the four of you were planning. He said they'd be skipping school, and you and Mom were fine with it. You said that good grades meant nothing if they were unhappy, and you urged them to have more fun, to hang out with their friends, to go out more often. It triggered me...because you never said anything like that to me. You didn't even notice how tiresome it was for me, how I was gasping for air some days because of the pressure I put on myself. You never pushed me to just be a girl my age. The immense feeling of hate was like a tsunami, overwhelming me, drowning me until I was ignorant to everything around me except the feeling of injustice. I wanted to punish you, to make you pay for your ignorance. Partying, almost getting kicked out of college for my horrible grades, and *being* kicked out of the dorm."

"Baby, look at me. Look at me, Angie." My tears are falling, reminding me of the raindrops that are trickling down the windowpane. It's a release of the storm raging within me, and it frees me from the weight on my soul. "I'm so sorry you went through that. For all the pain and struggles you had to deal with. If only I knew you felt like that, I'd have stopped you. I thought you loved studying—you told us you did. Don't you remember how many times your mom and

I tried to convince you to quit some of your activities and give yourself a break? Your answer was always no."

"Nev helped me realize that it wasn't your fault. That it was all me." I sob, trying and failing to smile. "My senior year of college was my path to redemption, my way to make things right and improve my grades. It was one of the most draining periods of my life, but knowing that I wouldn't let you down kept me going. Even if I knew you were disappointed in me because of my behavior, when I was skipping holidays, not coming home, all the parties where I was so drunk I couldn't move. I wasn't going to come back home after all that. I wanted a fresh start, and that's why I stayed with Nevaeh and then moved to Santa Clara."

It was also because my self-loathing phase wasn't over. But that's definitely not something I want to talk to my dad about. He doesn't need to know all the shit I did trying to punish myself for my mistakes.

"Angie, you're one of the most hardworking women I've ever met, and considering I'm your mom's husband, that says a lot. You're successful, smart, and very funny. Don't get me started on how beautiful you are, how naturally you attract people. Your high school boyfriends didn't appreciate you because they were kids. Fools who weren't able to see what a gem they had in their arms. Idiots who thought that breaking my little girl's heart would get them anything." Dad takes my hand between his two big palms. "You're the most precious gift my life gave me. You're my firstborn, my little baby, and I'll always love you. No matter your grades, your choir results, or even your career. I'm proud of everything you've achieved, even if I hate how difficult it was for you. Please, Angie, never do something like that again. Just be yourself, and be happy. And don't forget about your parents. Let us in from time to time; share your life with us."

I nod, my tears leaking down my face. "I love you, and I promise I'll do better...with my communication."

Dad drapes a hand over my shoulder and pulls me to his side, hugging me hard and kissing the top of my head. "Good communication sounds amazing. Especially since I really want to know about your boyfriend."

"Dad!" I squeal, pushing him away and wiping my tears with the heels of my palms.

"Okay, keep him a secret for now, but at least tell me—is he a good guy?"

My lips curl into a smile despite all the emotions that are still raw inside my chest. "He is."

Dad smiles and winks at me, taking his coffee from the cupholder. Looking at me over the rim of his cup, he mulls over his next words. "That's nice to know. You deserve a good one."

I hope I do...because I like Drake way more than just my neighbor, or even my fake boyfriend.

Drake

TWENTY-EIGHT

eyes on me

"Any plans for tonight?" Layla asks, trying to snatch a big pink teddy bear from Maya's hands. My niece is stubbornly shaking her head and pressing her toy tighter to her chest with a cute pout.

"Why are you taking her teddy?" I lean toward my phone screen; my cheek is propped on my fist.

"I need to get her to take a bath. There was a little accident, and she's stinky and sticky!" my sister exclaims, finally succeeding. A bloodcurdling screech leaves my niece's mouth, and for the first time in my life, I question whether I want to have a baby. It's like I can't hear anything anymore; my whole brain is ready to explode. "Maya, please..." Layla coos, but her daughter's scream only intensifies, her face reddening.

"I'll call you tomorrow," I blurt. I get a curt nod from my sister and end the call. Leaning back on the couch, I put my phone beside me and run my fingers through my hair. For absolutely irrational reasons, I don't feel calm. A whole damn storm is boiling within me and putting my mind in total disarray.

Thoughts about Angie buzz in my head, becoming louder with each move of the minute hand on my watch as I stare at it. The need to see her intensifies, taking over all my thoughts and feelings. The question I want to ask her weighs on me like a ton, making me feel like a hopeless fool.

The second she started to feel like something more permanent, I should've known I was a goner. She's like a thief in the night, quiet and fast, and after her, no one else could mean a thing. Evangelina wrecked me to the foundation, rebuilt the world around me, and filled in the space with her presence in such a short period of time, it really feels like something straight out of the TV show we're watching.

I'm hers. Devotedly and completely. She's ruined me for everyone else, and I don't feel bad about it. Not even for a second. It's absolutely out of my control, because not falling for my fake girlfriend has never been an option. If I don't ask her to be mine, I'll sentence myself to the loneliest life full of sorrow and regrets. And I don't ever want to be alone after knowing what it means to be with her. To be with the one who sees me as just Drake Benson, the guy next door, a man who loves his family and friends, who values honesty over pretense and doesn't care about all the fancy places, who chooses to stay in and do something fun together...even if it's just watching movies or reading books side by side.

Evangelina is like a devastatingly beautiful fire: captivating and dangerous, but absolutely impossible to ignore. She's untamed passion and intoxicating vulnerability, a paradox that possesses the power to destroy me, and yet it's not fleeting attraction between us. No one is more perfect for me than she is.

I stand up from the couch, pocket my phone in my jeans, and head to the front door. My shoulders are squared, and my breathing is steady, even if my heart beats insanely fast, pumping adrenaline through my veins. I brush aside all my doubts. There is nothing more pitiful than a man who's afraid to take chances because of his fear of failing. Some people are worth taking a risk for, and Angie proved to me with each day I got to spend in her company that she is worth the risk.

I knock lightly on her front door and loop my thumbs through my belt loops, waiting. Her house is too quiet—not even the tiniest sound of Cooper's paws near the door reaches my ears. Looking over my shoulder, my gaze sweeps over her Aventador, which is parked near my car. She should be home. Releasing a breath through my mouth, I knock once more, louder this time. Is she avoiding me for some reason?

Shifting from my heels to my toes, I stand here like a statue. What are the chances that I missed her, that I didn't see when she left to get Cooper from Marcy's? It's possible, but I'm not sure it's the case...her car is still here. I lift my hand, ready to knock one last time, but then the door bursts open. Angie's green eyes lock onto mine, and her breathing hitches. A slight shrug of her shoulder catches my attention when she grasps the door and uses it for balance, propping her hip against it.

"Hey."

"Hey," I echo, staying put and studying her face. No makeup and a cute little bun on top of her head, while the rest of her hair cascades down her shoulders like a heavy curtain. "How was your flight?"

"Good." Another barely noticeable shrug makes me furrow my brow. She seems off, and I'm clueless about why. Does it have something to do with her visit home? "What about you? How was your time with *Janelle*?"

The way she purposefully drawls Janelle's name hits me right in the face like a sucker punch—unexpected and sudden. Then realization dawns on me, making everything glaringly obvious. Angie is jealous, and knowing that, I want to smile.

Taking a step forward, I cup her cheek with my hand and lean down, my eyes searching hers. A mix of excitement and stupid pride settles in my chest when I notice her dilated pupils and the embers in her gaze. *Mine.* The feeling spreads over my skin, and all I want is to touch her.

"Who is Janelle?" I tease, my nose brushing hers.

Angie huffs, her eyes narrowing. "Your ex."

"Oh, her? My time with her consisted of twenty minutes on the porch, in which I made it clear I wanted nothing to do with her." My lips hover over hers, my nose brushing hers again. I sink my teeth into her bottom lip, sucking on it gently, my arm wrapping around her waist. "We're not going to watch anything tonight." I peck the corner of her mouth. "And we're not going to stay home either. We're going out."

"What?" she breathes.

"Go get dressed, Cupcake. I'll be waiting for you near my car in twenty." I kiss her lips sweetly, take a step back, and stroll down the stairs. Her stunned silence doesn't last long.

"Where are we going?" Angie's voice catches up with me when I'm by my front door.

"To the club," I reply and walk inside my house. It's not what I had planned for tonight, but improvisation feels right in this situation. I'm going to get the most out of it.

THE MUSIC REVERBERATES through the air, creating a rhythmic thump that envelopes the space. People dance with abandon, swaying and twirling to the infectious sounds, their laughter and cheers mingling with the lyrics. I feel at ease here, carefree and relaxed.

Strobe lights sweep across the dance floor, bathing the room in a dreamlike atmosphere. Navigating through the crowd, I hold Angie's hand, our fingers laced. Nevaeh and Pashkevich are waiting for us at the bar, arguing about something but still wearing the broadest smiles on their faces. This unplanned pairing is absolutely unreal, and I've wondered why I even suggested inviting some of our friends out with us. I never expected my teammate to be constantly bantering with Evangelina's best friend, and Nevaeh encourages it while also saying he annoys her.

"You're saying it all wrong," Roman bites out. His brows knit together as he pins Nevaeh with his stare.

She rolls her eyes, taking a long, exasperated breath and saying slowly, "*Spasibo.*" Then she arches her eyebrow at my teammate and crosses her arms over her chest. "What's wrong? I nailed it. Admit it."

Pashkevich glances at me and Angie, then focuses back on

Nevaeh. "That time it was good, but you definitely need more practice."

Her jaw drops, and she gapes at him without uttering a word. Angie shifts beside me, stepping closer to her best friend. "You're..." Nevaeh falls silent for a second and points a finger at Pashkevich. "A jerk. That was my first time trying to say anything in Russian—of course I need more practice."

My teammate shrugs, grabbing his drink from the bar. "Saying 'thank you' in Belarusian would've been way harder, doll."

"Doll?" Nevaeh snatches his drink from his hand and downs it in one go. "Buy yourself another one." Her eyes roam over Angie's face, and then she jumps off the barstool. "We're dancing."

"But Drake and I—" Angie's objections die in her throat as her best friend wraps her hand around her wrist and drags her away from me. So much for taking a break with my girl.

I plop onto the barstool, facing Pashkevich. He gestures to the bartender, and the guy pours him a glass of whiskey. "Sorry, Drake. She stole your girlfriend because of me."

"You sure know how to push Nevaeh's buttons." I laugh, peeking at the dance floor in hopes of seeing where they went.

"She told me that you and Angie are only fake dating, then she got irritated because she let it slip," Pashkevich mutters quietly, but it sounds as if he's screaming in my damn ear. I peel my gaze to him, and he lowers his glass onto the bar. "It's none of my business. Sorry."

"Nevaeh is wrong. It's not like that."

"Drake, you don't need to explain anything to me. I haven't known you for long, but I know a couple in love when I see it. I haven't noticed anything fake between you two."

I roll my lips together, finding Angie in the crowd. Her red dress clings to her curves like a second skin, the fabric shimmering under the club lights. Its neckline plunges daringly, and one of the thin straps slips down her shoulder. The fitted bodice accentuates her slender waist, highlighting her feminine silhouette. She's a divine sight, full of elegance and sensuality. I'd always notice her, even in the most chaotic of settings, like this dance floor.

She's smiling, moving effortlessly with Nevaeh, who has her arm wrapped around her waist from behind. It's intimate, and it draws attention to them. More and more men glance in their direction; some are openly staring. I sink my teeth into my tongue. The music and conversations fade into a distant hum as my eyes meet hers.

My girl. So fucking mine.

Wetting my lips, I stand up from the stool and look down at Pashkevich. He smiles, lifting a glass in salute. "Go get her, Benson." He sneaks a glance at the dance floor and mumbles, "I'll make sure Nevaeh is fine."

"She has a boyfriend," I tell him, and he snorts, shaking his head.

"Nevaeh is gorgeous and all, but I'm not looking to be snagged and eaten alive. I don't like being prey."

I nod and head straight to Angie and Nevaeh. Stopping in front of them, I snake my hand around Angie's waist and pull her into me. Her best friend's hand drops away, and she takes a step back. A wicked smile lights up Nevaeh's face, and she winks at me.

"Bye, Drake."

"Bye, Nev. Roman will look after you."

"In his dreams." Nevaeh giggles, slaps Angie's ass, and brisks past us, back to the bar. "Have a good, sweaty ride, baby."

"Oh God," Angie blurts, her eyes finding mine. "Are we going home?"

"Almost," I reply, and without another word I make her follow me through the crowd of dancing people, down the narrow hallway, and right to the bathroom. I let her walk in first, then I step inside, lock the door, and turn to face her.

"We won't have much time in here," she whispers, backing away from me a little.

"Just need to refuel my body with my favorite type of nourishment, one I've been deprived of for days." I stalk over to her and curl my hand around her waist, making her stumble backward. "You."

Lifting her, I set her on the countertop, standing between her thighs. Angie slowly winds her hands around my shoulders. I lean forward, and on an inhale our lips collide. Nothing about the way I'm kissing her is slow; it's raw and possessive. I nibble on her bottom lip, and she opens her mouth for me, welcoming my tongue with hers. Slipping my hands down her hips, I pull her toward me until her butt is on the edge. A moan escapes her lips when I push my erection into her pussy.

"Angie, you're perfect."

I lick the length of her neck, sucking and nipping, adding more pleasure and building up her arousal. She grinds herself over my dick again and again. My fingers reach under the skirt of her dress, and I pull her panties off and hide them in my pocket. I give her a long, lingering kiss and then distance myself a little, wrapping my arm around her knee and setting her leg on the counter, spreading her open for me. Holding her gaze, I lower myself onto my knees.

The sounds from the dance floor are barely audible in here, but I don't think I'd have heard anything even if it were booming inside of this room. She's all I want, and it's clouding my brain. I press my index finger to her clit, and she jerks forward, shuddering from my touch. Cupping her butt with my palm, I haul her closer to my face.

"I want you to come all over my fingers, on my fucking tongue, Angie...and I want you to look at me. Your pretty little cunt, glistening with your wetness, belongs to me...every moan. Every shudder of your body. Every breathless sound...it's all mine. Only mine. And I want to see it."

My lips brush her clit, and she quietly whimpers. Plunging one finger and then another inside her, I slowly fingerfuck her. I'm lapping my tongue over her sensitive nub, speeding up and then adding just a little suction. I suck and lick her folds, moving faster and harder with each stroke of my fingers. Her eyes snap closed, and I stop, leaning away.

Angie's eyelashes tremble. "Why..."

"Eyes on me, baby, or I'm going to stop."

Then she focuses her hooded eyes on me. Her chest is rising and falling rapidly, and she licks her lips, bobbing her head up and down in agreement. I grin, burying my face in her pussy again, sucking her clit inside my mouth and then releasing it, teasing it with my tongue, moving in little circles. My speed intensifies with each second as my fingers slide in and out of her. She watches me, and her fingers dig so hard into the countertop, her knuckles become white.

"Such a delicious little cunt you have," I murmur against her clit, enjoying how she reacts to everything I do to her.

"Oh my God!" Angie cries out. The buildup to her orgasm wracks her body. She lets go and comes, shaking and trembling. I lick her clean, not averting my eyes for even a second. Watching her come for me is one of the most beautiful views in the world. And I can't get enough of her.

Standing, I smile and help her to her feet. Her pupils are still dilated when she steps into me, her hands locking around my neck. Angie stands on her tiptoes and presses her lips to mine. Then she leans away, and her eyes roam over my face.

"Thank you."

"For what?" I ask, pinching my brows together and smoothing my hands down her dress.

"For my orgasm," she says, stepping back.

"You're weird," I comment with a smile. "I have no idea where that's coming from, but you don't need to thank me for making you feel good. I'm ready to spend my life on my knees with my face buried in your pussy if it would make you happy. Am I clear?"

"Very," Angie whispers, biting her bottom lip.

Taking her hand in mine, I unlock the door and walk us out of the bathroom. Luckily, we only meet one guy on his way to the bathroom as we go down the hallway. My whole body is buzzing with excitement, and the music sounds even louder than before. The strongest hard-on makes my jeans feel too tight, and I mentally pat myself on the back for choosing one of the closest nightclubs. A long ride home would've killed me.

Once we're outside, we head to my Lexus. I help Angie inside, wait for her to put her seat belt on, and only then close her door. Then I quickly start the engine and drive.

"Did you have a good time?" I ask her at a traffic light.

"Yeah, it felt great to be out. Sometimes I need it. Thank you for suggesting it," she replies, her fingers playing with the hem of her dress. "I hope you still like my best friend. She was a bit capricious tonight, like a kid."

"I think she totally matches Roman. They make a murderous combo," I joke, debating whether I should bring up Nevaeh blurting out our secret. Angie needs to know, but it's also a good opportunity to talk about the nature of our relationship.

"Too accurate." Angie giggles, then falls quiet almost instantly. "She said something to Roman."

"He told me."

Angie sighs, putting her hands on her lap. "I'm so sorry. Your teammate is the last person who needed to know the truth about us. Obviously, you never needed this farce, and you're just too good of a guy to say no to a girl in trouble. And you didn't deserve anyone from your closest circle to find out about my absurd idea." She turns her head to look at me. "I don't think we should continue. With your teammate knowing, what are the chances someone else will find out? What if my best friend gets too chatty again? It's not worth it."

I tsk, clicking my tongue. "Yeah, you're right."

Her face falls, and she looks away, staring out the window. When we get to our houses, I park beside her Aventador. Without another word, I jump out, but instead of going to her side and opening the door, I climb into the backseat. No way I'm leaving my car without making her understand how I feel.

"Come here," I tell her.

She glances at me and unfastens her seat belt, saying, "Drake, I better—"

"Come here." Reaching over, I wrap my arms around her waist and pull her to me. Angie draws in breath, a surprised whimper springing from her lips. It takes a minute, but now she's straddling my lap, her eyes locked on mine. "Don't run away from me."

The corners of her lips twitch a little, and she raises her hand, cupping my cheek. "I just didn't know what to say. You said you wanted us...wanted us to stop pretending."

"There's nothing to stop, because I wasn't pretending. What we have is real." I swallow my nerves, feeling my Adam's apple move up and down. "I don't want to be your fake boyfriend, Angie, because I want to be with you. You're everything I've ever dreamed about, and I think I've known it since our very first fake date. The moment you opened your door in that little black dress, I didn't have a chance." Tucking strands of her hair behind her ears, I trace her cheekbones with my fingertips. "Will you be my girlfriend?"

"Drake, I... You deserve so much more than I can give you. At least, this version of me."

"Every version of you is perfect for me. Sad. Angry. Happy. Excited or moody. I want them all," I urge, my eyes never leaving hers. "Will you be my girlfriend?"

The moment I see her nod, I don't hesitate anymore. Smashing my mouth onto hers, I assault her lips. Sucking and nibbling, making her open up for me. A wave of consuming passion overwhelms me the second my tongue curls around hers. The feeling is euphoric, reminding me of the ecstatic sensation I get after a successful game. She's my most precious and important win for sure, because I think I just won the prize of a lifetime.

She's panting, her hands sliding down my lap, unzipping my fly. I help her, taking my hard cock out of my jeans. Angie wraps her hand around my dick and gives me a few hard strokes. *Jesus Christ, she's going to be the death of me.* Angling my cock, she slowly lowers herself onto my lap, taking it inside her. A loud moan slips out of her mouth and makes me close my eyes. It's just too good.

Angie rides me deep and slow, bringing me to the edge with impossible speed. I've been hard since we left the club, and it takes all my willpower to hold off my release. Her pussy is warm and so wet, and she's taking me deeper with each move up and down my cock. The feeling of my dick stretching her cunt is exhilarating. The moment I'm balls deep inside her, I hiss and wrap her hair around my fist, yanking it down. Her head tips back, her moans increasing.

"Just like that, baby.... You take me so deep," I praise her. My other hand cups her ass. "You riding me and in control is the hottest thing ever; I'll never get tired of looking at you."

"That feels so good," Angie confesses, her eyes half closed. "Oh my fucking God..."

Her cries echo through my car. I release her hair, cupping her butt with my palms and pounding inside her faster, pulling her down onto my cock over and over. My release is overtaking me, warming up my skin; my blood is pumping in my veins.

"Be a good girl for me, baby," I growl. "Scream for me...."

Bouncing on my dick, Angie presses her open palms to the roof of my car. Her hair is sticking to her sweaty forehead, but she doesn't stop. She fucks me so good, I'm losing my mind. I'm literally holding on by a thread, but it won't last long.

"Drake... I'm gonna... I'm coming, Drake!" She screams my name, and her walls pulsate around me, choking my dick and skyrocketing my pleasure.

It takes three deep thrusts, and I'm spilling my cum inside her. My release combines with her orgasm; our lips are glued together. We kiss and kiss, our hands roaming over each other. There is nothing I want more than to take off her clothes and fuck her from behind.

"I've never been fucked that good before," she whispers, pressing her forehead to mine. "No one will ever stand a chance against you."

I grab her chin between my thumb and index finger, forcing her to look at me. "Your pussy is mine. There won't be anyone else," I state, and she smiles, her eyes crinkling with silent laughter. "And to make sure you know it, I'm going to fuck you all night, until my name is the only one you remember."

Angie stares at me. Her skin is glowing, and her eyes radiate warmth. "Will you stay the night?"

"Always," I whisper and kiss her again, losing myself in her.

Angie

TWENTY-NINE

self-destructive tendencies

Some days are like a blur, full of lazy mornings and goofy, joyful moments Drake and I spend outside, going for walks with Cooper or having lunch at our favorite Italian restaurant. There are movie nights and late-night talks in bed, when we can't stop sharing stories about our pasts.

Those days are my favorite. I can't even tell what I love doing most, because every minute I spend with him fills me with so much happiness. I finally feel as if I'm somewhere I belong. He sees all of me, all my scars, my mistakes, and my naivety, and still makes me feel worthy. Worthy of someone so kindhearted and with an absolutely beautiful soul.

It's been a month since Drake asked me to be his girlfriend, and my anxiety no longer bothers me the way it did before. Sometimes I still feel uneasy, hiding behind my walls and choosing darkness instead of reaching out for light. He's always the one who comes to my rescue, his deep, velvety voice telling me that everything is going to be okay, his strong arms wrapped around me and my back pressed to his chest when he holds me close. He doesn't ask questions about my reasons, just helps me to gain control of my troubled mind. With him by my side, I start to believe that everything is possible. I think I finally found a place where I can rest my head and feel safe.

I hope he never lets me go.

Sitting on the couch, I extend a glass of wine to Nevaeh. She takes it with a grateful smile. "You're positively glowing, Angie. It makes me incredibly happy for you. Your fake boyfriend turned out to be the most perfect real boyfriend you've ever had."

"It's true." I grin at her, taking a sip of my drink. "I've broken myself so many times, I didn't believe I could be whole again until him. Drake makes me feel seen and cherished; he doesn't judge, just lets me be my crazy-ass, weirdo self with messy thoughts, who feels confident one second and is ready to hide under a rock the next. I'm still his favorite. His girl, as he always reminds me, even if it's already tattooed on my brain and in my heart."

Nev reaches forward and takes my hand in hers. "You finally found a man who appreciates you for who you are and doesn't try to change you for his own selfish wishes. It's who you deserve, Angie." She squeezes my hand, her eyes welling with tears. "Love you so much, babe."

"Love you too," I murmur, pulling her to me and hugging her tightly. We sit in silence, locked in a warm embrace. Nevaeh is the first to lean away, smiling at me from ear to ear.

"Where is he, by the way? I seriously started to wonder if you glued yourselves to each other, because you're always with him. Even at your shop."

"That's not true. He comes to my shop a few times a week. He's always with Marcy in the kitchen, trying new recipes for cupcakes and donuts." I laugh to myself, remembering the time Drake walked out of the kitchen with his jeans covered in flour because he accidentally dropped the bowl on the floor. My pastry chef wasn't happy; she kicked him out and told him not to expect any new recipes. "He's with his best friend."

"And with Roman?" Nevaeh probes, hiding behind her glass as she takes a sip.

"No, just with Colt. He needed Drake's help with something at his house. To quote my boyfriend: 'They can obviously hire someone to do all the work, but it's more fun to try and do it ourselves.'" I study my best friend with my eyebrows knitted together. "Did you sleep with Pashkevich?"

"What? No. I'm with Travis." She bats her eyelashes at me, feigning innocence. "I swear, Angie, I didn't sleep with him. We flirted a little because I was drunk, but it was harmless. He's a very nice guy. He even dropped me off at Travis's place, waiting till I was actually in the building before his Uber drove away."

But you don't flirt with other people if you're happy in a relationship. These words hang on the tip of my tongue, but I chase them away with a sip of my drink. Even though she hated Asher and begged me to leave him, she was never judgy. I should be like her.

"Okay."

Nevaeh and I stare at each other. The only sound in the room comes from Cooper drinking his water in the kitchen. I open my mouth, ready to suggest we watch something together, when a knock on my door rattles the quiet. It's loud and impatient. Frowning, I set my glass on the table and head to the front door, hearing Coop's paws on the tile.

"Are you expecting someone?" Nev calls out.

"Drake must be back early," I reply, opening the door and coming face-to-face with Asher.

"Hey, Evangelina," he says, his eyes stormy. With how dilated his pupils are, he's either high or drunk. "Can I come in?"

Unease seeps through my veins, and I swallow a lump in my throat. "No."

A low growling sound becomes louder when Cooper stops by my side. I put my hand on his head, slide it down, and hook my fingers around his collar. "You should leave."

"But I don't want to," Asher grumbles, swaying a little and placing his hand on the wall for balance. Now it's clear he's drunk. "I just stopped by because...I miss you. And I'm...I'm trying to understand what I did wrong. You wanted me to be sober? I am. You wanted me to stop fooling around? I did. What else do you need, Evangelina?"

"For you to leave her alone." Nevaeh comes closer, her voice radiating anger. "Just accept she doesn't want you and get lost."

"No one's asking you, slut. I'm talking to Evangelina."

My hands are trembling so hard, I'm ready to fucking kill him. "You're talking to *me*? Then listen carefully, or read my lips—I don't care. I don't want to be with you. You're a worthless jerk who almost ruined everything for me. I should've never been with you, Asher."

He glares at me in silence, gritting his teeth and balling his fists.

I stand my ground, even if all my fears are coming back, resurfacing at a crazy speed. "You're—"

He surges forward, and Cooper instantly starts barking. He's baring his teeth, his ears drawn back. If I let him go, he could hurt my ex, and I'm holding him, wishing with all my might for Asher to give up and leave. The sound of car tires screeching catches me off guard, and I look over Asher's shoulder to see a Lexus coming to a stop beside my car.

Drake hops out of his SUV and slams the door shut. Determination crosses his features as he barrels toward my house. His jaw is set hard, and his eyes are narrowed on Asher. My ex spins around just as my boyfriend stops in front of him.

My heart is ready to jump out of my chest, and my hands shake harder. I'm holding my breath, not knowing what to expect.

"What are you doing here?" Drake demands, his voice full of fury.

"I came to visit my girl—"

Drake grabs Asher's collar and slams his back into the wall. "I dare you to finish that sentence. Just give me a fucking excuse, and I'll destroy you."

"What's your problem, man?" The high-pitched squeal that comes from my ex's mouth amuses me. I never expected to see him so scared.

"My problem is you standing on my girlfriend's porch. If you don't want your face smashed into this wall, I suggest you leave her alone. Starting right now, and for fucking good," Drake snarls, the veins on his arms bulging. "She's with me, and she's happy. Get fucking lost."

Asher's eyes run back and forth between Drake and me. He raises his hands in front of him, and my boyfriend lets him go. My ex takes a few deep breaths, sliding his hands through his hair.

"Okay, I'm leaving," he mutters, and Drake steps aside, closer to me.

"You'll regret this, Evangelina. You just lost the best man you've ever been with." He turns and dashes down the stairs, stopping just a step away from my house. "I was the only guy who didn't care that you were a frigid Snow Queen, because I loved you for other reasons. When this dude leaves you, don't try to look for me. You lost your chance."

I'm too stunned to speak. My jaw drops, and I blink in disbelief. The sound of Drake's laughter rolls through my body as he snakes a hand around my waist and pulls me to him. I stumble forward, dragging Cooper with me because I'm still afraid to release his collar.

"She's not frigid, you asshole. She orgasms just fine. Don't blame a woman for your shortcomings!" Drake exclaims pointedly.

Asher's face pales and then becomes as red as a tomato. "You'll pay for that," he spits and stomps away from my house.

I watch his figure slowly disappear from view, feeling relieved. Of course, I might be wrong, but I think it's the last time he will bother me. Drake's words were a fatal blow to his ego, and he's too self-centered to forget something like that. My chapter with Asher is finally closed for good.

Nevaeh's loud laughter breaks the silence, and Drake and I turn to look at her. This is definitely not how I expected my night to go.

"ANY CHANCE you want to tell me about your ex?" Drake whispers, his arms wrapped around me.

My bedroom is dark, enveloped in the moonlight that casts shadows across the walls. My relationship with Asher is the only thing I've kept to myself, even after I told Drake about my childhood and my rebellious years in college. How much I hated myself isn't something I'm proud of, and it isn't something I wanted him to know. But after today, I think he deserves the truth.

"How did you end up with such a jerk?" he asks. "I'm trying to find an explanation, and I'm failing." His fingers skim down my hip, and he splays his hand across my ass as I think of an answer.

"I think they're called self-destructive tendencies. I knew he was bad—a red flag. I met him when I finally realized I was the problem. It wasn't my parents who were ruining my life. It was me.

"In school, when I was exhausting myself to be the best at everything, and then later in college when I was rebelling against my parents, thinking they deserved all the stress I caused them—all of that was on me," I say quietly, my gaze focusing on the soft moonlight on the wall. "All the hate I felt toward my mom and dad was actually directed at me. I started to believe I didn't deserve anything good to happen to me. I felt like I wasn't good enough to be loved, wasn't good enough to be with someone who would respect me. I wanted to punish myself for my decisions, for all the problems I caused my family. And at that moment, Asher came into my life."

Drake chews on the inside of his cheek, his eyes glued to my face. "Remember how I googled you?"

I chuckle, nodding.

"There were other guys before him, and they weren't good for you either."

"Well, yeah, but no one could top him. He was the worst, and despite how it sounds, that's probably why I stayed with him the longest. Sometimes it felt like I was trapped in self-sabotage, unable to escape the damage, leaving a trail of chaos wherever I went."

He presses his knuckles to my cheek, caressing it gently. A sad smile ghosts over his lips.

"Before Asher and I became a thing, we spent time with our friends. I saw how manipulative he was with the people closest to him, how rude and stuck-up he was with strangers. His problems with alcohol also didn't go unnoticed—sometimes he was high. But I brushed everything aside when he asked me out. He was exactly what I deserved."

"And you stayed together for a year?"

"On and off, but yeah. It was an incredibly codependent relationship. He was cheating on me, and I was justifying it by convincing myself that I was a bad girlfriend. Manipulations, gaslighting, shifting the blame all the time. I was taking all the hits like a pro; it was becoming my armor. You get what you deserve, right?" I snort, hiding my face in his chest. "Nevaeh tried to make me leave him, and when she succeeded, I was the happiest girl ever. Until he came back, claiming he couldn't live without me. She convinced me to move to California because she hoped he would stay behind, but he didn't. It's hard to let someone go when you know the power you have over them. It becomes an addiction."

"But what made you leave him? Because when you told me about your scars, you said you were ready to break up with him for good."

"My shop was bringing me a lot of joy. I was doing something I was good at, and it helped me believe in myself. My modeling career was also blossoming; I was invited to fashion shows in Europe. Little by little, I started to fight for my confidence, for being able to make my own decisions without looking back at my toxic boyfriend. It was the beginning of my freedom and the end of my relationship with Asher. I knew his addictions were becoming a big problem, and despite everything he did to me...I wanted to help him. And that's how he ended up in rehab, which I paid for, and I ended up with scars I'm still afraid to talk about with my family."

"You're such a strong girl, Angie," Drake whispers, putting his chin on top of my head. "You endured so much shit, but it didn't take away your kindness, your willpower."

"I'd been in therapy for a few months. The girl you met that day is the product of my hard work and dedication to be better. When Asher came back, my anxiety popped up again, but thanks to you I was able to beat it—not completely, as you probably noticed. But I'm doing better."

"And I'll be there for you no matter what. Always." Drake tightens his arms around me, yawning. "Night, Angie."

"Night, Drake," I whisper, closing my eyes and letting myself relax in his embrace. He's my harbor in the chaos surrounding my life, my shelter from the storm. The sense of security he gives me makes me believe that the world outside can't harm me.

Just because he's with me.

Angie

bonus chapter

WALKING WITH COOPER, I STUMBLE OVER A ROCK I DIDN'T notice. Additional proof of how lost in thoughts I am. Meeting Drake's sister and niece for the first time in person is the only thing I can think about. I really hope they're going to like me...because it'll be a disaster otherwise.

They already like you. Drake's words from last night flash in my head as I get closer to my house. Well, he's not wrong, but there's a difference between seeing someone only through video calls and finally meeting them face to face. Especially when that someone is a one-year old, who my boyfriend adores. What if Maya doesn't like me?

My dog huffs, climbing the stairs, and my gaze drops to him. Coop is always friendly and gentle, but he doesn't really have any experience with such a small child. He's been spending a lot of time with my chef Marcy and her family, but her kids are six and ten. Goodness, I'm getting in my head so deep, I want to crawl under my skin and hide. A very familiar itching in my fingertips returns, and I ball my fists, only to prevent myself from chewing on my cuticle again.

Everything's going to be alright. It has to be.

Opening the door, I walk inside and glance at the plate with cupcakes I made last night. I needed to distract myself with something, and it turned into almost fifty chocolate cupcakes with buttercream frosting and sprinkles. Good thing Drake has practice today. He took some with him to treat the team to something delicious. Bad thing? There are still ten cupcakes left, and I'm not sure who's going to eat them. I haven't eaten anything since I woke up, and it's already lunch time.

The sound of 'Cruel Summer' rings in the air, and I pull my phone out of my pocket. Pressing it to my ear, I answer, "Hey, Drake. Are you on your way home already?"

"I wish..." He mutters, and the honking of the cars fills my ears. "There's a huge traffic jam, and my car hasn't moved an inch in the past fifteen minutes."

"Damn, I'm so sorry." I take off Cooper's leash, and he runs toward the bathroom. "You think you'll have time to hop home before going to the airport?"

"I don't think so. At this point, I'm not even sure I'll be on time to the airport."

I halt in my tracks, my heartbeat intensifying. With sweaty palms, I press my phone to my other ear. "You want me to go to the airport to pick them up?"

"Only if it won't be a problem."

"It's not. I can leave the house in ten minutes and drive to the airport," I reassure him with my voice sounding firm, despite the feeling of a tornado full of pricks and needles in my chest.

Drake sighs in relief. "Thank you so much."

"It's nothing. After so many months of Layla refusing to visit, we don't want her and Maya to stand in the middle of the airport waiting for you."

Walking into the bathroom, I glance at myself in the mirror. My hair in a high ponytail with a red ribbon around it, no makeup except red color painting my lips and a black dress with the skirt covering my knees slightly. At least I don't need to change, so it will save me some time.

"I'll try to be there."

My eyes land on Cooper standing in the shower cabin, head tilted to the side as he watches me. Chuckling to myself, I walk closer and say to Drake, "Better go home and take a shower, I'm sure your muscles will thank you for that. I'll bring Layla and Maya to your place, don't worry about it."

"You're incredible, Angie," he murmurs, and a warmth spreads through my veins, a smile blossoming on my lips.

"You're praising me way too much," I joke and put my hand on the tap. "Coop is waiting for me to wash his paws, so I better go. See you later."

"See you later, Cupcake."

Finishing the call, I continue smiling. The happiness I feel prevails, pushing my nervousness to the darkest corner of my mind. It's going to be alright. It can't be any other way.

Even from afar I notice them. Layla stands with Maya in her arms. The girl's hand is curled around her mom's neck. My boyfriend's sister is impatient. The tapping of her foot catches my attention, and I make my way toward them. I have no clue if Drake has warned her that I'm going to come for them.

My eyes wander over Layla's form, her blue oversized hoodie and black jeans with white sneakers. Her hair collected in a messy bun on top of her head, a few locks have escaped it and now are framing her face. I shift my gaze to Maya and can't help but smile. The cutest, smallest ponytail I've ever seen makes her look adorably sweet, just like her light blue knitted sweater and dark blue jeans. Such a stylish little girl.

Slowing down, I come to a stop in front of Layla, still giving her space. If Drake had been here, I'm sure he would've scooped his little sister in his arms, giving her the strongest bear hug he's capable of. I settle for a small grin on my lips and my hands at my sides.

"Hey, Layla," I say, and Layla focuses on me, her eyes boring into mine. “I’m Angie. Drake got stuck in a traffic jam, so he asked me to come pick you up.”

Maya hides her face in Layla’s neck, her hand clutching her mom’s hoodie. My smile drops. Did I scare her? I feel the hair on my arms stand on end and nervously lick my lips.

“Hey, Angie.” Layla’s voice sounds a bit raspy and deep. When I bring my eyes to her face, she’s smiling at me. “It’s so nice to finally meet you in person.”

“You too.” A relieved sigh springs from my lips, and my shoulders drop, releasing the tension. “You’re even more beautiful in real life,” I tell her. Her chocolate brown eyes framed with thick eyelashes are instantly narrow, and she twists her lips. It doesn’t last long, because no more than a few seconds later, an open smile graces her features.

“Thank you, but look who’s talking.” She laughs heartily, readjusting her arms as Maya presses herself even closer to her. “Maya, baby, this is Angie. Don’t you want to say hi to her?”

The little girl shakes her head, her face still hidden in her mom’s neck. My heart sinks, and I awkwardly shift, looking down at the suitcase beside Layla. “Is that all? Or do you have some other bags?”

“Only my backpack,” Drake’s sister says. I nod and step forward, putting my hand on the suitcase’s handle.

“Let’s get you out of here.” I keep my voice even, trying to sound enthusiastic. The way Maya doesn’t even want to look at me is like a punch in my gut. “Drake should be home already; he texted me when I was parking my car. Your brother has so many plans for your visit, including going to the games.”

“He’s always been like that. Though now he’s more overprotective than before, and it says a lot.” Layla laughs, following me. “I’m honestly looking forward to going to the Thunders’ game. I miss watching Drake play in person.” She glances at me, our eyes meet, and she gives me a reassuring smile. “She always reacts like this to new people. Don’t take it personally.”

An invisible knot unties, and I take a deep breath, nodding. “Thank you. I started wondering if maybe it’s because of me.”

"Maya likes you, and Cooper." The name of my dog gets Layla's daughter's attention, and she slowly turns to look at me. Her chocolate brown eyes, the same as her mom's, are sparkling. "Angie is hard for her, so I told her she can call you Eva. I hope it's okay."

"Absolutely. Eva is more than fine," I murmur, winking at the little girl. "I'm so happy you're here, Maya. Coop can't wait to meet you too."

Her lips suddenly stretch into a big almost toothless smile with the exception of four front teeth. Warmth washes over me, and something very pleasant forms in my belly. Happiness is the only emotion I can use to describe how I feel.

Shaking my head at myself, I lead the way, talking with Layla about their flight and about her own plans for this trip, since I'm sure she's dying to spend some time with her best friend, Ava. The warmth becomes only stronger, and I even feel dizzy.

I can't believe I was so nervous about finally meeting the most important girls for my boyfriend. Drake loves them...and simply this alone should've been the only sign I needed that everything was going to be alright. How could it not?

Drake is the swooniest and the nicest guy I know. The one who will do absolutely anything for his people. No surprise his sister and his niece's presence makes me feel the same as I feel around him – happy and content. And loved...so loved it still blows my mind.

"OHMYGOD." Layla moans, swallowing the last piece of one of my cupcakes. "Why is it so tasty?"

"Anything Angie does is tasty, especially her desserts," Drake coos, pulling me closer and kissing my temple. "Wait till you try her Red Velvet cake. That one is my personal favorite."

"God, please no." His sister groans, plopping herself on the couch and closing her eyes. "I'll never lose weight if I continue to eat such delicious pastries so often."

"Why do you need to lose weight?" Drake asks, furrowing his brow. "You look amazing."

His sister purses her full lips and averts her gaze to Maya. Her daughter sits on the floor on a fluffy rug, playing with the LEGO Duplo Drake got for her. To not overwhelm her, we decided to wait until tomorrow to introduce her to Cooper. So now we're sitting in Drake's living room after a very delicious dinner with some pasta and a little wine for Layla and me.

"Layla?" Drake calls out to her again. "Where is this coming from? Your body–"

I pinch his side. *Hard*. He gasps and looks at me, confusion marring his features. I curtly shake my head no. "Stop," I whisper.

Drake gapes at me in silence, holding my gaze with his eyebrows etched together. Suddenly, Layla's laughter fills the space, and we both turn to look at her.

"Thank you, Angie," she says once she's calmed down. "My big brother has no idea how to read the room from time to time."

"What did I do?" Drake asks, glancing between us.

"You don't ask a girl about her reasons to lose or gain weight. It's none of your business, or mine, or anyone else's," I tell him sternly. "It's Layla's choice, and you don't need to question it. She does what she feels right for her; you need to respect it."

Drake rolls his lips together, looking annoyed for a moment. Then he turns his head to his sister. "Sorry, Layla. I'll do better next time."

Her eyebrows shoot up in surprise, and her mouth forms a little O. She stares at Drake for a moment, then glances at me, and a big satisfied grin blooms on her lips. "She's a gem. I hope you'll keep her."

"Don't ever plan to let her go," Drake murmurs, drawing me even closer to him and planting a kiss on my forehead.

"Good," Layla says and stands up from the couch, heading toward her daughter and lowering herself beside her on the floor. "Seeing you two happy makes me unreasonably happy myself." She looks over her shoulder, eyes glued to her brother's face. "I'm so glad we decided to visit."

"I'm glad too," Drake replies, and a comfortable silence settles between us, as we watch Layla help Maya to build a little elephant. He's been waiting for his sister to agree to come here for so long, so the smile on his face now seems deeper, his skin warmer. His happiness is contagious and everyone feels it. Especially me.

Drake

THIRTY

hat trick

THE ARENA BUZZES WITH ELECTRIC ENERGY AS THE FINAL seven minutes of the third period start. The crowd roars with anticipation, their voices echoing throughout the space, fueling the adrenaline coursing through my veins. It's the first home game of the season, but more than that, it's a game against the Chicago Hawks. Playing against Clay's team is a total blast.

As the clock ticks down, the intensity of the game heightens. Skates carve deep into the ice as a Hawks player darts towards Thompson, trying to steal the puck. He doesn't succeed; Colton sends it flying in the opposite direction to Pashkevich instead.

I scored two goals in the second period, and it helped our team take the lead and focus on the only possible outcome—our win. We're leading six to four now, but our opponent doesn't give up. Each pass and shot carry the weight of the game's final score.

Gauging my chances, I feel my heart pounding in my chest. Every move is calculated, every decision purposeful. Tonight's game is eventful; the fights for possession of the puck are fierce. Every player from our team is pushing themselves to their limit. Hours spent on the ice in shared dedication bind us together and make us feel a part of something incredible.

My eyes meet Thompson's, and he nods curtly. Swiftly maneuvering through the Hawks defense, we move forward. It didn't take us long to remember how to play as a whole again, our years in college acting in our favor. I've never felt other players the way I feel Colton. We're on the same wavelength, understanding each other from one simple glance.

Suddenly the Hawks defense covers Thompson, and he shoots the puck in my direction as we're nearing the net. The puck dances on my stick, and I skate faster to the net as if my life depends on it.

Time seems to slow as I release the puck, shooting it toward the net with all my might. At this moment, I have a feeling that the whole arena is holding its breath. All eyes are fixed on the puck as it soars through the air and collides with the net, landing in the right corner, just behind Rodgers's back.

The crowd erupts in a thunderous uproar, their cheers reverberating through the air. My teammates are skating toward me, and I can't help but feel elated. A surge of happiness spreads all over my body, and I don't even register at first what's going on. Hats falling on the ice make my jaw drop. I've been so focused on the game, I didn't even realize I just completed a hat trick, making the score seven to four.

"Sorry, man," I say, moving past Clay. He shoots me a look, shaking his head and dismissing me with a wave of his hand.

It takes a moment to clear the hats from the ice, and I use the opportunity to skate to my favorite girls, who are sitting in the first row of section 114. Pressing my hand to the glass, I smile at Angie. She leans forward, pressing her hand to mine from the other side. Her hair is collected into a high ponytail, secured by a red ribbon with a little bow on top. Seeing my jersey on her makes my smile broader, and a feeling of immense pride settles in my chest. *My girl.*

She's grinning at me from ear to ear, her eyes roaming over my face. She forms half of a heart with her thumb and index finger and presses it to the glass. I form the other half and complete the heart, my emotions swelling inside me, ready to explode. The warmth of seeing her coats me in her unwavering support and belief. With her by my side, I feel ready to conquer the world, not just win a game against the Hawks. Angie is a never-ending source of inspiration for me, and I'm—

A knock on the glass breaks the spell I'm under. I barely register what's going on around me; the feeling is overwhelming and astonishing. Squinting at my sister, who's sitting beside my girlfriend with my niece on her lap, I smile. My mind is elsewhere. I wave at them, shift my gaze, and wink at Michael, who's standing in front of Ava. All my movements are robotic, because the storm in my chest makes it hard for me to breathe. In the very depths of my soul, I think I've known it for some time already. I just wasn't fully ready to acknowledge it.

Turning around, I glide away from the stands, and a lopsided grin forms on my face as I reach my position. Only two minutes left, and we will be celebrating our first win of the season. Though I have many reasons to celebrate, and being in love with my girlfriend is definitely one of them.

"IT WAS A GREAT PLAY…EVEN though we lost," Clay says, hugging me and clapping me on my back. "Who were you trying to impress, Benson? Completing a hat trick in the first game of the season against your *best friend*."

"His girlfriend," Colton comments, a sly smile lighting up his face. "Don't you follow him on social media? She's all over his feed."

"That's not fucking true." I feign offense, stepping back from Rodgers. "We don't post much. There isn't a single picture with our faces."

"Okay, if you say so." Rodgers runs his palm over his face and down his beard. All his playfulness is suddenly gone, and his stare hardens. Thompson and I exchange a look.

"When are you flying back? Any chance you can stay and fly home tomorrow?" Colton asks, hiding his hands in his pants pockets. "We thought it'd be nice to get together. Our old gang is—"

"I'm going back tonight, with my team," he huffs, shifting his weight from one leg to another, his yellowish-green eyes scanning the place. When he finally brings his gaze back to us, I know something is wrong. "I thought we were friends."

"We are," Thompson and I say in unison.

"Then how come neither of you told me Layla has a baby? Not on the phone, not in your messages, not even when I visited this summer for a week. Why were you hiding it?"

Fuck. I roll my lips together, my fingers raking through my hair. "It's just that we knew—"

"You knew what? That I was still hoping to get back together with the girl I haven't been able to forget? Didn't want to take away that little fantasy?"

"Layla asked us not to tell you about Maya."

Hearing me say it, Clay's eyebrows reach his hairline.

Colton mutters quickly, "We wanted to tell you, but—"

"No." Rodgers raises his hand, stopping him. "You should've told me. I should've known she's happy with her boyfriend and that they were having a baby. It would've helped me move on."

He glances between Colton and me, exhaling a long breath and stepping back from us. "I hope next time I see you two, I'll be able to look you in the eyes and not feel resentment."

Clay heads to the exit, his shoulders slumped, his hands deep in his pockets. Thompson and I stay still, our eyes never leaving our best friend. The deepest turmoil permeates my soul, and bitterness fills my mouth. This is why I never wanted to hide the news from him. It was a mistake.

"We fucked up," Thompson says, his voice hoarse.

"We did," I confirm, poking my tongue into my cheek in exasperation. "I have no idea how to tell him she's a single mom."

Colton's eyes radiate sadness. "That should come from your sister. He's not going to listen to any of us."

A feeling of uncontrollable sorrow settles within me, heavy and suffocating. The weight of Layla's secret no longer burdens my shoulders; it's been replaced by regret. I'm grasping the consequences, the hurt we unintentionally caused our best friend. Hiding things is never an option because the truth always finds a way out. Just like the importance of words that have been said on time.

Missed opportunities are like bullets that shred the target to pieces with each hit. Something that might not look like a big deal becomes one over time.

There is only one person who can help me deal with these emotions. My personal heaven. The girl who holds the power to make me the happiest person alive, but also to destroy my heart if she doesn't feel the same.

Angie.

QUIETLY CLOSING the door of my house, I head to Angie's place. Layla is putting Maya to sleep, and my niece hasn't wanted to let me go. It took some convincing and a promise to take her for a walk with Cooper tomorrow morning. Thankfully, Angie's dog loves Maya, and I'm sure she's not going to say no to that.

I knock on the door and loosen my tie. I'm still wearing my suit; everything that happened after the game took a toll on me. All my plans went down the drain, and my happiness after the win disappeared. I'm not in the right mindset to even think about confessing my feelings tonight. The only thing I want to do is forget.

The front door opens, and my mouth waters on instinct. My eyes coast down Angie's body, devouring her from head to toe. Her long brown hair streams down her shoulders, hiding the Thunders logo on her chest. My jersey is the only thing she's wearing, and this sight is a thousand times better than any fantasy I've ever had.

"Nice game," she says, grinning at me with the cutest smile and stepping aside to let me in. Cooper is patiently waiting behind her.

"Nice jersey," I reply, looking her up and down again as I pass her. Stopping to pet Coop, I look at Angie over my shoulder. "Where did you get it?"

Angie pushes the door closed and turns to me. I straighten my back and peel my gaze to her face. Coming closer, she bites her bottom lip. "My boyfriend gave it to me. He's the best."

"Is that so?" I ask, winding my hands around her waist and slipping them down to her ass. *Jesus Christ, I'm gonna lose my fucking mind right now.* She's not even wearing panties.

She nods, rising onto her tiptoes and bringing our mouths closer. "The title of best boyfriend I've ever had easily goes to him."

Groaning, I squeeze her butt, my lips covering hers. The sweetness on her tongue makes my head fog. I press her closer to me, the scent of vanilla becoming stronger. She moans into my mouth, her hands locking around my neck. It's just a kiss, but I'm ready to drop to my knees and make her come all over my face. Whatever she wants, I'll be there to fulfill her wishes.

"How was your dinner with Clay and Colt?" Angie sighs as I slide my lips down her neck, pushing my hips into hers.

"It was a fucking disaster." I nibble on her skin, making her dig her nails into my scalp when I suck on her neck.

Angie leans away. Her eyebrows knit together, and a worried expression crosses her features. "What happened?"

"Can we..." I lick my lips, breathing heavily. "Can we talk about it later? I've been fantasizing about you in my jersey for months, and right now fucking you is the only thing I want. It will cheer me up for sure."

"For months?" she questions, arching an eyebrow at me. An amused smile plays on her lips.

"Yeah, since our first kiss," I confess, watching her intently.

Angie extends her hand to me, and I take it, entwining our fingers. She leads me to her bedroom, closing the door once we're inside. Stopping just beside her bed, she lets go of my hand and reaches up to my tie. Untying it, she drops it to the floor and helps me take off my jacket. Her fingers fly across my chest, and she starts to unbutton my shirt. One button after another, and it becomes harder and harder to control my breathing. I'm dying to touch her, but I'm letting her take the lead.

My shirt lands on the floor, and I swallow with difficulty. My throat is dry, and I'm thirsty, but not for a drink. For her. Unbuckling my belt, Angie holds my gaze. Fire dances behind her irises, and her chest rises and falls with quick breaths. Her fingers skim over the skin just above the waistband of my pants, and shivers spread all over my body. The emotions she causes me are powerful and unique, something I've never felt in my life until meeting her.

I step out of my pants and my briefs and stand in front of her completely naked. Her eyes sweep around my face and slowly trail down my chest and to my cock. Angie presses her index finger to her bottom lip, tracing it slowly, her eyes never leaving my body.

Skirting me, she goes to her bed. I watch her with my hand wrapped around my dick, slowly jerking off. Angie climbs onto the bed, plops herself down on her back, and scoots until her head hangs off the edge.

"You did a hat trick tonight," she whispers, beckoning me with her finger. "Now it's my turn." I stop right in front of her. "Fuck my mouth, Drake, and don't you dare stop before you shoot your load inside. I want it all. Every last drop."

"Show me your tits and I'll fuck your mouth, baby," I tell her. My cock feels hot in my hand. Smirking, Angie arches her back and lifts up my jersey, revealing her full breasts to me. "Good girl," I murmur, reaching down and pinching her nipple. "Keep your little mouth open for me."

Positioning myself, I slide my dick inside her mouth. *Shit.* It's so fucking warm. Her full lips circle my shaft, her tongue teasing me as I slowly fuck her mouth. She moans even with me in her mouth, her eyes half closed. It feels so good, I start going deeper. Angie opens her mouth wider for me, and my cock almost hits the back of her throat. Her gagging mixes with the slurping sounds she makes, and I slow down, not wanting to hurt her. Her teeth scrape the sensitive skin on my cock's head, making me hiss. She doesn't want me to slow down or stop going deeper. She lets me fuck her mouth the way I want to.

"Be a good girl, Angie, and touch yourself," I command, watching as she slides her hand down to her pussy, spreading her legs open. My eyes zero in on her fingers moving slowly around her clit. "That's it, baby, suck my cock, and let me watch you play with yourself. I'm going to come so hard for you."

Her movements are unhurried and erotic, and I lose myself in the moment. My gaze is fixed on her fingers playing with her pussy as I continue to fuck her mouth. Slowly, I start thrusting harder; the gagging sound intensifies, but I don't stop. My forehead is sweaty, my brows pinched together. It feels better than anything, coming undone because of her.

"Fuck," I growl. My eyes shut as my cum slides down her throat. "So fucking good, baby."

Stepping back, I look down at Angie. She swallows my cum and smiles, her hand freezing over her clit. "One down, two to go." She slaps her pussy and closes her legs, depriving herself of an orgasm. Her legs are wobbly when she stands up. "Come here and sit."

I do as I'm told, sitting on the edge of her bed. Angie climbs onto my lap, her mouth attacking mine. The taste of me on her tongue sends a blinding energy down my cock, making it even harder than before. Her kiss is teeth and tongue, sucking and biting, and I'm here for it. Her little ass grinds against my cock, making my brain empty. Grabbing her hips, I squeeze them hard and slowly lower her onto my dick. It slides inside her, and her head bobs back. A moan leaves her mouth; it's my favorite sound in the world.

I take my jersey off of her and toss it onto the floor, adding it to my pile of clothes. My mouth closes around her nipple; my tongue swirls around her sensitive bud. Moans and whimpers fill the air. She's never silent, always giving me what I want. I pump inside her, lifting her up and down on my cock. It's electric. Delightful. And so thrilling, my mind is foggy.

Licking the length of her neck, I suck on her skin again. Leaving my mark on her always sends me off the handle. I'm making her mine in every way possible, even if I don't want anyone else to see. Wrapping my arms around her waist, I let her take control. Her green eyes are hooded with desire, and her lips are parted. She rides me deep, rotating her hips in circles.

I release a breath; my mouth opens. "Oh, fuck, baby..."

“Your dick makes me feel so full,” Angie moans, riding me faster and faster.

“Tell me who owns your little pussy.” I collect her hair and wrap it around my fist, holding her in place. Her body arches, and I suck the hard point of her nipple into my mouth, grazing my teeth around it.

“You!” she cries out, her hips moving frantically. “Oh my... I’m coming....”

Grabbing the back of her neck, I press her forehead to mine. Our eyes lock, and that’s when I feel it. Her pussy closes around my cock, her walls suffocating me. It triggers me, and I come too, shooting my cum deep inside her. There is something absolutely out of this world, something transcendental, when the pleasure hits us both at the same time. I’m levitating, completely ruined by this woman, with no chance of going back.

I sink my teeth into her bottom lip and suck it into my mouth. Mischief swims in her eyes when I finally release her. “Two down, one to go, right?”

“You learn fast,” Angie teases.

I smile, tightening my grip on her. She’s relaxed and soft in my arms. Nudging her nose with mine, I cover her lips and kiss her slowly. My cock inside her is still hard as fucking wood. She’s like the strongest aphrodisiac, always making me insanely horny when she’s around.

Standing up from her bed, I make her wrap her legs around me. Her eyes snap open, and a gasp escapes her mouth when I slam her back into the wall.

“I played by your rules, but right now we’re going to play by mine,” I whisper, leaning into her ear. “I’m going to fuck you so hard right now, so fucking hard, until you scream my name.”

“I love when you talk to me like that.” Her hot breath gusts over my cheek, and I lean back to get a better look at her face. “Fuck me.”

A crooked grin slips onto my lips. Sliding my hands down to her ass, I pull her pussy onto my cock. When I’m balls deep inside her, I suck in a breath. With how tingly she makes me feel, I know I won’t last long. And yet, I’ll do anything to give her what she wants.

Deep and hard, I fuck her slow, burying my cock inside her pussy to the hilt. She moans into my ear, clinging to me, her hands snaking around my shoulders. Her body trembles; we are both covered in sweat. My fingers are digging into her flesh, clouding my mind, and my own skin hums from the pleasure I feel with her.

"Harder," Angie begs. "Please, Drake."

Smashing my lips onto hers, I drown her moans in our locked mouths. I pound into her faster and rougher. My hips are rotating as I slide inside her pussy again and again. My cock is ready to explode, and I feel it in my fucking bones. The pleasure flows throughout my veins, pumping my blood. I come first; my cum spills inside her. Without stopping, I continue to thrust into her until I feel her fall apart in my arms. My name leaves her lips as she orgasms too, her walls circling my shaft and milking me till I'm finally empty.

"Damn." I lower her to her feet. Pressing my hand above her head, I balance myself. Even my legs are trembling. I came three times in a row.

Angie chuckles, wetting her lips. "Your cum is dripping out of me."

"We need to put it back."

"We need a shower, or a hot bath." Angie taps on my nose, pushes herself from the wall, and instantly tumbles forward. She looks stunned. "My legs gave out."

"That's what happens when you are a good girl; you get fucked like one." Wrapping my arm around her waist, I pull her to my chest and walk us to her bathroom. "Bath or shower?"

"Bath. We can talk about your disastrous evening while we're there."

"Sounds good." I kiss her shoulder as she starts the water. "What do you like more? Baths or showers?"

"Baths." Angie shrugs, checking the temperature of the water with her hand.

"Hm. I was sure you'd prefer the shower."

"You don't know a lot of things about me, Drake." She looks at me over her shoulder, throwing a wink my way.

She's right; I don't know everything about her yet, but I'm looking forward to puzzling out all her secrets. I'm sure they will make me love her even more.

Angie

THIRTY-ONE

screwed

My kitchen is so quiet, I hear cars honking in the distance. A mug of chamomile tea sits on the table in front of me, along with an apple-spice cupcake with salted caramel frosting. My right knee is pressed to my chest; my chin rests on it, and my left hand is locked around my leg. Shifting my gaze to my phone on the table, I sigh, grab it, and quickly unlock it.

Noticing the time, I involuntarily smile. 12:12. An opportunity to make a wish. Even a silly one. I close my eyes, and Drake's image pops up in my head. He's always there, as if he imprinted himself inside my brain and made himself at home. His five-game road trip isn't something I'm a big fan of. I want to see him so much.

The sudden buzz of my phone and Drake's face on my screen causes my heart to rattle in my chest. Answering his FaceTime, I smile; the butterflies in my stomach are going crazy. I'm a lost cause, but I don't have any regrets. He's all my soul thinks about.

He's the wish I made years ago, hoping to meet someone who'd make me happy, and he came true.

"Hey, Cupcake," Drake says, the brightest smile playing on his full lips. His hat is backwards, hiding his curls under it. "I miss you."

"Hey, I miss you too," I murmur. My eyes roam over his handsome face, and I feel a pang in my chest. Just one more day, and he'll be back for a four-game home stand. "You played outstanding yesterday. It sucks that you lost."

"Well, yeah, but one day you win, and the others you learn from your mistakes. It's just the beginning of the season, and we're doing pretty well. We've won five games out of eight, and we're hoping to win tonight. Though this is hockey we're talking about. Anything is possible." He props his cheek on his knuckles and grins at me. "How are you doing?"

I mull over my answer, looking around my kitchen. Cooper catches my gaze and lifts his head from his paws. He misses Drake too, always pulling me to his porch and trying to climb the stairs on our walks. In just a few months, this man won over every single part of my body and soul, filling my house and my life with his presence, not leaving me any choice except to surrender.

"Angie?" Drake coos, and I focus my attention on the phone screen. "How are you?"

"I'm okay, just a little bored. I read one thriller and listened to an audiobook about a girl who falls for her stepbrother. Things at the shop are good, just...I don't know. Movies used to help, but not anymore. Everything I want to watch, I don't want to start without you."

"We just finished *One Tree Hill*. All nine seasons. I thought we were taking a break." He laughs wholeheartedly, my favorite dimples on full display.

"Not really. It took us several months to finish, and I got used to watching things with you."

"Maybe it took us so long because since we started dating, we've had more fun things to do."

Shaking my head, I stand up from my stool and head to the living room. "Wait a minute...is that my T-shirt?"

I lift the phone higher, so only my face is visible. *Dammit*. The back of my neck warms up as I sit down on the couch. "No."

"Angie, it's my tee. I'd recognize it anywhere. Where did you get it?"

Beaming, I move my phone away from me so he can get a better look. "Remember when you asked me to take Layla and Maya to the airport?" He nods, his eyes coasting over my body, sending tingles all across my skin. "I kinda snuck into your bedroom and borrowed this T-shirt. It smells like you."

Drake snorts, lifting his hand and showing me his wrist. A red ribbon is tied around it. "I also wanted to take something of yours with me."

We're so screwed.

"Will you have it on during the game tonight?"

"It's my lucky charm, baby." He winks at me, eyes glimmering with joy and happiness. "Just like you, according to *Sports Today*'s Instagram."

I roll my eyes, groaning quietly. "'Everyone thought she loved football, but apparently hockey players are her thing.'" Pouting, I rap my fingers on my thigh. "They need to hire someone to write better captions."

"You looked stunning in those pictures. In my jersey, with my arms wrapped around you. I don't think anyone cared about the caption," Drake states with conviction.

Another compliment from my boyfriend, and I'm melting. The way he makes me feel appreciated and seen blows my mind every single day. It's so genuine and effortless, weakening my knees and making my heart full. His words carry a little magic, one I've never really believed in, but he proved me wrong. He makes everything real; even the smallest moments are special with him.

"Based on the comments, you have a real fan club, and they all want to be me," I tease him, twirling a lock of my hair around my finger.

"Maybe, but I only want one Evangelina Jones, and it's you. I don't care about anyone else."

This feeling is so familiar and so foreign at the same time. As if he's saying "I love you" without actually saying the three little words.

Suddenly, I hear men's loud voices, and Colton's face appears on the screen. He smirks and waves his hand. "Hey, Angie. Sorry, but I need to steal your boyfriend."

"Practice isn't something you can skip, buddy." Roman's face pops up on my screen wearing a big, radiant smile. "Hey, Angie."

Chuckling, I wave at them, watching as Drake tries to shoo them out of the room. When he returns to his phone, his hat is nowhere to be seen, and his curls fall into his face. He says he needs a cut, but I love threading my fingers through his hair, so I never insist or remind him to make an appointment. He's pretty perfect as he is.

"Sorry, baby, I need to go."

"Of course, see you on the ice. I'll be watching the game with Nevaeh."

"Say hi to your best friend for me...and Pashkevich," Drake says and looks over his shoulder. The door of his room opens again, and Colton stops in the doorframe. "Gotta go. Bye."

"Bye," I whisper, continuing to stare at the dark screen. The butterflies in my stomach dance to a song I never hoped to hear again. It's a song about love. It's a song about Drake and me.

"I SHOULDN'T HAVE LISTENED to you," Nevaeh mutters, putting the plate of cheese on the table. "Why couldn't we fly to Washington to watch the game?"

"Because it's not the first time he's on the road, and it's not going to be the last. I don't want him to think I'm so clingy that I can't even let him breathe," I counter, reaching over the table for my glass of rosé. "There'll always be games, Nev. Next time, we can plan a trip together."

"That's better."

"Is this about me and Drake though? Or is it about you and Pashkevich?" I watch my best friend with curiosity.

"It has nothing to do with Pashkevich." Nevaeh frowns, plopping a cherry tomato into her mouth. "I'm trying to make my relationship with Travis work, so I'm staying as far away from your boyfriend's teammate as possible. The attraction, the sexual tension...it's all there, but I don't want to ruin what I have with Travis."

"What matters most is your happiness," I point out, grabbing a cheese cube from the plate.

"I'm happy with Travis. Promise." She smiles at me.

"That's nice to..." I fall silent, hearing my phone ringing in the kitchen. "Sorry. Need to check it."

Putting my glass back on the table, I head to the kitchen. The sounds from the TV indicate the start of the game, making me hurry up. The second I see my brother's face on the screen, I grin. Since my siblings' Euro-trip lasted longer than they planned, Ethan didn't have a chance to visit me. The last time we talked, he promised to come during his winter break. I miss the goofball to no end.

"Hey, little brother," I greet, pressing my phone to my ear.

"You need to fly home." He sounds out of breath, his voice trembling.

"Did something happen? Are Mom and Dad alright?" Fear settles in the pit of my stomach, and my index finger instantly starts circling my thumbnail. I slap my hand on the kitchen counter, balling my fist and digging my nails into my skin. "What about Emma?"

"Angie, there are pictures of you using cocaine all over social media."

This can't be happening. My legs shake, and only my hand on the counter helps me keep my balance. Panic fists my heart. My gaze wanders over the kitchen, not settling on anything, my mouth falling open.

"Articles are popping up at lightning speed. They are talking about Dad, about your modeling career and your new boyfriend. It doesn't look good, sis."

"I..." It feels as though the walls around me have been torn away, leaving me exposed and vulnerable. Dread coils inside my chest, tightening its grip with each passing moment. The deepest sense of shame washes over my consciousness, leaving me gasping for breath. "I'll look for flights."

"With Dad they're taking it easy. Like, you live on your own, and he can't control you—"

"Ethan." I stop him, brushing away my tears with the heel of my palm. "I'll look for flights. Our parents deserve an explanation."

"Okay, Angie. You know I'm always here for you, right?"

"Yeah. See you soon."

"Text me your flight details. I'll come pick you up."

I don't say anything, just end the call.

An unread text on my screen draws my attention, and I open it.

UNKNOWN NUMBER:

Now we're even. Be happy, Snow Queen.

I should've known he wouldn't let it go. I should've known he was too selfish to let it slide.

I look at the screen of my phone, tears streaming down my face. The mistakes of my past have finally caught up with me, threatening to ruin my future—the future I wanted more than anything in the world.

Quickly opening the browser, I type my name into the search bar and wait. When the results load, my breath hitches in my throat. Ethan was right; the articles only briefly mention Dad, but they talk a lot about my relationship. It's only the start of the season, and it's all about Drake's reputation.

A warm hand wraps around my wrist, forcing me to turn around, and I come face-to-face with Nevaeh. Her eyebrows are pinched together, and her eyes are distressed. She tucks away my hair, her thumbs wiping my tears.

"What's wrong?"

"Asher leaked some old pictures where I was...using cocaine. Journalists are using it against Drake. They're saying being with someone like me jeopardizes his career."

"What? When were these pictures taken?"

"I tried it twice, Nev, when we were still in Philly. I didn't like it, but it was a good way to make me forget about my problems when my mind wouldn't shut down," I mumble. My hands are trembling as I start looking for flights home. Messages from Mom and Dad appear on my screen like an avalanche, one after another. My parents are beside themselves with worry and concern. They're asking me to come home. Swiping away their texts, I quickly book a flight that leaves in two hours and slip my phone in my back pocket. "Can you please look after Cooper? I'll call Marcy; can you take him to her?"

"Wait...what are you doing?" Nevaeh steps back as I rush past her to the living room. The sounds of the TV are just white noise to me right now.

In my bedroom, I pull out my suitcase and start tossing clothes inside. The sound of Cooper's paws and Nevaeh's footsteps stop near the door, and then they both step inside.

"Angie, what are you doing?"

"My parents deserve an explanation," I mutter, tossing two pairs of jeans into my suitcase and stomping to the bathroom for my skin-care products. "I should've told them the truth a long time ago. It was a mistake—"

"What about Drake?" Nevaeh asks, staring down at her phone as I skirt her to return to my suitcase. "They make you look like an addict, speculating whether he should be tested for drugs too."

My heart sinks to my feet; the floor I'm standing on doesn't feel so solid anymore. They say no publicity is bad publicity, but not when it's about sports and drugs. Drake is innocent, and it'll be easy to prove that. And yet, it's still awful for Drake's reputation to be associated with someone like me.

Every story has a villain, and it looks like I'm the villain in his. I don't deserve him, and I never should've thought I did. Broken girls don't belong with nice guys. They tend to ruin their lives.

"I'll make a statement the instant I'm home with my parents. Dad's agent can help." I close my suitcase and straighten my back, meeting Nevaeh's gaze. "It'll be better if I keep my distance from Drake."

My best friend puts her hands on her hips, eyeballing me from under furrowed eyebrows. "Are you going to break up with him?"

"I just need to make sure he doesn't face speculation." I grab a black hoodie from the shelf and put it on. I'm ready to go; I'll call Marcy on my way to the airport. Bending down, I take my suitcase and pull it to the door, feeling Nev's and Cooper's eyes on me. "I'll text you Marcy's address."

"Sure, I'll take Coop to your chef's or look after him myself. It's no big deal." She follows me closely as I make my way to the front door. "Angie, what are you going to do about Drake?"

"Make things right," I tell her, letting my answer linger. Then I open the door and walk out of the house. "Bye, Nev."

As I slide into my car and start the engine, I finally say the words I left unspoken. The ones that keep me sane in this chaos. "I just hope he'll still want me."

Drake

THIRTY-TWO

philadelphia

Winning a game after our last loss feels nice. Even if it was pretty tough, it still ended in our favor. Four to three—and a very nasty bruise on my left side, right under my ribs. I got it slamming into the boards as Washington's left defenseman bumped into me at full speed in the second period.

The only thing I want now is to fly back to my girlfriend. Take a hot bath to soak my sore muscles, tend to my bruise to make it hurt less, and just hold Angie in my arms. That's pretty much everything I plan to do tonight once I'm home—in addition to doing her.

As I make my way down the tunnel toward the locker room, the cheers of the crowd still echo in my ears. My heart is galloping, and a feeling of accomplishment surges through my veins. Happiness about my team's success and anticipation of seeing Angie pour inside my chest, spreading over my whole body. Two days off in addition to four home games. What could be better?

A woman holding a microphone halts me in my tracks as I'm approaching the locker room entrance. The reporter flashes me a smile, her eyes glued to my face. I furrow my brow, my confusion mingling with the lingering adrenaline still fueling my body. What is she doing here?

"Congratulations on the win, Drake. Can we get a few words

about the game?" the reporter begins, her voice a mix of composure and eagerness.

My initial puzzlement slowly dissipates, and I nod, readying myself to answer the usual questions about the team's performance and my individual contributions.

Then a subtle shift in the reporter's demeanor draws my attention. She plays with her perfectly styled hair, her manicured fingers rapping on the microphone. Something is wrong, and the longer she keeps quiet, the more this feeling settles in the pit of my stomach.

"So what's your question?" I demand, staring her down.

A flicker of uncertainty dances in her eyes. "There's been some buzz on social media regarding your girlfriend. Can you comment on the recent scandal?"

"Um..." I take a step back, blinking rapidly. Her question astounds me, and I suddenly feel out of place. Being asked about my personal life is the last thing I expected after a successful game. The cheers and other sounds from the arena fade into the background. I struggle to grasp reality, trying to understand the meaning of her words.

What scandal is she talking about? How does it involve Angie? What the fuck started it?

Dragging my palm down my face, I glance around without seeing anything. I have no clue how to answer the reporter's question. Frustration simmers in my brain, mixing with an undeniable desire to protect Angie and shield our relationship from the prying eyes of the public. No matter what, we'll deal with it together, without other people's involvement.

Taking a deep breath, I muster a smile and gather my composure. Determination inflames my body as I take a step forward, leveling this woman with a glare.

"Thank you for the congratulations. As for the recent speculation surrounding my girlfriend, I want to emphasize that my personal life is not up for discussion."

The reporter frowns; a deep wrinkle appears on her forehead. She tsks, shifting her weight from one foot to the other. "So you don't have anything to say—"

"No comment," a man's loud voice thunders behind my back, and I whip my head around, seeing Coach Reed approach us. "If you have questions about the game, Ms. O'Brien, you can ask them during the postgame press conference. It's already starting." He wraps his arm around my shoulder and guides me to start moving. "Have a good night."

My initial shock has vanished, but Coach's intervention weirds me out. It doesn't take me long to put two and two together, and when I edge inside the locker room and slump onto the bench, I already know the team is aware of whatever scandal is involving Angie. It must be something serious. Deep disturbance engulfs my whole being, and the only place I want to be right now is with my girlfriend. She's all I care about; the rest can go to fucking hell.

"Drake, how long have you and your girlfriend been together?" Coach Reed asks, stopping in front of me, his thumbs hidden in his pockets.

I take my helmet off and set it on the bench beside me. Running my fingers through my hair, I meet Coach's eyes. "With all due respect—"

"There are pictures of Evangelina Jones using cocaine circulating on multiple sites. Do you know anything about it?"

A sharp intake of breath, and my eyebrows go up. The rattling sound scatters over the room after my stick falls on the floor. My teammates are throwing curious glances in my direction, keeping their distance. What is said and done in the locker room always stays in the locker room, but that doesn't mean they don't want to know what's going on.

"I'll take that as a no," Coach Reed mutters and claps his hands together in front of him. "There will be a short call with the team's management after the press conference is over. We want you to join it."

"Of course."

"Thank you, Drake." Coach eyes me from under furrowed brows.

Then his expression softens, and he gives me a small smile. "You worked hard tonight. That snap shot to the goal in the third period was perfect." My face is like an emotionless mask; my chest is aching. The buzzing in my head doesn't stop for even a second. Coach Reed bends and puts a heavy hand on my shoulder. "Go take a shower, son. It'll help."

Stepping back, he turns on his heel and storms out of the locker room. I pull off my jersey and take off my elbow pads, followed by my shoulder pads. My movements are frantic, a thousand thoughts swirling around in my mind. Something about this story isn't right, but my head is too fucked-up to figure it out now. With a heavy sigh, I run my palm over my face and start untying my skates.

Hot water is exactly what I need to sort out my emotions. For my talk with management, I need to have all my marbles.

"What did they say?" Colton asks the second I slump into the seat beside him on the bus to the airport.

"We read almost every article we found." Roman hovers over us from his seat; his forehead is creasing with wrinkles. "They are all pretty much a copy-paste of the first post on Instagram. Evangelina is a former model with some shady stories in her past; that's probably where her addiction started."

I pinch the bridge of my nose with my thumb and index finger. "I spent my whole summer with Angie, and I didn't see her high even once. She's not an addict, and everything in those articles is total bullshit."

"What did the team say?" Thompson repeats his question.

"They believed me when I said I didn't know anything about this part of Angie's past," I say, and Colton's eyebrows shoot up to his hairline. I nod. "I was able to convince them that the pictures are old."

"How do you know they're old?" Pashkevich stares at me, running his hand through his sandy blond hair; his upper lip is quirked.

Rolling my eyes, I pull my phone out of my pocket, find the picture, and shove it into Roman's face. He lowers his head, eyes glued to my phone screen. A moment later, he looks up and arches an eyebrow at me.

"When I met Angie in April, she already had tattoos covering her left arm," I explain calmly, and Pashkevich's face lights up with a smile. "This was taken a long time ago, before me."

"I didn't even realize there weren't any tattoos on her arm. Roman and I studied this picture several times, and still..." Colton shakes his head.

"I just know her." I shrug, feeling unsettled.

Bitterness fills my mouth, and I swallow my nerves, staring at my feet. The realization that Angie kept such big secrets from me is a bummer. It was probably the strongest blow I withstood today.

"I suggested a drug test to show that I'm clean, and they agreed. I want this to be over, and I don't have anything to hide," I mumble, choosing to focus on my career to avoid more questions about Evangelina from my friends. "The team will issue a statement to express their full support for me, and they'll ask the public to respect me and my girlfriend's privacy."

Colton and Roman exchange a look, and then both their gazes bore into me. I keep silent, tapping my foot on the floor. My only desire remains the same—I want to see Angie. Hold her, talk to her, and make sure she knows she can trust me with anything. Her secrets aren't going to scare me away, no matter what she might think.

"How is she?" Thompson asks quietly.

"Have you talked to her?" Pashkevich adds.

I force a smile, fidgeting in my seat. "She's not answering her phone. My guess is that she turned it off."

"Call her best friend. If something big happened, she'd be by Angie's side. And I bet her phone would be on," Colton offers, nudging me with his elbow. "Your sister is the first person Ava calls all the time."

Nodding, I quickly find Nevaeh's number in my contacts and dial it. She picks up after the third ring, panting and huffing. "Hey, Drake."

"Hey, Nev. Any chance you know where Angie is?" A long pause follows. I even move my phone away from my ear to check if the call is still connected. "Nevaeh?"

"Cooper, I swear to God, stop trying my patience," she shrieks in my ear, and my frown only deepens. "Sorry, Drake. This dog is driving me nuts. He's been a nervous wreck since the moment Angie left, and I'm honestly counting the fucking seconds till Marcy comes to get him. He refuses to get out of my car."

"Angie left? Where did she go?"

"She...said she sent you a text. Didn't you get it?"

Pulling my phone away from my ear, I open my messages and scroll down to find her name, ignoring all unread messages as I do. The moment I open our text thread, it dawns on me that Nevaeh is right. I must have accidentally swept it away during the call with the team's management. There were just too many messages coming through, and I wanted them to stop.

CUPCAKE:

I should've been honest with you about everything. Sorry for all the mess my past is causing you. I'll fix it, I promise

"Nev, her message doesn't explain anything," I blurt, meeting Colton's heavy stare. My best friend is watching me with his lips pursed and his eyes narrowed. "Where is she?"

"On a flight to Philadelphia. She wants to explain everything to her family and make things right for you. Issuing a statement and..." Nevaeh trails off, uncertainty lacing her voice.

"And what?" I demand.

"Keeping her distance from you...for your own good."

It feels like she just tore me open, buried a knife deep in my gut and twisted it to make it hurt more.

Nev continues, "She believes being with someone like her is bad for your reputation. At least until she makes things right."

Clicking my tongue, I look out the window and notice that our bus is getting close to the airport. A plan quickly forms in my head. It's not in my nature to back down, and I'm not going to do it now. Not when it comes to the woman I love.

"Nevaeh, is there any chance you can give me Angie's parents' address?"

"Sure, I'll send it to you in a minute. Oh my God, Marcy is finally here. Gotta go." Another high-pitched scream, and she hangs up. To her credit, not even a minute later, I have the address in Philadelphia.

"Don't worry about your gear," Colton says confidently, a crooked smile playing on his lips.

"I'll help too," Roman joins, winking at me.

Gratitude for my friends overwhelms me. The feeling is strong and abiding, and my chest is full. Hockey is not just my passion that brings me joy. It also gave me the most priceless gift in the world—my friends, people I can call my family even if we're not related by blood. It's everything.

After a quick chat with the coaches to get their approval, saying goodbye to my teammates, and thanking my friends for their help, I take my bag and head inside the airport. Tonight, my team is flying home without me. I have somewhere else to be.

All roads lead to Philadelphia.

Angie

THIRTY-THREE

love is...

It's barely nine a.m., but I couldn't sleep a wink. Since my plane landed in Philadelphia, I've felt caught in the middle of a hurricane. I got home with Ethan, talked to my dad's agent and issued a statement, and watched as, one by one, the posts were replaced by articles based on the story I was willing to share.

Making mistakes is not a crime. It's human nature to do things when we're young and inexperienced and then regret them later. The worst thing we can do is not learn from our mistakes and failures. Slipups and poor choices, not our successes, forge our personalities. I've learned that the hard way, but looking back, I know that I'm where I should be because of the decisions I made, even if they were bad. All my fuckups are my own, and for the first time in my life, I'm not hiding anything from my family.

Last night was probably the hardest and the most liberating talk I've ever had. Sitting on the couch in my parents' living room, surrounded by Mom and Dad, Ethan and Emma, I let it all out. I started at the very beginning and didn't hide even the tiniest details. My eyes weary and red-rimmed from all the tears I cried—swollen eyelids were the best testament to my disturbance. And yet, I didn't stop. I explained all my reasons and confessed all the stupid things I've done. Overwhelming support from everyone in my family was all I got in response. They cried with me, they told me they loved me and reassured me they always would be there for me. My family has my back, and I was finally ready to accept it. I need them.

Plopping onto my back, I stare at the ceiling of my bedroom. My phone's still downstairs in my purse, and I'm trying to psych myself up to go get it. A sleepless night wore me out, and tiredness is all I feel now. I want to call Drake. I want to know how Cooper is, but I'm just lying here, not able to move a muscle.

Slowly, the door of my room cracks open, and my sister's head pops in. Our eyes meet, and she gives me a hesitant smile. Emma edges inside, closes the door behind her, and ambles to my bed. Not saying anything, she lowers herself beside me. With a sigh, I turn onto my right side, facing my little sister.

Emma has heterochromia; it's always been the only difference she's had from Ethan. Now her green and brown eyes are peeled to me as she stares at me in silence. Her dark brown hair is collected into two braids, and she's still wearing her pastel pink pajama shorts and tee. My heart stings a little, knowing that this is probably the first time my sister and I are sharing a moment like this since she became a teen.

"I'm sorry," she whispers, hiding her hands under my pillow.

I blink, knitting my eyebrows together. "Why are you apologizing, Em?"

"Because I've been hating on you for absolutely no reason. It didn't even occur to me to talk to you, to see things for what they are, like Ethan did. Instead, I imagined your life as a colorful kaleidoscope of perfection. Good grades, incredible at any sport you tried your hand at, a beautiful voice, and undoubted acting skills." Her voice trembles, and her bottom lip starts to quiver. "I wasn't good enough in comparison to you, and people around me always needed to remind me about it. You didn't deserve my anger. It should've been directed at all the idiots who were trying to pit me against you. I should've been proud of you, but I was bitter...."

Moving to Emma, I wrap my hand around her shoulder and pull her to me. She sobs; her whole body trembles. Hiding her face in the crook of my neck, my little sister cries, her tears streaming down her cheeks, wetting my tee. I close my eyes and hold her close, giving her comfort.

"I didn't try to make you understand me. I let you hate me because it was easier than explaining what I was doing with my life. I should've explained, Em. I should've given you a good example of what not to do if you don't want to ruin everything around you, including yourself." I hug her tighter. "I'll always love you, Wemmy." She chuckles, hearing her cute nickname we've used since she was a small girl. "I'll be the big sister you deserve."

"You already are, Angie," she murmurs, leaning away and gazing at my face, her eyes welling with tears. "And you went through so much, all your hardships only making you stronger. I admire you, and if one day I'm even just a little bit like you—I'll be proud of myself."

"Comparison is the thief of joy, as they say. Never ever measure yourself against others, even if they are your family. Look at your past self. At what you were capable of a month ago, a year ago, two years ago, and you'll see how far you've come." I brush her tears away with my thumbs. "You're an incredible young woman, and I'm so lucky to have you as my sister."

Emma smiles shyly and cuddles me, wrapping her arms around my waist. I inhale the scent of her perfume, with notes of bubblegum, and my heart is instantly full of happiness. Even in my wildest dreams, I didn't think my visit home would bring us closer.

We lie in the quiet of my room, both lost in our own thoughts. A light knock on my door makes us stir, and we sit up on my bed.

Ethan steps inside, a lopsided grin playing on his lips as his deep brown eyes land on Emma and me. He's dressed in blue jeans and a white hoodie, a cup of coffee from the local coffee shop is in his hands.

"Finally!" my brother exclaims, saluting us with his cup.

"Took us long enough," I jokingly reply, giving Emma a side hug and making her giggle.

"I've been patient," Ethan comments. Then he narrows his eyes at me. "I'm still your favorite sibling, right?"

Swinging my legs over my bed, I stand up and walk over to him. "You're still my favorite little brother."

Ethan snorts and takes a step back, sweeping his gaze over my face. He rubs the back of his neck with his palm, eyebrows pulled together.

"What?" I ask, not understanding his reaction.

"You should change. No way you're meeting our guest looking like that."

I look down at the red and white pj's I blindly tossed inside my suitcase yesterday, which are really more suitable for Christmas. Then I bring my eyes back to my brother. I freeze, and my jaw drops; the meaning of his words suddenly dawns on me.

"Guest?"

Ethan shrugs, pressing his cup to his mouth and taking a sip. After he swallows, he says, "Your boyfriend is here."

"Her hockey boyfriend?" Emma chirps from behind us, and I watch my brother nod. "Oh my God, I need to change too. I don't want my future brother-in-law to remember me as someone who wears Maleficent pj's."

"Brother-in-law? You don't even know Drake," I mutter as my sister breezes past me.

"Even if we weren't speaking, it doesn't mean I know nothing." Emma winks at me over her shoulder as she exits my room.

My brother heads out the door too. "Hurry up, sis. Mom and Dad also know he's here."

Dammit.

DESCENDING THE STAIRS, I listen carefully to the sounds coming from the living room. Mom's laughter. Dad's deep voice. And Drake's calm and velvety tone. The butterflies in my stomach are acting crazy, making my heart flutter. My happiness mixes with my fears, and I loiter near the door to take a deep breath before I step into the living room.

Mom sees me first; her face lights up with a gentle smile. Her dark green eyes, the same color as my own, focus on me, enveloping me in warmth and giving me much-needed confidence. She tucks a lock of her brown hair behind her ear, and her bracelet slides down her arm.

"Did you sleep well?" Mom asks, and Dad and Drake snap their heads up to look at me.

"Two hours is barely sleeping well," I reply with a lift of my shoulder, my eyes focusing on my boyfriend. "Hey."

"Hey," he murmurs. The corner of his mouth quirks up, and one of my favorite dimples is visible on his cheek.

"I found your boyfriend on my way back from my run," Dad states matter-of-factly. "He's a Red Lions fan."

"Logan," Mom warns Dad, her eyes rounding.

Briefly locking eyes with Drake, I notice how his gaze darkens, never leaving my body, even if a playful smile blossoms on his lips. My need to touch him escalates within a second, and I look away, pinning my dad with my stare. "Maybe that's because he's from Michigan, Dad."

"I didn't mean anything bad, Angie," my dad retorts, and Mom instantly puts her hand on his knee. "What?"

"We better give them some privacy." Mom stands up from the couch, and Dad scoffs grumpily. He stands as well, but I stop them. If I want some privacy, the living room of my parents' house is the last place I should be.

Tilting my head, I say with certainty, "We'll talk in my room."

Drake stands up from the couch as soon as those words leave my mouth. My eyes travel down his body, enjoying the view so much my knees become weak. He's wearing a gray and white hoodie paired with gray sweatpants and white sneakers, and his clothes fit him perfectly. Especially his pants—but I don't dare let my eyes linger.

Lining up with me, he takes my hand in his, lacing our fingers. Tingles spread across my skin, and his so familiar scent engulfs me. I'm ready to lose myself in him, but it needs to wait. Keeping him in the dark about some things from my past ends now. I don't want to hide anything from the people I care about.

I make Drake follow me. The second I put my foot on the first stair, my dad's voice catches up with us. "We'll have breakfast at eleven."

"*Logan*," my mom groans, making me shake from silent laughter.

"What, *Becca*? Don't you think they want to eat?"

"I think you're being an overbearing parent, and our daughter won't appreciate it."

Shaking my head, I start climbing the stairs, tuning out the conversation my parents are having in the living room. All that matters is the man who is quietly following me. His words are the only thing I want to hear right now.

Once we're inside my bedroom, Drake closes the door. I edge to my bed and sit on it; he joins me a moment later. Our shoulders are pressed together, and I shut my eyes, allowing my heartbeat to slow down and become steady. I have so much to say, but the words are stuck in my throat. A hopeless sigh bolts out of my parted lips.

"Why did you run away?" Drake's quiet voice slides under my skin, and I shiver.

"I didn't."

"Angie, we're in Philadelphia, at your parents' house. If you hadn't run away, we would've had this conversation at your place last night."

"After the news broke, and Ethan called me, I knew I owed my family an explanation. I just wanted for all my secrets and omissions to be out in the open." I lick my lips. "Plus, I knew Dad's agent could help me make things right, help me make a statement so they'd leave you out of it. It was about my mistakes, and I'd be damned if I let you pay for them."

"I'm fine," he says, and our gazes instantly clash. "I had a conversation with my team's management after the game. They believed everything I said, and they know the pictures are old. They were taken before we even met. The Thunders have already issued a statement, it's all good."

"How did you—"

"Your tattoos." Drake smiles at me, and my skin is searing. A tingling sensation rolls over my body. "The moment I saw the pictures, I knew it was long before me."

"I should've never hid something like that from you." I hang my head low. "It was so long ago, before I even moved to California. Seeing what it did to Asher, I knew I'd never try drugs again. I'm sorry it came to this, that you found out about my fuckups this way. You didn't deserve it."

"Angie," he croons. His warm palm cups my cheek, making me look at him. His deep brown eyes with honeyed flecks scrutinize me with intensity, taking hold of my heart. "Never ever think that there is something you should be ashamed to talk to me about. I'll never judge you, or make you feel less than you are. Don't be afraid to share with me even your deepest secrets if it's something you want me to know. We all make mistakes all the time, and it's what makes us human."

"I thought I was doing the right thing."

"Keeping your distance from me? Saving my image?" Drake asks, and my eyes open wider as I gawk at him. "Nev told me about your plans when I called her to figure out where you were."

"Drake, I—"

He silences me, crashing his mouth on mine. His lips hungrily devour me, making my head spin. I cling to him, my fingers curling around his hoodie. Drake hauls me to his lap, lowering us both until the back of his head hits my covers. The hard outline of his cock under me is exactly what stops us. I press my forehead to his, closing my eyes on an exhale.

"Angie, look at me," he pleads, a vulnerability I've never heard before weaving in his voice. I open my eyes, locking my gaze on his. "Just be honest with me, okay? I'll do absolutely anything to protect you. To make sure you're safe and happy, and to never let anyone bother you. I know how to fight my own battles, and I definitely know how to take care of the woman I love."

I suck in a breath, searching his face for any trace of doubt and not finding it. His honesty washes over me, blanketing me with joy and happiness. I'm so full right now, my chest feels tight.

"You're someone who stepped into my life unexpectedly, leaving me zero chances for escape. Letting you come in that night, agreeing to fake date you, I thought I was doing you a favor, and I hoped it would save me from my loneliness. And it did. It exceeded all of my expectations, because I can't even imagine my life without you anymore." His lips curve into a beautiful smile, his fingers combing my hair. "You're the Peyton to my Lucas, and there is no one and nothing in this world that will ever stand between us. I love you, Angie, and I think I've loved you for a very long time. Even before I realized it myself."

Taking a second to collect my thoughts, I peck his lips tenderly and smile, then lean away to have a better look at his face. "I kept saying that athletes aren't my thing, that sports guys aren't my type because a few jocks hurt me when I was young and naive...and it was true. Until you." My voice is trembling, and my eyes are welling with happy tears as I look down at Drake. "I thought I didn't deserve to be loved. That I wasn't good enough to be happy with someone who'd respect me. I was just going with the flow, trying to succeed in other areas of my life, compensating for the void I felt in my chest. I think I was waiting for you...only you. And I love you so much, even the tiniest thought that being with me might hurt you made me lose my mind. I was scared that I—"

"You as you are, with your flaws and your merits, are the only woman I'll ever want. Don't try to fit someone's idea of perfection, because you are perfect *for me*. Don't try to hide your insecurities or fear I won't understand you. I will, and I love all versions of you. I don't need anyone else."

"And I don't need anyone else either," I whisper against his lips, my nose nudging his gently. This almost-kiss is my favorite, making me always want more, building a fire within us both.

Drake grabs the back of my neck, forcing me to look him in the eyes. "Don't tempt me."

"Or what?" I tease, rotating my hips and purposefully dragging my pussy over his hard-on.

"Damn." He curses, turning us around and hovering over me with a serious expression on his handsome face. "I want your family to like me, and your dad is already not a fan. Fucking you in your bedroom when I'm sure the whole house is listening is definitely not something I should do."

"Okay."

"Okay? That's it?" Drake pinches his eyebrows together, eyeing me in confusion.

"I have no idea how to keep quiet when you're inside me, and I also want my family to like you. So makeup sex will have to wait till we're back home..." I trail off, looking expectantly at my boyfriend.

"Tomorrow. We need to fly home tomorrow." He bends his face down to mine slowly. "You think we can kiss a little at least? I'm sure it's not even close to eleven."

"That we can always do," I reply and close the distance between us, pressing my lips to his.

Kissing Drake, all thoughts leave my head little by little, until there is only one, and it settles deeper. He's not only made me fall in love with him. He made me fall in love with myself after so many years of self-loathing. Never asking me what I needed, he understood how I wanted to be loved, and he gave me everything.

The best things in life don't always come to us when we expect them, but they definitely come when we're ready. Sneaking up on me, knocking me off my feet, and just loving me the way I am. Falling in love with Drake is not even falling anymore. It's about building the world around us from scratch, creating our own reality...a place that feels like home only because we're together.

That's what being in love is.

Drake

THIRTY-FOUR

lucky charm

I'M SITTING ON THE BENCH, BREATHING HEAVILY. MY EYES are glued to the ice, and the roaring from the stands barely breaks through the tornado rampaging in my head. The more I watch Vancouver's left wing, Sokolov, the more my knuckles are itching. This dude not only wasn't letting me stand up when I tripped after colliding with their defense, but he was also chirping me. I'm all for good old trash talk, but not when he made fun of the whole scandal with Angie.

Talking shit about my girl was his worst mistake.

Ten minutes after the third period starts, I finally return to the ice, our team trailing by a goal. The atmosphere in the arena is electric; not just the players but the fans crave a comeback.

Bursting with speed, I move through the Vancouver players, my stick dancing across the ice with finesse. I look for an opening and spot Thompson. He's right near the net, ready for the pass that can change things in our favor.

With precision, I lift my stick and send a crisp pass sailing across the ice. The puck glides toward Thompson, and after, a thunderous shot hits the back of the net. The arena erupts in deafening shouts, cheering wildly as the goal ties the game. *Fuck yes.*

Like a breath of fresh air filling my lungs, determination surges through the team. I'm no exception, feeling confidence refuel my veins. Our chances are still strong. As long as the game is on, we can win.

Noticing Sokolov skate away in the direction of our net, I take off after him. My desire to make this jerk pay pushes me to move faster. He's focused on the puck; he doesn't see me circling him from his left side. Rushing forward, I collide with him, bracketing him into the board at full speed. He lands on his ass, his stick falls on the ice, and he loses the puck. I instantly steal it and send it flying to our left wing, Crowford, right from under Sokolov's nose.

"Next time, think about the bullshit that leaves your mouth," I growl, loud enough for him to hear me. He spits, not saying anything, and slowly stands up.

I return to the bench, a smile plastered onto my lips. Making my point with punches and blows is nice, but taking the opponent by surprise when he least expects it? Priceless.

The clock winds down, and I'm back on the ice, desperately trying to find a way to score. Exchanging a glance with Thompson, I finally see our chance. With a wink, we both skate to Vancouver's net. Weaving through their defenses, Colton creates an opportunity for a breakaway.

Maneuvering past the opponent's players, I find Crowford with my eyes. With an accurate wrist shot, I send the puck flying precisely where my teammate is. It falls on his stick, and a moment later, it lands behind Vancouver's goalie. Five to four.

We celebrate just as the arena erupts with the final buzzer, announcing our victory. The chanting from the stands is loud and contagious. Winning home games has a special charm, and I never underestimate it. It feels like magic—just like spotting my girl in the middle of the crowd, jumping and cheering for me.

Skating to the glass, I find Angie with Nevaeh in the first row of section 114. They are both smiling from ear to ear, and I can't help it. A huge Cheshire cat grin spreads across my lips when I stop in front of my girl and press my gloved hand to the glass.

Angie mirrors me, mouthing *I love you* as our eyes lock. She's not in my jersey tonight, but only because my last name and my number seven are sewn into the back of her bomber jacket. Her red knit sweater paired with black jeans look amazing on her, and her long brown hair spills down her shoulders in light waves. My girl is absolutely stunning, and my gaze zeroes in on her red lips. They would look so good wrapped around my cock...*fuck*. One wrong thought might cause me a huge hard-on.

"Your place or mine?" Angie asks.

"Mine," I tell her, and she nods.

I sweep my eyes over Nevaeh. She seems a bit lost, absentmindedly waving at me. I know who she's looking for, and I'm glad he already went to the locker room. Angie's best friend is in a relationship, and until she figures out what she wants, I hope she stays away from Roman. He's a great guy, and I don't want him to have his heart crushed because Nev hasn't made up her mind. Unrequited love is a bitch.

"Have a good ride home," I murmur and skate away from Angie and Nevaeh.

Before I go to the locker room, I stop in front of *Sports Today* reporter Kit Norman. He smiles, directing his microphone at me. "Congratulations on the win, Drake. The game was amazing, a real pleasure to watch. And you're one of the most valuable players on the ice. The Thunders made a great decision acquiring you last season."

"Thank you, Kit. I have very skillful teammates, and amazing coaches. That helps us win; so does a very supportive atmosphere among management," I reply nonchalantly.

"We all saw how the team advocated for you, pledging full support during the scandal you and your girlfriend faced. Do you have anything to say concerning all the articles and the statement Evangelina issued?"

A smile tugs at the corners of my lips, my happiness becoming harder to contain. Everything is going exactly as I hoped when I stopped to have a little chat with Kit. He's a nice guy, and very professional. And if I'm going to do something crazy for my girl, I want him to cover it the way only he can.

"I'm in love," I say simply, and Kit chuckles knowingly. A smile mirroring mine forms on his face. "As you probably know from my girlfriend's statement, she had her share of mistakes in her past, but who doesn't? The important thing about mistakes is that we learn from them. We all have our flaws and imperfections, and honestly? Evangelina is perfect for me. I'll always be there for her, and I'm beyond grateful for all the support the team and fans have shown us. Thank you."

The reporter smiles. "Thank you, Drake. Have a nice evening."

"You too, Kit," I say and stroll into the locker room.

A feeling of accomplishment fills me to the brim, and I continue smiling even when I'm already in the locker room. Looking down at Angie's red ribbon tied around my wrist, my heart is ready to explode. She's my lucky charm indeed.

"I BOUGHT SOMETHING FOR YOU," I coo, my lips trailing down Angie's throat. We're in my bedroom; she's straddling my lap as I sit with my back pressed to my headboard.

Soft, muted moonlight spills gently from the window. The air is tinged with a familiar scent, her favorite perfume mixed with coffee and sandalwood. The faint sound of rustling leaves and the distant sounds of the city carry into the room, but we barely pay attention to it. We're too absorbed in one another.

"A gift?" She moans, arching her back and rolling her hips deeply, rubbing her sweet little cunt over my dick.

"Make it two." Threading my fingers through her hair, I give it a little tug, and her head tips back. I suck on her skin, tracing the mark I left with my tongue.

Angie leans away despite my grip on her waist. She studies my face, her eyes sparkling with curiosity, one brow quirked in a question. "What is it?"

"Check my bedside table. The first drawer."

She hops off my lap, scoots away from me a bit, and reaches over to the first drawer, pulling it out. I don't see her face, but I watch as she takes out one little package and a wand. When she turns around, her lips are slightly parted as she gazes at me in silence.

"You told me your wand broke, so I bought you a new one," I tell her with a nod of my head. "And the other one is a bit for me, because my first away games proved to me that I can't stand the idea of not being able to satisfy you. We'll need to install an app on our phones and adjust all the settings—"

Dropping both toys on my covers, Angie lunges at me. She climbs on my lap, her arms wrapping around my shoulders. Our mouths mold into one as she kisses me, leaving me gasping for air. It's passionate and uncontrolled, her tongue curling around mine, dominating and making me fucking moan for her. She humps me dry, her fingers skimming over my neck and up my hair. Twisting my curls on top, she tilts my head and slides her lips down my throat. Teasing and sucking, licking the length of my neck, she makes me so hard, I see stars behind my closed eyelids.

"Fuck, baby," I hiss, feeling her teeth sink into my skin. "Who knew buying you toys would turn you into a little wild thing?"

"We promised not to talk about other partners," she whispers in my ear, her hot breath on my skin making me all tingly. "But you're the first man who sees sex toys as friends, not enemies."

Angie leans away, her eyes roaming over my face. She sticks her tongue out and moves it slowly between her teeth. I watch it, mesmerized, my patience disappearing into thin air.

Wrapping my hand around her throat, I take control into my own hands. "Get rid of your clothes and lie open for me."

A sexy smirk plays on her lips when she nods. Letting go of her throat, I watch as she undresses herself, tossing aside her tee and then standing up to pull down her shorts. She starts taking off her lacy panties, but I stop her, my hand covering hers. I cock my head, nodding at my bed, and she obeys, lowering herself beside me. I tower over her, admiring how beautiful she is, how her hair spills over my pillow like a dark cloud coating it.

I press my finger to her clit through her panties and slowly move it along her folds, feeling her wetness. My mouth goes dry, and I exhale sharply. Tugging on the waistband of her panties, I drag them down her legs and toss them aside, my eyes zeroing in on her glistening pussy.

Bending her legs at the knees, I settle my head between her thighs. I curl my tongue around her clit, circling it and sucking it into my mouth. A breathless moan rumbles from her throat, her hands fisting my sheets. Lapping my tongue, I tease her clit, my breath gusting over her sensitive skin.

"Such a delicious pussy," I murmur, burying my finger inside her.

Angie moans; her eyes fall closed. Adding another finger, I suck her clit into my mouth. My fingers move in and out, stretching her for me. I could eat her every day of every week, feast on this little cunt twenty-four seven, and I would still be hungry for her. Being with her takes being obsessed to another level; it's a lifelong addiction.

"You going to come for me, baby?" I ask, plunging another finger inside her.

"Yes..." she breathes. Opening her eyes, she holds my gaze, and it sends a blast of sizzling energy down my cock.

Fingerfucking her, I continue to ravish her clit with my mouth. She moves her hips, wanting to take more of me, and my dick swells in my shorts. It longs to be deep inside her, but it can wait. I want her to come all over my tongue and my fingers.

Her thighs clamp around my head; her fingers dig into my hair. Angie comes, and my name escapes her mouth with a long moan. She tries to push me away, but I stay put, sticking my tongue inside her pussy and licking her until she's empty.

I move away, letting her catch her breath. I take off my shorts, fling them to the floor, and wrap my fist around my cock. It's hard and hot, trembling in my hand when I give myself a long, slow stroke.

I grab the wand from the bed and turn it on. My eyes meet Angie's, and she smiles. I coast my gaze over her body, the hard points of her nipples drawing my attention. Bending my head down, I twirl my tongue around her nipple, popping it into my mouth and gently biting it. She whimpers, lifting her hips for me on instinct.

The second I align the wand with her clit, Angie shuts her eyes. Her eyebrows pinch together. I lick my lips, angling my cock and sliding inside her. "Jesus Christ, you're so warm...."

I fuck her slow and long, rotating my hips to slide deeper, until I'm balls deep inside her. The buzzing sound of the wand is nothing compared to Angie's rapid breathing and her moans. She's dripping, and the slopping sounds of her pussy clamping around my cock fill the room.

"Holy shit, don't stop..." she begs, cupping her tit with her palm, massaging it and pinching her nipple between her fingers. "Please, Drake..."

Taking the wand away, I put it on my bed. Her eyes fly open, but the surprise flickering behind her pupils doesn't last long. I hook my hands around her knees, spreading her wide open for me. I pound harder; the sound of our bodies slapping together rings in the air.

"I think I'm in love with your cock... God...it feels so good..." Angie moans.

Smirking, I slide my hands up and curl my fingers around her ankles. I draw her legs together, my eyes traveling down her pussy. It's soaked, my dick sliding inside faster and faster. I'm captivated by her bare little cunt, her lips glistening with her wetness.

"You take me so well, baby," I praise, slowing down a little and guiding her legs onto each of my shoulders. My eyes roll inside my head when I grip her ass with my palms. She arches her back, hips lifting to take more of me. "What a good girl you are, letting me ruin your pussy."

"Please, Drake... Har...Harder..." She's breathless, her hands gripping the sheets.

I draw her hips to me with my hand, pulling her down onto my cock again and again. My other hand trails up her perfect tits and curves around her throat. I squeeze my fingers, thrusting into her roughly. I'm about to explode, but I want her to finish first.

"Come for me, baby... Come for me..." I tell her, controlling her breathing and watching her cheeks redden.

Her back arches, and she slams her eyes shut. Her pussy pulsates around my cock, suffocating me with her orgasm. She trembles in my hands so much, I let go of her throat and drive myself inside her to the hilt. My cum spills inside her as I continue moving my hips until I'm spent.

Giving her a long and languorous kiss, I move away and lower myself beside her. We are both breathing hard, and my heart beats like crazy against my rib cage. I finally turn off the wand and look at Angie.

"I have no idea how I'm going to walk Coop in the morning—or how I'm going to move at all. I'm about to pass out from the pleasure you gave me," she confesses, a little smile adorning her face.

Grazing my index finger over her forehead, I brush away her hair. She's breathtakingly stunning, and my heart aches with how full of love it is for her. Even one minute away from her feels like a missed opportunity. And I hate letting my time go to waste.

"Move in with me," I blurt out.

Angie turns around, plops onto her belly, and props herself on her elbows, her chin resting on her open palm. I wait, watching her in silence.

"Move in with *me*," she says, raising an eyebrow at me. "If Layla finally moves here from Michigan, she'll be staying at your place, and we'll need to look for another house. So...move in with me now, and keep this place for your sister."

Snorting, I shake my head. "Why do I have a feeling you already thought about this?"

"Maybe I have." Angie smiles. "Plus, I might know something about Layla that you don't." I frown; uneasiness seeps into my veins. "Nothing bad, relax. She's applying for jobs here, in Santa Clara."

I prop my head on my knuckle, mirroring Angie. "She told you before she told me. My sister likes you."

"She does, just like my family likes you."

"Not sure about your dad," I joke, and she swats me in the chest with her palm. We both laugh, and then I inch my face closer to hers. "So, I'm moving in."

"You are," she whispers and presses her lips to mine.

Falling asleep, I think back to her words when we were at the Thompsons' place. I'm right on time with my life...because with her it feels complete.

One year later

ANGIE

"ARE YOU SURE?" I PRESS MY PHONE TO MY EAR WHEN THE sounds of busy streets become louder. "I can always call Marcy and ask her to look after Coop. Or even Nevaeh. She lives with Travis, and he also has a dog."

"Angie, you're even worse than my brother. Stop worrying. Maya loves Cooper, and he loves her; they're having the time of their lives," Layla chirps, laughing heartily. "You're in the City of Love. Enjoy Paris. It's all good here."

"Thank you." I sigh, glancing at Drake. He lifts a cup to his lips and takes a sip of strong black coffee, his eyes never leaving my face. "Just call me if you need anything, okay?"

"Bye, Angie. Tell Drake I said hi," she says and ends the call.

Putting my phone on my lap, I look to my right, admiring Jardin des Tuileries in the bright sunlight. After we spent the whole morning going from one beautiful masterpiece to the other at the Louvre, I needed a place to recharge my batteries. The gardens, which separate the Louvre from the Place de la Concorde, are a perfect place to do so. Beautiful and full of history. Sitting around the fountain and discussing our plans for dinner, I feel happiness filling my every pore.

I have no idea why, but this city really has a magical effect on me. Just like the man sitting beside me.

Inhaling, I breathe in the scent of freshly baked pastries, almond, caramel, and vanilla mixing into the sweetest aroma. Taking my cup of herbal tea, I focus on my boyfriend. His deep brown eyes radiate warmth; golden hues are dancing behind his irises. He has an impressive stubble, but it only favors his natural charm. Running his fingers through the short locks on the top of his head, he gives me a crooked smile.

"So?"

"You were right. They are fine," I tell him, poking my tongue out at him. "You're not the only person who's allowed to be nervous."

"Such a mama bear to Cooper." Drake winks at me. "I can only imagine how overprotective you're going to be with our child. Whenever it happens."

"We'll see about that," I reply nonchalantly, flashing him a smile.

If he only knew my reasons for postponing our trip till August, we would've stayed put. No way I would've missed my date with summery Paris. Especially with Drake by my side. My favorite man in my favorite city—what could be better?

"What did Marcy say? I saw you reading a message from her when we were placing our orders."

"My shop is fine. We have a lot of customers, and pretty much all of them want to try your favorite red velvet cupcakes. Who knew a post on your Instagram would bring so many people to my place?"

"I'm a marketing guru," Drake states with a serious expression.

I inch forward, taking his chin between my thumb and index finger. "You're amazing. Thank you," I say and press my lips to his for a sweet kiss. He tastes like coffee, and when I lean away, the butterflies in my stomach erupt into a crazy dance. The feeling is so familiar and wholesome.

"You don't need to thank me. If I can help you, I'll do it in the blink of an eye. Your place is fantastic, and you deserve every bit of your success."

"I'm doing my best, even if, with my modeling gigs, it feels like I'm lacking sometimes."

"You missed being a runway model, Angie. A few gigs here and there doesn't mean you're lacking. Don't feel bad about doing something you love," Drake coos, reaching over and entwining our fingers.

"Well, you're right. It's mostly for fun, and to help some of my designer friends." I smile at him. "Where do you want to go next?"

"Wherever you want. Though I don't think I'm ready to see any more artwork in the foreseeable future," he exclaims, taking a bite of croissant with almond filling.

I pout. "I thought about going to Musée d'Orsay. *Starry Night Over the Rhône* is my favorite Van Gogh painting. I always go there."

Drake chews his croissant, eyeballing me from under furrowed brows. I keep my face neutral, knowing perfectly well he's not going to say no to me. The past year I've spent with him has made me realize I have the best boyfriend in the whole world. Attentive, caring, and so loving, he makes me feel cherished and happy, and I'd do anything to make him feel the same.

"Fine, but I get to decide what we're going to do after dinner."

"Deal," I tell him, feeling gratitude and overwhelming love.

HAND IN HAND, we stroll along the charming streets of Paris. The city comes alive before our eyes, embracing us with its timeless elegance and vibrant energy. I share my stories of this place with Drake, and my cheeks hurt from smiling so much.

The soft breeze carries the melodies of street musicians and the sounds of busy city. The Seine's gentle flow mirrors our pace as we wander along it, taking in the breathtaking views of the historic architecture, the grand boulevards lined with elegant cafés and boutique shops.

"Are you excited for the start of the season?" I ask as Drake drapes a hand over my shoulders, drawing me to his side.

"Of course. We made it to the playoffs last season, to the conference finals. I'm sure the guys will be more than motivated to make the Stanley Cup final."

"Especially with a very talented goalie joining the team." Nudging him to talk about things that bother him is something I always do. Very gently, without pushing him to open up to me if he's not ready.

Drake chuckles, tightening his grip around my shoulder. "I'm happy Clay is joining us. He's going to be an amazing addition to the team. I feel like he's exactly what we need to reach our goals and make our Stanley Cup dream come true. I'm happy my friend is going to be around way more often. It's a great opportunity to make things right and fix what was broken." He hides his nose in my hair, inhaling and kissing my temple. "But I have no idea how it's going to be with him and Layla in Santa Clara."

"They're both adults, and they're fully capable of making their own decisions. We just need to let them be, and they'll figure everything out on their own."

"Just like you let Roman and Nevaeh be?"

Rolling my eyes, I try to wiggle out of his embrace, but he's not letting me. His wholehearted laughter reverberates through my body, and I giggle as well. "I did nothing. The first rule of being a good friend is to not interfere with your friends' lives. Meddling with other people's love lives is taboo."

"Your best friend helped me win you over. I have no complaints about that."

I stop, and Drake halts in his tracks too. He dips his head, so our eyes are on the same level. "Me neither."

My boyfriend covers my lips with his, kissing me deeply and slowly. Closing my eyes, I let myself get carried away, enjoying every brush of his tongue against mine. After so many shared kisses, every new one still feels like something out of this world. My skin warms up; my heart beats faster, and I'm losing myself in the arms of this man.

"I love you," I whisper once he presses his forehead to mine.

"I love you too, Angie," he says, arms snaking around my waist and holding me close.

We stand still on the Pont Alexandre III as people pass by us. The majestic arches, intricate sculptures, and golden accents that reflect the sunlight with a captivating glow lured us there, even if initially we had other plans for our day.

Drake suddenly leans away, glancing at something over the railing. Turning his head to me, a boyish smile lights up his face. "How about going on the Seine River Cruise?"

"*Oui, mon chéri.*"

Interlacing our fingers, we hurry to buy tickets and board the boat. With Drake, Paris feels like a fairy-tale city full of secrets I want to uncover, full of history hiding behind every corner and on every cobblestone street, and full of love—all-consuming and magnificent.

There is no other place in the world I want to be to give him the news he's been longing to hear.

DRAKE

Angie was sound asleep when I left an hour ago, and now I step into our hotel room, trying to close the door as quietly as possible. It's nine p.m., and I don't want to wake her up. Suggesting the Seine River Cruise turned out to be one big disaster. I had no idea she would get seasick.

Putting the package on the table, I tiptoe to the bedroom. She's peacefully sleeping, tucked under a blanket. I bend and kiss her forehead, stepping back as soon as she stirs. Slowly moving around the room, I change into only my sweatpants. A heavy curtain blocks all light from the street, and the room is dimly lit.

Once the bedroom door is closed, I go to the table and pour myself some of the whiskey I bought last night. Proceeding to the balcony, I step outside and sit on a chair. The Eiffel Tower sparkles in the distance, the perfect view I wanted when I booked our hotel.

Taking my phone out of my pocket, I open a text from Angie's dad. It's very old-fashioned, but I wanted to get his blessing before we came here. Having a good relationship with my future in-laws always seemed like something very important. I did my best to make them like me, and now I'm grinning as I read her father's text again.

LOGAN JONES:

I warned you, women in my family and a proposal in Paris aren't a good combo. Good luck, Drake.

Everything definitely didn't go how I imagined. The only good thing out of all this mess is that I was able to sneak in my gift for her. I hope she likes it; it'd be a bummer otherwise.

"Why didn't you wake me up?" Her soft voice behind my back makes me jump in my seat. Snapping my head in her direction, I lock eyes with Angie. She smiles, sashaying over to me. "Sorry, I didn't mean to scare you."

"I was sure you were asleep." I slip my phone in my pocket and wrap my arms around her waist, pulling her onto my lap. "Did I wake you?"

"No. I just feel better now," Angie reassures me, winding her hands around my shoulders. "Where were you?"

"Is it even possible to hide anything from you? You were asleep when I left."

"I woke up an hour ago, found the room empty, and fell asleep again." She cups my cheek with her palm, her thumb caressing my skin. "Sorry I ruined your plans for tonight."

"It's okay. The most important thing is that you're feeling better. I'll never invite you on a boat again," I tell her, and she giggles. "I brought you a gift."

"Can I see it?"

"Can't you wait till tomorrow?" I ask teasingly, and she scoffs.

"Drake, I thought I was going to throw up my lungs. A gift from the man I love would definitely make up for it."

I watch her, smiling affectionately. She knows all the buttons to push to get what she wants. Not that I have anything against it, because I love doing things to make her happy. No matter what it is. If she wants it, I'm going to get it.

"Fine. Just wait for me here." I haul her to my chest, stand up, and lower her to the seat. "One moment."

Dashing into the suite and right into the bedroom, I quickly grab a little box out of my suitcase and snatch the ring out of it. My fingers tremble a little when the realization of what I'm about to do settles in. It's the moment I've been waiting forever for, and even if it's not as picture-perfect as I imagined, it's still perfect for me.

Back in the suite, I grab the package and return to the balcony. Angie is standing near the railing, staring off into the distance. The skirt of her simple red cotton dress sways in the warm breeze. I set the package on the table and walk up to her, winding a hand around her waist. She puts her head on my shoulder, sighing deeply.

"I can't believe we're leaving in two days."

"Well, yeah, but I think we spent a perfect week in France. Nice and the French Riviera were amazing, and Paris with you exceeded all my expectations."

"I thought the same. You make everything a thousand times better, even things I loved before you."

"Hold that thought, okay?" I blurt out, stepping back to the table and taking the package in my hands. Sauntering to Angie, I extend it to her. "I hope you like it."

A mischievous smile crosses her lips when she takes the package from me. She tears it open and slowly pulls out a painting. Her jaw drops, and she tumbles back. Angie grasps the railing with her hand, drawing the painting into her chest. I watch her, following her every move with my eyes.

"It's Louis. How did you... How did you find him?"

"Ethan and Emma helped me," I reply, noticing her legs wobbling. Scooping her into my arms, I edge to the table and sit down, then haul her to my chest. "When they were on their Euro-trip last year, they made some friends here in Paris. I sent the picture of your painting to the twins; they sent it to their friends. It took about a week, but they found Louis and gave me his phone number. He recognized his work right away, just like he remembered you. He figured out why I was calling and promised to have this painting ready whenever we came to Paris."

Angie holds the painting in front of her, and the happiest smile plays on her lips. It's similar to the one in our living room, with a few exceptions. Now it's a sunny day, the Eiffel Tower bathed in the golden colors of the sunrays. A man and a woman stand right in front of it, their lips locked in a kiss. A folded red umbrella hangs from the woman's hand.

"It's us..." she whispers. Her voice cracks with emotion. "I finally found someone to share my umbrella with."

"You did," I say, taking the painting away from her and putting it down on the table. Angie's eyes well up with happy tears. I take the ring out of my pocket and show it to her. An audible gasp leaves her lips, and she blinks rapidly.

"It's not how I wanted it to be. Not how I *planned* it to be. But honestly? I'm dying to see this ring on your finger. I want to spend every moment of my life with you, because you're here..." I point at the veins in my arm. "Here." I point to my forehead. "And here." I press my finger to my chest. "You're everywhere, and there isn't even an hour when I don't think about you. You're my happy ending, Angie. Will you be my wife?"

"Yes... Yes, I will." Angie nods, and I quickly put the ring on her finger.

A brilliant round diamond with a platinum band fits her perfectly, and I can't help but marvel at it. She's going to be my wife...and hopefully, one day, the mother of my children. I won't try to speed up the process, just enjoy every minute of my life with her. My timeline is no longer a reason for my worries; it's the source of my inspiration and excitement.

Angie wiggles on my lap, turning around to face me. She smiles and leans forward, kissing me deeply. Her hands wrap around my shoulders, her tongue dancing with mine. Feeling her in my arms is absolutely blissful, and I'm slowly losing myself in her. This moment, as it is, is flawless.

"I'm pregnant." A whisper caresses my skin, and at first I don't even register the meaning of her words. Angie leans away, looking down at me. "You're going to be a dad, Drake."

I pause, a billion fireworks erupting in my chest. Jumping to my feet, I hold her close, making her wrap her legs around my hips. She laughs; the sound of her melodic voice permeates my veins and swims straight to my heart. I'm so happy right now, I think I forgot how to breathe.

"Say it again," I demand, desperate to hear those words. "Please."

"You're going to be a dad, Drake Benson, and I can hardly wait to share this journey with you," Angie murmurs gently.

Smashing my lips onto hers, I kiss her again. I'm full of happiness and love for her.

All my life, I'd been looking in the wrong direction until she and her dog barreled into me. Meeting her turned my world upside down. Angie is the fire I tried to keep my distance from, right until I realized she's the only woman I need. Her flames aren't here to burn me; they're here to bring me warmth and comfort, coating me to my very bones with her love and affection. She's strong and vulnerable, anxious and calm, funny and sad. Every day I love her more and more, falling deeper and harder for the girl of my dreams.

Every relationship is different. Every love story is different, beautiful in its own way. But ours is my favorite.

Drake

bonus chapter

I LOVE HOCKEY. LOVE THE THRILL OF EXCITEMENT DURING the game. The buzz of the arena, and people's happiness when the team wins, and even their disappointment when we lose because it shows how much they care about the game. The start of the season always brings a lot of euphoric feelings, but this time nothing compares to how I feel when I come home to Angie. Seeing her growing baby bump, I can't keep my hands to myself, and all I want is to spend every minute of every day with her.

This is everything I've dreamed about and more. So much more, I often wonder how I got so lucky.

"Any plans for tonight?" Roman asks as we go down the hallway to the parking lot.

"Not really. Just want to spend more time with Angie before we go on our stretch of away games." I glance at him. His hair is disheveled and sticking in every direction. When I first joined the team last year, he was that broody guy with a mysterious persona, who only opened up to his friends. I am his friend now, but I can't really say I know a lot about him. "You?"

"I promised Nevaeh to take her out for dinner and a movie."

"Things are okay between you two?" It's been two months since they got married in Vegas, and while I'm one hundred percent sure that Nevaeh would've loved for things to turn into something real, with Roman it's not that easy. The guy has mastered his poker face to a T, hiding his feelings and emotions, unless he's on the ice. No surprise Thompson is his best friend on the team.

Roman shrugs. "We're fine." *What an insightful answer.*

I roll my eyes and head to my car, not bothering to ask more. He's not going to say anything–

"I'm not going to hurt her, Drake," he suddenly exclaims, and I halt in my tracks, looking over my shoulder at him. "I like my wife."

This statement brings a smile to my face, and I chuckle, holding his gaze. Who would've thought he would be calling Nevaeh his wife after getting drunkenly married to her? Definitely not me, but I'm glad to be wrong. "Good to know. Nevaeh is not only Angie's best friend, she's my friend too, and I don't want her to have her heart shattered."

He shifts awkwardly and unlocks his car, pushing his sports bag in the trunk. "I don't want that either," he says, and a crooked grin stretches across his mouth. "See you tomorrow, Benson."

"See you tomorrow, Pashkevich." I mimic him, and he bursts out with laughter. "Tell Nev I said hi."

Roman nods and gets in his car, closing the door and driving away a moment later. With a sigh, I open the backseat of my car and put my things there. When I'm already behind the steering wheel, I notice Colton and Clay walking to their cars. They're talking and laughing, while I twist my lips, eyes zeroing in on Rodgers. He's not over my sister, and no matter how hard he tries to hide it, I see it. It's written all over his face when he looks at her, thinking that no one is watching...and it makes me sad for my friend. Layla isn't going to get together with him. At least that's what she told me.

And she can be easily lying, simply because she wants to protect herself and Maya. Oh, thank you so much, my inner voice, it's exactly what I need.

God, I need Angie. With her by my side, everything seems so much less problematic.

STEPPING INTO THE HOUSE, I'm met with the loud sound of the TV, and then the sound of the dog's paws slapping on the tile follows. Cooper rushes out of the living room, jumping around me with his little tail wagging. I crouch to him, petting his head between his ears. "Miss me, buddy? I missed you too, boy," I murmur with a smile on my face.

"Hey, you." Angie's voice draws my attention to her. My fiancée stands in the doorframe, her hip propped against it. She's in a red oversized hoodie and black sweatpants, her hair in a bun with a little braid wrapped around it. "How was the practice?"

"It was good," I tell her, standing up and taking a step closer to her. "How was your day?"

"It was good," she murmurs as I wrap my arm around her waist and pull her to me for a kiss. "I missed you."

"And I missed you too, Cupcake." I tenderly kiss her, the scent of vanilla and chocolate sliding under my skin. "Have no idea how I'm going to leave you tomorrow."

"You love hockey, and so far, you have a really good start to the season, so I'm sure you'll be fine." Angie winds her hands around my shoulders, eyes glued to my face. "Even if I'll miss you terribly."

Chuckling, I scoop her up in my arms and carry her to the living room, my eyes falling on a cardboard box on the small coffee table. Is it a cake? What's the occasion? Usually, she doesn't need one, bringing home new desserts and pastries she has at her dessert shop, but recently, it has become incredibly rare. Mostly because her OB-GYN advised her to be careful with sugar and sweets.

"Are we celebrating something?" I ask, putting Angie down on her feet.

She slides her hands down her baby bump, the sweetest smile on her lips. "I have a surprise for you. Layla helped me to organize everything."

"Really? And where is it?" I look around the room, eyebrows arched. My veins are filled with warmth, the feeling of comfort blanketing my body. It's true what people often say. Home is not really a place for me; it's so much more than just this house we live in. It's the immense happiness and all consuming love, embodied in this very girl who stands in front of me with her palms on her belly.

Jesus, how much I love her. I never even thought that such strong feelings were possible.

"We need to go outside for it," Angie says, winking at me. "The cake is for later."

"Fine, let's go outside then." I grab her palm in mine and pull her with me to the backyard. Angie's laughter is contagious, echoing around the place and making me smile broader. The click-clack sound of Cooper's claws on the wooden floor indicates that he's following us outside too.

Once we're in the backyard, Angie pulls her hand away from mine and trots to the small table. She takes something from it and comes back to me, hiding whatever she took from the table behind her back.

"So?" I tip my head to the side, hiding my hands in my pockets.

"Remember I went to the ultrasound, and the doctor promised not to tell me the gender of our baby?" I nod, my heartbeat skyrocketing in an instant. "They sent me the results yesterday, and I gave them to Layla, without checking what's inside." Angie shows me her hands with two cannons. "She bought these smoke cannons for us, so we can do a little gender reveal party for just ourselves."

"And my sister kept it a secret?" I furrow my brow, my eyes trained on the cannons.

"Layla knows how to keep a secret." Angie flashes me a smile. "You're underestimating her."

Laughter bolts out of my mouth, making Angie roll her eyes at me. I step forward, invading her personal space. "Which one is for me?"

"You choose." I look down at the cannons and take the one from her right hand. "Cool."

Rounding me, she pulls out her phone from her pocket, launches the camera and places the phone on the table, leaning it against the table lantern. She points her finger in front of the table, and I follow her instructions without even a word said. Angie checks where I stand and that it's totally visible on the camera and then comes to me.

We stand side by side, grinning at each other. The birds chirping and Coop's huffs are the only sounds that reach my ears. "You sure you don't want a big party? With our friends and family?" I ask her.

"Absolutely."

"Don't you think your parents and twins will be disappointed? Or Nev?"

"I'll send my family a video. As for Nev, she'll come to our place tomorrow." I open my mouth to ask another question, but she beats me to it. "Layla and Maya will be here soon, but only after I call your sister. She said for her it was enough that she knew first."

"You have everything figured out, don't you?"

"I always do, Drake," she murmurs, getting ready to pop the cannon. "On the count of three?"

"One." I glance at my fiancée.

"Two." Angie continues.

"Three," we say in unison, popping the cannons at the same time. The pink and blue colored powder explodes in the air, and Cooper starts barking, while my jaw drops.

Blinking rapidly, I turn to look at Angie, who stares at me with an absolutely calm expression on her face. A gentle smile curves her lips, and her eyes glimmering with warmth and something that is really close to mischief. She knew...she knew for the whole time?

"But... How... Are you...?" I blabber, my eyebrows etched together. "How is it possible?"

"Do I need to explain to you how I got pregnant?" she asks sarcastically.

"No, Cupcake, I totally know how that happened." I deadpan. "Your brother and sister are twins. How come we're having *twins* too?"

Giggling, Angie bends and presses her hands to her knees. Coop dashes to her, trying to lick her face, happily barking. When she finally straightens her back and faces me, I notice something I haven't seen before tonight. Her annoyance.

Angie sighs and crosses her arms over her chest. "Yes, Ethan and Emma are twins, and supposedly, I shouldn't be pregnant with twins, but I am." She purses her lips tighter, as she glares at me. "You're kinda forgetting that your dad has a twin brother."

Shit. She's absolutely right. With a click of her tongue, Angie stomps to the table, turns off the camera and stalks into the house, without even a glance in my direction. Fuck.

I run after her with Cooper following my steps. Catching her by her elbow, I halt her in her tracks and twirl her around to look at me. Her teeth are sunk into her bottom lip, eyebrows knit together. She's angry and she has all the rights to feel this way. I ruined my own gender reveal party.

"Cupcake," I coo, framing her cheeks with my palms. "I'm sorry. My shocked state got the best of me, and I didn't react how I should have."

"It was an honest reaction, I suppose." She avoids looking me in the eyes, so I gently tilt her head up so our gazes clash. "The doctor told me at the first ultrasound, but I wanted to keep it a secret. Till we knew the gender." A dejected sigh leaves her parted lips. "I should've told you."

"Angie, I'm not angry with you. That thought didn't even cross my mind," I tell her, bending my head down to look at her more closely. Her deep green eyes are full of intensity. "I was just stunned because I didn't even think it would be possible for us to have twins. But here we are..."

"But here we are," she echoes me, and my favorite cutest beam lights up her face. "Are you happy?"

"I'm over the moon." I pull her to me and lay a tender kiss on her lips. "A boy and a girl, it's like all my dreams come true...simply because you're with me."

"Or because you are with me." She sighs, enjoying the warmth of my embrace with her eyes closed. "You make me the happiest, and your love makes me feel so powerful... Even having twins doesn't scare me, although it probably should since I watched my siblings grow right in front of my eyes."

"Let's keep the stories about Emma and Ethan under wraps. Our kids won't be like them," I tell her with conviction, not really sure if I'm trying to convince only her or myself too.

"They won't. They will be ours," Angie says as I hug her tighter, my chin on top of her head. She smells so sweet and so familiar, I close my eyes, and a vivid image of my future pops in my head.

It's bright and happy. Full of love and joy. Of kids' laughter, and our never-ending talks.

Of course I know there will be bumps on the road. Small hiccups and big ones. But I'm not afraid of them. With Angie by my side, I know I'll be able to withstand anything and that I will do even the impossible for her and our children's happiness.

Because they are my home...and I've never been more excited about what's to come.

about the author

Anastasija is an indie author who spends her days creating swoon-worthy and steamy stories that will make your heart race. Her writing is filled with flawed and relatable characters that you'll find yourself rooting for. Whether you're in the mood for angsty drama or steamy romance, her stories take you on a rollercoaster ride of emotions with guaranteed happy endings.

When she's not writing, she loves to lose herself in reading books, rewatching her favorite tv-shows and spending time with her son. She loves traveling and exploring the world, and then including places she visited in her novels.

If you're a fan of romance that leaves you breathless and begging for more, Anastasija is the author for you. Connect with her on Instagram and TikTok, where she loves to hear from her readers and share sneak peeks of her books and upcoming projects.

Made in the USA
Las Vegas, NV
10 May 2024